TANDEM

We Rendezvous at Ten

The formation of Hurricanes and fighter-bombers flew steadily on. "Line astern. Line astern. Go." The Hurricanes had sighted their target, two tankers surrounded by flak-ships. Before the anti-aircraft gunners could fire, Whelan and his men were on them. A fury of cannon-shell swept the decks, and the flak-gunners fell, crawled and rushed for cover.

Then the Hurricane bombers swept in upon the tankers. Little firing met them, for Whelan's vicious, searing attack had blasted the path open for them to bomb and hit and soar to safety. Fountains of foaming sea rose in the clear air, then the bombs hit clean amidships. Above the destruction the Spitfire escort circled.

Thistle Squadron had spent all its ammunition. The bombers had dropped their bombs. The Hurricanes were darting, weaving like gigantic dragonflies, across the water and away. The Spitfires stayed for one more moment before turning to shepherd the Hurricanes in their charge. Then they were homeward bound.

"Hallo, Tartan. Thistle Leader calling. Job finished. Quite successful."

Also by Wing-Commander Ronald Adam

READINESS AT DAWN Tandem edition 5/-

We Rendezvous at Ten

Wing-Commander Ronald Adam, OBE

TANDEM

14 Gloucester Road, London SW7

First published in Great Britain by
Victor Gollancz Ltd

Published by Universal Tandem Publishing Co. Ltd, 1970

Made and printed in Great Britain by
The Garden City Press Ltd, Letchworth, Herts.

Author's Note

The R.A.F. Fighter Station depicted does not refer to any particular station, except that, for the purposes of the story, it must necessarily be somewhere near London.
The Squadron call-signs do not refer to any particular squadron.
While the characters are imaginary, the incidents are based on fact.

CHAPTER ONE

AT FOUR o'clock in the morning Roger MacMurray pushed back his chair, opened a tin of tobacco, filled his pipe and looked across at Havering.

"Any more of them?" he said.

"I shouldn't think so," Havering told him. "Just before the last one went off they said the weather was closing down, but I'll ring them and ask."

"It's been a good evening's practice," Roger remarked to the Sergeant at his side.

"A pity the Hun wouldn't oblige, Sir," the Sergeant said.

"They'd like to speak to you," Havering called to Roger.

"Hallo," Roger said into the telephone to the ear listening to him at a distant aerodrome. "You're not proposing to do any more, are you?"

"We'd like to," a cheerful voice replied, "but there's a mist up to about a thousand feet and it makes landing very tricky. If there's anything important we can go; but as the whole squadron has had plenty of practice tonight we propose packing up, Sir, in the meanwhile."

"Of course," Roger said; "and thanks very much for the co-operation."

"Good night, Sir."

"Good night—or rather, good early morning."

He lit his pipe and began to enter up the log-book with details of the night's flying, the many and varied courses undertaken, the work with searchlights and with anti-aircraft guns, the constant watchfulness for enemy raiders and the equal watchfulness for any British bomber that might need assistance.

Havering had walked up beside him and was standing waiting for him to finish writing.

"Are you going to try to get some sleep?" he asked Roger.

"It hardly seems worth it. What time's readiness?"

"In about an hour and a quarter."

"Then there's no point in sleeping. I'll get a rest after

breakfast. Does the weather look dud?"

For an answer Havering produced the signal that had arrived on the teleprinter. Roger read it carefully.

"Not too hopeful," he said.

George, the Army's representative in Operations Room, arrived from his end of the dais to make a third at the Controller's desk.

"What's it going to do?" he asked.

"Looks like a poor day beginning."

George failed to conceal a prolonged yawn. "If flying's off for the night I might as well get some shut-eye—unless . . ." and he looked round with anticipation, "there's a cup of tea coming." And at that moment, up the stairs and on to the dais came a W.A.A.F. with a large tray and rows of welcome cups upon it.

"Sweet at the back, unsugared in the front, Sir," she said to Roger, holding out the tray precariously so that the cups danced to a little jingle.

Roger took his cup and deposited a penny on the tray. Havering and George took theirs, and the W.A.A.F. continued on her rounds to the others of the night watch who were looking for her coming. The three Officers sipped their tea silently. There had hardly been a pause in the controlling since ten o'clock the previous night, when they had relieved the preceding watch. While Havering had taken and given information from and to many distant points, had answered Group and given the Station Commander news of all activities, and while George had kept his batteries of searchlights and guns fed with news from minute to minute and received their reports almost as frequently, Roger and the Sergeant beside him had sat with telephone hand-sets close to their ears and talked with the night pilots high in the blackness remote from them.

There had been momentary difficulties—pilots losing themselves for a short time and having to be homed in safety; one machine with a faulty engine, liable to fail at any moment, leaving the pilot the only alternative of jumping into the inky well below, and another whose radio had failed completely but who, with the help of the watchful men manning the many searchlights, had been directed back to his aerodrome. For hours the sky had presented a cubist's dream of long, slender pencils of light groping and grouping in every direction.

Not so conspicuous, but just as intense, had been the work of the gunners finding range and height and practising all motions of their drill, to be ready for such real target as might present itself. And in Operations Room the plotters had sat round the huge map, marking with coloured counters and arrows the tracks of aircraft as told to them by the Royal Observer Corps, the members of which, out in the fields and on the roof-tops, were keeping that same vigil which had warned Great Britain of the approach of its enemies since the outbreak of war.

The floor supervisor, a Corporal, had walked round and about every now and then, listening-in himself to check the plotters' accuracy, arranging reliefs at periodic intervals when headphones were becoming tight and ears numb with the pressure and the constant messages. Occasionally a tea-carrier put in her appearance, and throughout the hours the noise of operations had been made up of a confusion of voices talking into mouthpieces, the teleprinter clattering and the clock with a loud tick, inexorably beating the seconds away.

From time to time a Signals Officer or N.C.O. would come into the room and glance round to see whether any detail of the communications needed his attention. The Army signallers, too, were busy plotting from the information gained from their own network spread from coast to coast.

The Navy would add its quota of information, and even the unruffled voices of distant policemen would come to the Controller's ears. Not an unusual light could be shown, not an unusual sound be made, but Operations would know of it almost within the instant of its birth.

The enemy had left the English shores alone. Periodically the night-fighter pilots had called from their eyries to say that they could see anti-aircraft fire, but Roger had reassured them.

"It's not ours," he had said over and over again. "It's over the other side." For the British bombers had been going and coming like trains.

George was the first to finish his tea, and he put down his empty cup. "Shut-eye," he said laconically, and walked out of the room.

Havering returned to his seat, and now, after the subdued and concentrated chatter of the previous hour, the room was silent.

"Which squadron is readiness at dawn?" Roger asked.

"Cygnet," Havering answered.

"If the weather really does close down between now and then, Group might relax them a bit, instead of bringing the whole squadron to readiness."

"I'll ask them," Havering replied, "in about half an hour's time, just before the night waiter begins to waken people."

Roger puffed his pipe. He had been completely unaware of any tiredness until now. It was always the hour from four to five in the morning that engulfed him in huge waves of slumber if there were no activity. He propped his chin on his clenched fists as he leaned on the glass-topped desk in front of him, but he knew that if he persisted in this attitude for more than a few minutes the pipe would drop out of his mouth as he lost consciousness, so he stood up and began to walk up and down the dais behind the figures at the telephone keys. He paused to look at files and order-books, or to concentrate on maps and charts or notices. After a time he found a newspaper of the previous day in a waste-paper basket, but the shrunken size of its war-time edition gave him only ten minutes' reading.

"I'm going to sniff the air outside," he said to Havering, "so you know where I am if I'm wanted."

The picket at the front entrance rose from his chair as Roger approached and stood quietly to attention. Roger opened the door and went out. The stars were obscured. A blackness more intense than the earlier hours of night had preceded this hour before dawn, but, gazing upwards, Roger could feel rather than see that clouds were now rolling across the sky. For many minutes he could distinguish nothing. He drew in the air, which was sweet after the stuffiness of Operations with its curtained windows and the tension of its efforts. There was now no sound from anywhere except the rising wind.

He found a wooden bench alongside the wall and sat on it, resting his elbows on his knees and enjoying the last embers of his pipe. He must have been there a long time, for he recovered his full wits to hear borne on the wind the first faint crow of a cock and to feel a slight rain blowing in his face. He realised that he was cold, and standing up suddenly, he almost fell over with the stiffness of his limbs. As he came in at the door the picket said to him, "I was thinking of coming out to look for you, Sir. I thought something must have happened."

Roger smiled at him. "I think I must have gone to sleep," he said. As he sat down at his desk once again, Havering spoke to him.

"Group say the weather reports from everywhere are wretched. It will be sufficient to have a flight at readiness only in the meanwhile. I've told the Officers' and Sergeants' Messes not to waken more than are necessary. The flight will be at readiness in about fifteen minutes."

Roger looked at the blackboard on which a W.A.A.F. had chalked details of recent weather at many distant places. Low cloud, rain, high wind . . . the story was the same everywhere. But that was not to say that the enemy would not send out reconnaissance machines or early bombers in the hope of finding gaps in the cloud and the chance of a target below. So, filling his pipe again, Roger sat down to wait for the little time before the dirty grey of dawn.

He fell into a trance for this short period before the daylight activities of the Station began. He was unaware of Havering's many telephonings as he ascertained the number of aircraft and pilots available, the condition of various aerodromes for landing, the latest positions of convoys and the final assembly of complete reports from the night-flying aircraft whose pilots had now gone to bed.

Havering called to Roger, who did not hear him. He was still drawing at his pipe, but his eyes were fixed in a stare at the large map, through and beyond which he was looking into some distance which vanished and was no longer identifiable when Havering spoke to him from his elbow.

"Cygnet Squadron is now at readiness. . . . Were you asleep?"

"No. I don't think so," Roger answered, and puffed a cloud of smoke from his pipe. "I seem to have passed out for a few minutes, but my pipe's still alight."

"It gets a bit trying in here, doesn't it?" Havering remarked, "especially in the early morning."

"I don't know that it's that," Roger answered him. "It's the complete absence of rhythm to life. Morning, noon, afternoon and night—they all seem the same. The time on the clock means nothing. The day of the week is unknown, and almost the month of the year. Dash it! I sometimes find myself wondering whether it's 1940 or 1941. I have to say to myself, 'France, Holland, Battle of Britain—1940. That was last year, so this must be 1941'."

"It's a bit different this year, isn't it?" Havering said.

"Yes. Different in its setting; different in its tempo; different in its orchestration. But sometimes I think it's a much greater strain on the fighters."

"My wife sometimes says to me when I go on leave," Havering said, " 'What do they all find to do these days?' "

"That's just it," Roger answered. "The ordinary folk don't know. But last year, when the boys were fighting like inspired furies, they were defending their own doorsteps against an enemy all could see. They knew that every bomber they brought down might mean saving a friend or a relation from annihilation. If they were unlucky themselves, and could bale out, they fell in friendly hands. There's a wonderful tonic effect in fighting over your own land. That's why I think they have a tougher proposition now. The fact is that they've pushed the enemy's front line back, but there's colder comfort fighting over France and Belgium than over Kent and Surrey."

"What about us?" Havering asked. "In our day we were flying over anywhere but our own land, and we hadn't got radio and parachutes and dependable engines."

Roger puffed some smoke at him. "My dear old Bunny," he said. "Surely you've learned by now that nobody wants to hear about us. It stands to reason. What was your attitude in the last war towards the bloke who wanted to talk about the scrap with the Boers?"

"I thought him a long-winded old gas-bag," Havering said.

"That's precisely what we are to the lads today," Roger told him, "if we open our silly mouths to talk about our flying days."

The telephone startled Havering into activity, and he gave a sudden leap to his end of the room. He listened for a moment or two.

"Very good, Sir," he said. "I'll tell him.... No. He's here, Sir." He rang off and grinned. "Group were asking if you were asleep," he said to Roger. "They told me to pass you a message. There's an enemy reconnaissance machine off our map to the North. He seems to be drifting southwards a bit. Can you be ready to put a section up?"

"Is Ogilvie at readiness with his squadron?"

"I'll ask," Havering answered. "Hallo, Cygnet dispersal. Is Squadron Leader Ogilvie there? ... Could he speak to Controller? ... They're fetching him," he told Roger.

"Good morning, Roger," Ogilvie's cheerful Scottish voice said. "I can't stand these early hours. They're not good for my constitution."

"Good morning, Scottie. What's it like for flying?"

"Is that a polite enquiry, Roger, or is it in aid of something?"

"It might be in aid of something. There's a hostile recco a long way away at the moment. He might make a pass in our direction."

"That being so," said Ogilvie, "it's a beautiful morning for flying. If you'd asked me if I wanted to fly for pleasure I'd have told you the weather was filthy. In fact, the cloud's pretty low, visibility's poor, I haven't had a shave, I want my breakfast and my tummy's rumbling. Do you want a section to stand by?"

"They'd better be on their toes, Scottie, just in case."

"All right, Roger. I'll go myself if necessary. Cheerio."

A W.A.A.F. plotter at the far end of the map pressed her headphones to her ears for better listening. Then, acting on the details she had heard, she picked up a little painted arrow and put it pointing southwards on the map. Next she took a metal holder and placed in the slots provided various numerals in different colours, and this complete, she put the holder beside the arrow, with its information facing Roger.

"There it is," Roger said to Havering. "One bandit at three thousand feet. He's presumably cloud-dodging as he collects details of whatever shipping he can see as he hops in and out."

The W.A.A.F. placed arrow after arrow as the enemy hugged the coastline, coming South.

"Group for you," Havering called.

"Sector Controller here," Roger said into his mouthpiece.

"Can you get a section off to look after that raid?" he was asked.

"Yes, Sir. I don't know that they'll have much luck."

"I know," the Group Controller replied. "It's an outside chance in this weather, but have a shot at it."

"Very good, Sir.... Havering, get Ogilvie and his Number Two off. Tell them the bandit is sticking to the coastline and coming South. Tell them to steer East and keep just below cloud, and I'll keep them informed."

Ogilvie had wasted no time. He and his second pilot must have been sitting in their cockpits waiting for the word to go, for even as Roger was noting that Operations Room was very still, Lookout was broadcasting that two aircraft of Cygnet Squadron had left the ground.

Roger and Ogilvie exchanged messages, but reception was not faultless. The Sergeant listening with another telephone beside Roger shook his receiver as if it displeased him.

"Possibly the weather, Sir," he remarked to Roger. "I never did understand wireless."

"Listen carefully," Roger told him. "I expect they'll be flying low, and I hope they don't get out of range. Hallo, Cygnet Leader, Tartan calling. Are you still receiving me? Over."

"Hallo, Tartan . . . crackle . . . crackle . . . crackle. Over."

"Damn!" said Roger. "It's going to be difficult. Hallo, Cygnet Leader, Tartan calling. There is strong interference. Please say again. Over."

"Hallo . . . crackle . . . crackle . . . receiving . . . crackle . . . but not . . . crackle . . . crackle. Over."

"Hallo, Cygnet Leader, Tartan answering. Still receiving you with interference. Can you gain height? Over."

"Hallo, Tartan, Cygnet . . . crackle . . . answering. Am just . . . whee . . . whizz . . . crackle."

"Did you get that?" Roger said wearily to the Sergeant.

"I think, Sir," the Sergeant answered, "he must have said he was just below cloud.... Meaning, I suppose, that he can't go higher unless you want him to."

"Hallo, Cygnet Leader, Tartan calling. Gain height. Gain height. Over."

There was silence for a little time, and then faintly, but

more distinctly than before, Cygnet Leader's voice called.

"Hallo, Tartan. I am flying in cloud. How high do you want me?"

"Hallo, Cygnet Leader, Tartan answering. Bandit may be flying between layers of cloud. Over."

"Hallo, Tartan, Cygnet Leader answering. Bandit must have found a better pitch than I have. What height is bandit?"

"Now reported two thousand feet, Cygnet Leader."

"O.K., Tartan. I'm going down again."

From then on the battle was not between Cygnet section and the enemy, but between Roger and the atmospherics. With studied pedantry he mouthed his messages without result. Sometimes it seemed as if Ogilvie must be receiving them, for the position of the Spitfires came very near that of the plots as shown by the arrows pointing the enemy's course. Roger and the Sergeant screwed fingers into their free ears, turning their heads from side to side to try to catch the whisper of information from the air. Sometimes they could just head Ogilvie's voice, but it faded before they could distinguish what he was saying. Then the plots on the enemy ceased and the indications of Ogilvie's position jumped so wildly, and for minutes were missing altogether, that it was impossible to tell where he might be.

"Any luck?" Group asked Roger.

"Wretched luck, Sir. I can't get R.T. contact, and I'm not a bit sure where our aircraft are."

"I think the enemy's got away," the Group Controller said. "You'd better get your boys back."

"If I can," Roger muttered despondently. "Hullo, Cygnet Leader, Tartan calling. Return to base and land.

Over and over again he repeated the call, but nothing happened. There was not a sound from the Cygnet aircraft. There was not a sign of their existence. It was as if they had flown into the cloud and disappeared for ever.

Roger walked over to a W.A.A.F. sitting beside a row of telephone keys.

"Get the Royal Observer Corps and see if they've any news of two Spitfires. Anything will be helpful." He waited anxiously while she telephoned.

"They say that about five minutes ago," she reported, "two

aircraft sounding like Spitfires seemed to go over the coast, but they could not see them for cloud."

"Go on calling them, Sergeant," Roger told his assistant. "They may hear you even if we're not hearing them. Give them a course of two hundred and eighty degrees. If they can pick that up it's bound to bring them nearer home."

"Don't worry," Havering comforted him. "Ogilvie's much too old a hand to get lost. Remember our days. We didn't have R.T. and all these modern aids, and we got home all right."

"May be," said Roger, "but we were flying aircraft that we could land on a pocket handkerchief if we knew our business. Spitfires need a good bit more than that."

"Observer Corps," the W.A.A.F. telephonist reported, "say they've heard what sound like two Spitfires coming back over the coast, but they still can't see them."

The Sergeant's voice had a pleading note in it. He was still repeating at regular intervals the course for the Cygnet aircraft to fly.

"Observer Corps," the W.A.A.F. called eagerly, "say they've just seen two Spitfires flying West."

One plotter beside the map had begun to busy herself with arrows and details.

"Ask Group," Roger told Havering, "if there's anything else up in that area. If not, that should be Ogilvie for certain." He watched the plots steer an erratic course.

"Nothing else up," Havering said to him.

"Thank God!" Roger remarked.

"He's calling, Sir," the Sergeant said.

Roger grabbed his telephone. "Hallo, Tartan, Cygnet Leader calling. I say again, are you receiving me?"

"Hallo, Cygnet Leader, Tartan answering. Receiving you very faintly. Are you O.K.?"

"Hallo, Tartan, Cygnet Leader answering. Coming home now. Quite useless."

"Bunny, let Group know he's coming home. It's obviously been a washout.... Hallo, Cygnet Leader. Do you know your position?"

"Hallo, Tartan. I do now, but I've been a whale of a time finding it."

And so the aircraft came home. Ogilvie telephoned Roger

when he had got back into his dispersal hut.

"Not a pleasant trip, Roger. I have seldom been so frightened in my life. When we broke cloud we found we were diving straight into the water. It shook us a bit. In fact, Number Two has not properly recovered his speech yet! What about the Hun?"

"He just disappeared."

"Well, let's hope he dived into the water. I'm going to have some breakfast, Roger. My tummy's rumbling worse than ever. Good morning."

"Good morning, Scottie. Thank you for your effort."

"Not at all, Roger. Anything I can do at any time to oblige."

"I think we'd better tell Group," Roger said to Havering, "that it's not much use trying anything in these conditions."

But apparently the enemy had come to that conclusion too, for as the morning advanced the map in Operations Room remained blank and uninteresting.

At eight o'clock Roger rose stiffly from his chair to greet Placket, pink-faced, bright-eyed and scrubbed and shining almost offensively to those for whom the long night and dawn watch was now ending.

"Anything doing, Roger?" Placket asked.

"No," said Roger, "and not likely to be."

He collected his tobacco tin and the book which he had brought with him but had had no chance of reading, and he and Havering went out into the sombre morning and walked silently towards the Mess.

He had breakfasted comfortably, had eaten his porridge, herrings, eggs and bacon, toast and butter and marmalade, and now his second cup of coffee was beside him while he read the morning paper. There had been only one paper left on the polished oak table beside the hotplate, and Roger and George Cardew had had a scramble to secure it. George, a young Flight Lieutenant with a mop of light brown hair, suddenly abandoned the struggle, and drawing himself up to attention, said with some solemnity: "Squadron Leaders first, Sir."

George's hair showed some form of cohesion only on such formal occasions as guest nights or Mess dances. He grinned now with a friendly impudence and went off to the hotplate for his porridge. The D.F.C. he wore was a further step towards his great ambition, which was to be the youngest Squadron Leader in the Royal Air Force. Exactly a year before this morning, Roger had greeted George at the same spot.

"I've got a key now, Sir," George had said.

"What do you mean?"

"I'm twenty-one today . . . twenty-one today"—and George had burst into song and a little dance. He was a Pilot Officer then, with the battles of 1940 yet to come. Remembering this, Roger called to him: "Is today your birthday, George?"

George, on his way to another table with the plate of porridge in his hand, stopped suddenly and looked at Roger in surprise.

"How on earth did you know that, Sir?"

"I remember a year ago," Roger told him.

"What a memory, Sir, if I may say so—what a memory! I'm an old man, Sir: I'm in the sere and yellow, Sir—I'll soon be a lot older than you."

Roger had one of the sudden mental jerks that occasionally assailed him when talking to these young men. It always filled him with amazement to think that he was old enough to be the father of a George.

"Are you going to celebrate this time?" he asked.

"Much too old, Sir. But I shall be delighted to give you half a can of beer this evening." Springing to attention again and imperilling his porridge, George then passed on to his table.

At this hour the dining-room had few people in it. The pilots of the squadron which had been maintaining the state of early morning readiness and who were being relieved by another squadron had not yet arrived back in the Mess. The third squadron, which had a more relaxed state, was still invisible, and its members were no doubt contemplating from the comfort of their beds the dreary day outside their windows. Except for a few on duty, all those other people necessary to put an operational pilot into the air were getting up and preparing themselves for the day's work. Intelligence Officers, Administration Officers, Doctors, Engineers, Ground Defence staff, Equipment Officers, Operations Officers, Dentists and Padres and Accountants, were still shaving, or complaining of the temperature of the bath-water.

George had sidled up to Roger's table. He removed the milk-jug, against which Roger had propped his paper. Roger propped it up again in front of the sugar-sifter. George removed the sugar-sifter.

"You won't get the paper that way," Roger said to him.

"Oh! Sir!" George answered in reproachful tones.

"And by the way," Roger said, "what happens to all the papers in the mornings?"

"Can't say at all, Sir," George answered blandly.

"You know perfectly well that they all find their way to Dispersal Points and nobody in the Mess ever sees them again."

"Oh! Sir," said George again. "Who would ever dream of such a thing?"

"I'm going to ask the Mess Secretary," Roger told him, "to send an Orderly round to Dispersal Points to collect the hundreds of weekly papers, knives, forks, spoons, and cups and saucers, blankets and pillows, that must be there."

"That being so," replied George, making for the door, "I'd better telephone Dispersal Points and tell them he is coming round."

Roger went on sipping his coffee.

The W.A.A.F. waitresses stood round the servery door in their pink smocks. Amongst them was one rather harassed-looking waiter in a white coat. His main problem was to see that the W.A.A.F. waitresses performed their duties efficiently, but the problem was increased because the W.A.A.F.s were in charge of a woman Corporal. He was only a Leading Aircraftsman, or L.A.C.—the equivalent of a Lance-Corporal—and the senior members of the Mess still looked to him to preserve order in the dining-room; but the stony stare of the W.A.A.F. Corporal daunted him. He had become much thinner since the W.A.A.F.s had entered the Mess.

Behind the servery a Yorkshire Sergeant held sway over his kitchen. He was a round-faced, pink-cheeked young man with a passion for cleanliness. His attack on cockroaches had been one of the major actions of the war, and now his kitchen was spotless, and so were the cooks who served under him. The big pot of porridge bubbled volcanically on the kitchen stove, the herrings were in the oven, and passed from there to the hotplate in the dining-room. The bacon and eggs fried happily on the gas-range, and the toast browned and crisped under the electric grill. Round the huge kitchen table in the centre of the tiled space the cooks were already busy with preparations for the mid-day meal, and at the back of the kitchen and in the adjacent scullery the Mess and Kitchen Orderlies worked in the clatter of cutlery and china and the swish of hot water. The Sergeant Cook was a shy man; he could not be persuaded to serve in the Mess but left that duty to his Corporal, who, in his white chef's hat, coat and apron, stood behind the hotplate at mid-day and evening meals and served the queue that formed in front of him. But though the Sergeant Cook was shy, his views on the conduct of his kitchen and on the unsuitability of any food sent to him to prepare, could be concise and vigorous.

A few more people were coming in to breakfast now. First, the Intelligence Officer, tall, fair, very quiet, and, as befitted his temporary profession, eager for information on all subjects, from the result of last night's snooker game to the possibilities of action for the day. Next, the Station Adjutant, a fair man also, with a fair moustache and a reserved bearing. When he entered for meals, he usually looked round cautiously to circumvent the possibilities of sudden attack, for sooner or later some angry individual would express his heated views about petrol coupons, and the Adjutant would become even more reserved, look straight in front of him, grow pale, and get indigestion in consequence.

"Good morning, Harvey," Roger said.

"Good morning, Sir," the Adjutant replied quite genially, for Roger did not possess a car.

At the end of the table, the Squadron Leader Administration had seated himself, and he too was on his guard for the individual who was sure to sit down beside him and open the conversation with the words: "About this question of establishment...."

But most of the refectory tables arranged in rows with their white table-cloths were still unoccupied, and from the large oil-painting hanging in the dais where the orchestra sometimes played, placid cows looked out from their byre.

Roger rose and, putting the paper purposefully under his arm, he made for the double swing doors. As he reached them, the Group Captain entered. Roger stood aside, and saw him again as he had seen him on many mornings—a man in his early thirties, just above medium height, broadly built, with a grim determined face, long upper lip, dark restless eyes, and a wide mouth which could snap over a jaw thrust forward as if it were ready to carve through anything on sea or land or in the air. Usually the face was set in lines of quiet pugnacity, not of ill-humour or vindictiveness, but watchfully belligerent for anything hostile that might cross its path. He was a man of few words and of immediate decisions. And then, suddenly, all those lines in the face could readjust themselves into delighted laughter; the nose would crinkle and the eyes screw up, and Group Captain Faversham would suddenly look twenty years old again. Then the wide mouth would snap down once more and the jaw thrust forward and the dark eyes restlessly resume their watchfulness.

"Good morning, Roger," he said as he passed. "Anything likely to happen?"

"Very doubtful, Sir," Roger said. "The weather report is pretty dreadful."

The Group Captain nodded and passed on to sit at the end of the table. The harassed waiter darted forward, looking happy at last, for this was where no W.A.A.F. Corporal could interfere.

Roger made for an easy-chair in the anteroom. Someone had left the wireless switched on after the eight-o'clock news, and a brass band was blaring strident marches. Roger turned it off and settled down, the paper in his hands and a determination in his mind to keep awake until a suitable time had elapsed between breakfast and a bath. It was always the same—a few minutes after settling down in the deep leather chair with the tired springs, the bottom lines of print on the newspaper would begin to climb upwards and march one into the other in an increasing rush, until Roger's head fell back and Roger's mouth fell open and he was asleep—a revolting sight for all who might enter to see.

The cleaners were now busy in the passage-ways, brawny young W.A.A.F.s with their shirt-sleeves rolled back as they polished and swept and dusted yesterday away. It always seemed as if there were somehow a difference about the nature of work on an Operational Station—a something of greater readiness, of greater cheerfulness, as if those on the ground mixing with those of the air were determined that they too would do their part, however unexciting it might seem. Here indeed was a fantastic life—a Fighter Station on the doorstep of a great city, with its own impressive buildings, its amusements and flower-beds, with its aircraft soaring within sight of the heart of the Metropolis and disappearing south-east into the blue haze, into a whirlpool of cannon fire and machine-gun fire and coming back for tea and buttered toast and an evening at the pictures. Even those of the meanest imagination could feel something of these astonishing opposites, and the cleaners picked a crushed cigarette stub off a floor with greater cheerfulness than ever they would have shown in some large hotel, redolent with the odours of countless well-fed civilians. They breathed on the silver inkwell lying on the ceremonial table in the entrance where the visitors' book was kept; they dusted the carved wooden emblems of the squadrons, and they whisked away the last dejected tankard from the window-sill. In the east and west wings, where the bedrooms lay, the batmen scurried about, filling baths, polishing shoes and buttons, brushing and folding clothes, and recounting the exploits of the owners of those tunics which bore wings. In the billiard-room a little Orderly was sitting re-tipping cues, and in the card-room a big Orderly was using a vacuum cleaner. The door to the bar stood open, for the bar waiters were bringing in supplies from the cellar, and the Corporal in charge was writing up his stock-book. The inside of the cupboards showed cigarettes, tobacco, toothpaste, soap, aspirin, fruit salts, toothbrushes, safety razors, notepaper, and the many odds and ends that might be forgotten on shopping expeditions outside camp. In the Mess Secretary's office the book-keeper had already begun his troubled hunt for an elusive three-and-ninepence difference in his cash balance.

George Cardew had entered the anteroom and, seeing Roger asleep, had secured the paper by pulling it gently from his limp fingers. Just outside the window, Tom, the gardener, was busy at a flower-bed. He was a thickset, red-faced man with a little bristling moustache and very candid eyes. He had always seemed one of the happiest men Roger had ever met. He loved his work, he loved Nature, and he had an absolute faith in the rightness of its workings. He had watched over the Mess garden for six years, and now in war his pride was the account-book which he kept, and in which he noted day by day the market value of the produce which he delivered to the Mess kitchen from the vegetables he had planted and nurtured. He seldom spoke to anyone, and if asked his opinion on gardening matters, he would sometimes answer: "I'll have to wait another forty years before I've any experience." Placed in a colony of cheap modern houses, Tom's garden was an oasis, for all around the Station was evidence of the enlightened civilising influence of the last twenty years—row upon row of cheap little semi-detached dwellings thrown together with immature wood and ill-mixed plaster, but appealing to the same eyes that gave so much trade to manufacturers of imitation jewellery. And when the bombing had come, the cheap little houses had split open, and the little gardens had returned to their earlier tangle of weeds, and the unmade roads had filled their potholes with muddy water. Those who had been buying their dream home for fifteen-and-sixpence a week could now return and see the handful of dust of which it had been created. Even on this dreary day, the garden shone under the grey sky, and Tom bent over his flower-beds helping the only beauty which he understood.

The hands on the electric clock standing on the mantelpiece above the fireplace were pointing to a quarter to ten when Roger wakened. His neck was stiff from the cramped position in which his head had fallen, and one arm imprisoned under his recumbent body was numb. He picked it up with his free hand and started to massage it.

Regarding him with amusement and with assumed disgust, were two figures standing with their backs to the empty fireplace. One was James Glebe. He stood in his characteristic attitude: legs a little apart, hands clasped behind his back, head lowered, and his steady eyes looking from beneath the heavy eyebrows. His hair was, as usual, immaculate. These immaculate heads, Roger thought to himself as he took in the vision of Glebe's face, seem one of the features of the R.A.F. Glebe had been flying operationally since a date in late winter some five months ago. Before the war he had been a member of a squadron famous in the old war, and now famous again in this. He had worked through those happy days of before-the-war, and gained the unrivalled training of the pilots who were to hurl back the massed might of the Luftwaffe in the 1940 days. But shortly before the war, James Glebe, to his own chagrin, had been appointed Operations Officer of the Station. Nobody particularly wanted the job; the thought of messing about with little coloured counters and then sliding numerals and letters into little holders and subsequently pushing them round a large map standing waist-high on the floor did not appeal to most people, who infinitely preferred to have their Wednesday afternoons free for their own amusement. So James Glebe found himself appointed as Operations Officer. Together with the Accountant Officer, the Engineer Officer and other unwilling but obedient spirits, the organisation of Operations Room took shape.

Recruiting for the R.A.F. Volunteer Reserve had opened, and in the evenings or at week-ends a team was assembled from the residents of the locality: bank clerks, insurance clerks, warehousemen, printers, tailors—some of all sorts, the volunteers of Britain who have always had to win her wars. They used to arrive straight from their work, from their gardens or allotments, and Flying Officer James Glebe would lecture them and train them so that when the eleven strokes of the bell sounded on September 3rd, 1939, Operations Room was manned, and James Glebe sat on the dais ready for what might come, with his bank clerks and his printers grouped tensely below him, easing their unusual collars and smoothing their uniforms to their assorted shapes. Then, after the first electric few days, things had settled down. Henry Clay had shortly joined from his Auxiliary Squadron; Placket and Havering and others arrived to learn and master the duties of Operations "B" Officers—the eyes, ears, dictionaries and encyclopædias of the Controllers. People had come and gone and early 1940 had found James Glebe and Henry Clay as Flight Lieutenants, with Roger as a Controller, and one other whose stay had been short until Placket took his place. Promotion to Squadron Leader followed, but James Glebe was not satisfied. At twenty-five his body and mind ached for the air—ached to be out of the office chair and into the cockpit. He would fly non-operationally when aircraft could be spared, and there was always an exultant ring in his voice when he called the Controller from ten thousand feet over the aerodrome. Quietly over a tankard of beer and puffing his pipe, he would urge the great fighter leader Bo'sun Spritt to get him back to the squadron to which he belonged.

"Any luck, James?" Roger would say.

James would answer darkly: "My Fifth Column is at work"—but he could not be spared. The great battles to come needed his knowledge and his organising powers on the ground, and the aftermath of the great battles needed his organising powers again. He withdrew more into himself; but for Bo'sun Spritt, he seldom spoke to pilots, as if he wished to avoid their coolly appraising look at the rings of Squadron-Leadership on his tunic, and their knowledge that he did not fly with them.

And then at last the day had come: he returned from leave to find he was posted as a Flight Lieutenant to one of the squadrons at the Station. Even as he was told, the brooding look fell from his face; the slim, alert figure seemed to stretch even taller than its tall height; the rare smile flooded and creased the face; the solemnity and caution of the voice vanished: James Glebe, aged twenty-five, was again a free man among his peers.

There stood Flight Lieutenant James Glebe, pilot, ex-Squadron Leader and, did he but know it, soon to be Squadron Leader again and to achieve his dreams.

Beside him was Wing Commander Romilly, second-in-command and Wing Commander in charge of flying under Group Captain Faversham. But where James Glebe's head was bent and brooding at this moment, the Wing Commander's was held high and tilted back. It was a face compound of Red Indian and Viking, a lynx-like face, eyes set wide with imperceptibly an upward tilt, high, wide cheekbones and the face narrowing past the arched nose to a pointed chin. It seemed always to survey the world from an aerial angle. He was older than James Glebe, but not much; he was twenty-nine.

Roger's bemused eyes took in the two of them until they could focus properly, while he still slowly massaged the dead arm.

"Roger," said James very gravely, "you've dribbled."

"Roger," said the Wing Commander, "you have dribbled on your tunic."

Roger grabbed for a handkerchief, but the accusation was not true; it was the standing joke against Roger when caught asleep in the anteroom. He began to struggle to his feet.

"Let me help you up," James said solicitously, coming forward.

"Since you went back to flying, James," Roger answered, waving him away, "you never seem to have anything to do. Suppose you come back to Ops, and do a job of work."

"I leave that to my seniors, both in rank and, if I may say so, in years."

Roger walked unsteadily towards the door. The Wing Commander called after him: "I should wear a bib in future, Roger."

The telephone was ringing in the cabin near the entrance, and as there seemed to be no Orderly immediately available Roger answered it himself.

"Officers' Mess here," he said.

"Can I speak to Squadron Leader MacMurray?"

"MacMurray speaking."

"Oh! Sir, will you speak to Squadron Leader Placket?"

"Hallo, Roger," Placket said to him. "Do you know anything about a bomber that came adrift at about eleven o'clock last night?"

"I believe one was in trouble," Roger replied, "just as he was crossing in on the other side, but that's all I was told."

"Well, it appears that he went in the drink about twenty miles off their coast. An early reconnaissance aircraft thinks he saw what may have been a dinghy. Group have got the approximate position, and they want Thistle Squadron to see what can be done. But I just wondered if you had any information."

"No," said Roger. "Sorry. I hope you find him."

"I'll get busy," Placket answered, and Roger rang off.

The air outside revived him. The rain had ceased, but the heavy, lowering clouds persisted, though a stronger wind was blowing. He passed Tom, bending over his flower-bed.

"How are the vegetables going, Tom?" he said.

Tom straightened up and wiped his hands against the legs of his blue dungarees. Then he pushed the peak of his cap a little up. These were always his preliminary actions before answering a question.

"Quite nice, Sir, quite nice. But of course I could do so much better if I'd the help. But these batmen—these batmen, Sir . . . you know how it is. If you're not brought up to love Nature—well, I suppose it doesn't appeal. Any help they're told to give me is more of a hindrance. Still, we've got some nice . . ."—and he rattled off his list of onions, potatoes, peas, beans, tomatoes, and the seasonal supplies to feed the pilots yet to come.

"What about fruit, Tom?"

The two of them stood regarding the surroundings of the Mess garden—the young trees, oaks and chestnuts, birch and may, that waved their summer foliage against the background.

"If only they had been fruit," said Tom.

"I know," Roger answered. "I suppose we've been so used to apples from Canada, pears from Australia and plums from South Africa that we never thought to plant fruit-trees when this garden was first planned."

He turned his back on the pretty uselessness of the birches, and made for the house where his room was. He went by the garden fence of the Group Captain's house, where the snorts of the Group Captain's pig erupted on the air.

"Pigs," the Group Captain had said one evening in the Mess. Everyone paid respectful attention. "Why don't we have pigs?" the Group Captain asked. "There's enough swill from the Mess to feed a score of them." "I'll show you," the Group Captain said a little later, after the heavy silence. "I'll get a pig myself. I'll show you."

The pig was now evidencing its existence as Roger passed. He turned in by the kitchen entrance of the house which he shared with James Glebe, Henry Clay and others.

One batman was cleaning buttons in the kitchen. Another, looking rather like a coy housemaid, was dusting the stairs.

"Bath!" said Roger in a loud voice, and to no one in particular, as he went up to his room. "Yes, Sir," replied two voices simultaneously.

Roger's windows looked out to the right over the C.O.'s garden, and to the left towards the Mess buildings—to the front and in the foreground to a patch of waste land, where a turfed air-raid shelter wound its labyrinthine way, then to some wooden huts, and beyond that to ploughed fields and the distant skyline. He had looked out of them so often, seen the changes of the seasons, seen the woolly balls of anti-aircraft fire come closer and closer, seen the aircraft streak across the limited vision, seen by night the enormous flash of bursting bombs as they wakened the dark exterior to vivid light. The room was clean, but impersonal. Roger neither loved it nor hated it; it was just somewhere in which to sleep and to keep his few clothes.

Those he was wearing he now took off. He rummaged in the drawers of the dressing-table for clean shirt and vest and pants and socks, and by the time he had put in his cuff-links and attached his sock-suspenders, the bath was ready. By the side of his bed he found an old copy of *Punch*; with it under his arm he went to the bathroom and gently lowered himself into the hot water. He dried his hands, picked up *Punch* and leant back. He was in danger of falling asleep again as the water and the waves of somnolence lapped over him. *Punch* was almost too heavy to hold. He dropped it over the edge of the bath, and with a moan he raised himself to see that he had not dropped it into a puddle. He soaped himself and brushed himself, and the fumes of heat and sleep intoxicated him. He settled back again and regarded a fly fixedly. It was crawling on the inside of the bath. A little ripple of water caught it, and in a moment it was swimming vigorously alongside Roger's body. He put a finger under it and lifted it on the ledge. It crawled up the wall, up and up, and settled down to dry out near the ceiling. Roger told himself he had been stupid. Flies breed fast, but the wretched insect had fallen in the "drink", and that was enough for one day.

It set him thinking of how the fighter pilots from the Station from time to time had "fallen in the drink", and how the fast little high-speed launches put out from the shores of Britain and picked them up and brought them home again. It set him thinking of their voices as they were about to bale out, and the adventures they recounted when they returned, and of those who did not return.

He remembered Mac, with the wild and rebellious eye, who pretended to resent all authority and who never failed to carry out the hardest of orders. Mac's most valuable possession was a silver flask that might have been made for Falstaff. He conserved in it some special brandy which he had picked up in France, and which he carried in his hip pocket for the final emergency of falling in the sea. The day came when Mac did fall in the sea. Nobody knew he had gone, and he had nothing but his life-saving jacket—his "Mae West"—to keep him afloat. No rescue boats were aware of his plight, no searching aircraft had been told to look for him. So he floated in the water, quaffing the contents of his flask as philosophically as he might. And then—with the water carved into curling foam by her bows—a destroyer, like a spirited horse drawn up short, had sighted him and stopped. Mac was fished out. He stood swaying dizzily on the destroyer's deck while puddles of water formed around him as the sea poured from his bedraggled figure. The brandy had taken effect, and it was that, and not the destroyer's motion, that caused the wavering of his arms and legs. The Commander of the destroyer eyed him good-humouredly. He had been pulled from a lingering death, and a little banter suited the occasion.

"I say," said the destroyer's Commander, "you're making an awful mess on my deck!"

Mac's rebellious eye looked up and concentrated on the naval man opposite.

"I never," said Mac, "stay where I'm not wanted." And he walked straight into the sea again.

But they hauled him out once more, and Mac's only regret was that he could not replace the brandy.

The wind was blowing with almost gale force when two aircraft of Thistle Squadron left the forward aerodrome to disappear into the cloud scudding low over the disturbed sea.

Placket had given them a bearing and the area of search, while the Navy had detailed two of its high-speed launches to set out for the same position. Two more of Thistle Squadron had hurried off to try to pick up the launches and escort them through the storm. They cruised about like well-trained dogs picking up the scent, and at last they found the two shapes below making high speed through the waves, with a strong South-west wind behind them. As long as they kept the boats in sight their task was the easier one, for they had not to trouble about courses, but only to protect their charges.

For the first section it was a different proposition. They had no mark upon which to position themselves, but only a waste of water with wretched visibility and poor radio communication because of their low height.

Placket's voice came to them in fading whispers, as if the gale were blowing it away, and he was standing in Ops. Room, too concentrated in his endeavours to sit down, as he tried to guide the aircraft in their search and not to lose touch with them altogether. His mind had seized on the plight of this lonely dinghy that had been drifting away North-east and from all chance of help for so many hours through the night and the miserable dawn.

Thistle Blue Section turned in wide sweeps and in figures of eight, scanning every wave and trough below them. The minutes passed by. Before long Blue Section would have to be relieved and the search go on. And still no report came from them.

"Is the next section ready to take off?" Placket asked.

"It will be off in about five minutes, Sir."

"Tell them to steer the same course as Blue Section and to carry out the same search."

"Blue Section's calling, Sir," the Deputy Controller said.

"Thistle Blue One calling," a thin voice was saying. "Have seen something. May be a dinghy."

"Hold the next section," Placket ordered Ops B. "We may be able to tell them the exact position.... Hallo, Thistle Blue One. Stick close to the dinghy, and we'll try to get your bearings."

"Hallo, Tartan, Thistle Blue One answering. It's very difficult. Visibility is so rotten. I can see the dinghy now. One occupant."

"Thanks, Thistle Blue One. Hang on. Your relief will be on its way."

One occupant, thought Placket. So the rest of the bomber crew had gone, and again his imagination played round this solitary member of an aircraft crew that had set forth with such eagerness and which had now been reduced to the man tossing in the North Sea with hope reawakened.

Rapid calculations had been made and the position of Blue Section ascertained. Placket gave detailed instructions to the relief.

"Get going as fast as you can," he said, "and tell the squadron to put another section up to relieve the one over the boats." He telephoned Group and gave them the same particulars.

"Good work," Group said. "We'll pass it to the Navy."

"I only hope the next section going out can pick up Blue Section," Plackett remarked. "It will be damnable if, having found the dinghy, we lose it again."

"It's Black Section going," Ops. B told him, "and White Section to take over the boats."

With extreme patience Placket guided the fresh aircraft, but while White Section had little difficulty in finding the launches, Black Section swept and circled for minute after minute until they had at last found Blue as it was calling that it must abandon the dinghy and come home.

A blank descended on Roger, and he came back to consciousness with a start in water that was almost cold. He levered himself up, and stepping out of his bath, put his wet foot straight on to the centre page of *Punch*. . . .

As he emerged from the bathroom door, he met Henry Clay.

"Have you only just got up, Havana?" he asked.

"Yes," Havana replied abstractedly. "Yes." But he paused amiably before going downstairs.

Roger, standing there in his dressing-gown and slippers, could see Havana with the light from the hall windows on him as he stood with his hand on the bannister. He was tall and fair, with an eager mobile face, strong lines of humour on each side of the mouth, and blue eyes that would gaze above the head of a speaker, only momentarily concentrating on him before they gazed away again into unseen distances. He was a man of alert mind, with a capacity for cutting through verbiage to the kernel of a problem, with a strong sense of the ridiculous, and with a point of view very often opposite to the obvious and very often right. The exterior could appear brittle, but not hard, as if to mask many emotions not to be shared. His sense of justice could be quickly outraged; his impatience with slow-wittedness quickly manifested; his annoyance at stupidity quickly voiced. But lurking behind the lines on either side of the mouth his sense of the ridiculous was always twitching to be shown, and in the midst of his ready vocabulary of scorn would come some phrase that would render him and his listener helpless with laughter. He cared little for his outward personal appearance, and he carried with him something of an eighteenth-century elegance that even his very old cap and his much too small overcoat could not hide. He was never seen to travel on leave or on any long journey with luggage other than a diminutive leather case about the size of a large envelope. His delight was an assault on pomposity of all kinds, and the axe of his iconoclasm feared nothing.

Standing there in the light of that watery day, Roger could transpose his figure to Operations Room when, alongside one another, James Glebe and Havana and Roger had controlled the squadrons as the screech and blast of bombs had filled the air around. Roger, with some sub-conscious reaction from the old war, had descended to one knee and, telephone in hand, had called his messages to the aircraft from the proximity of Havana's left leg. He could remember trying to amuse himself by unhitching Havana's suspenders from his socks, and the vague little kicks that Havana had given as he, too, concentrated on his work. Havana was now the senior Controller and the Operations Officer, which work he had taken over when James Glebe went back to flying.

"When are you on again, Roger?" Havana asked.

"Five o'clock this evening. Do you want me for anything?"

"No," said Havana, still looking out of the window. "No."

"Are you going up to Ops.?"

"Yes," Havana answered. "Is there anything in?"

"Nothing urgent," Roger told him.

"Any operations?"

"Nothing yet. There's not likely to be anything today.... Maybe tomorrow," Roger said, making for his bedroom.

"See you at lunch," Havana called as he went downstairs.

A batman had cleaned Roger's shoes and buttons and had laid out his clothes for him. The trousers and the tunic were very shiny, and the elbows and cuffs of the tunic sleeves were bound with leather where rubbing on hard desks had frayed them. Roger sat with a pair of scissors and trimmed the whiskers off the rings of rank, ruefully deciding that money must be spent on a new uniform. He contemplated his bed, but found that the overmastering desire for sleep had left him; so he decided to be social, and to spend his hours before the next day watch pottering about the Station, at the risk of interfering with people at their work. At last, washed and shaved, hair brushed, cap on, respirator slung in the correct fashion, hands properly gloved, Roger stepped out of the house for his walk round the Station before lunch.

Thistle sections had taken off one after the other, and still the boats crept towards the last member of the bomber's air crew. There was one agonising period when the dinghy had been lost to view and it seemed as if the whole effort was to be fruitless. For long stretches Placket could get no contact with either of the sections and was left in fearful doubt lest everything had gone wrong. Successive positions of the rescuers, when they could be recognised, showed that they and the dinghy must be drifting farther and farther away. The little rubber boat was bound on a long, unhappy voyage if it could not be saved in time.

"Heaven knows," Placket said to the Sergeant, "what those boats are going through. It must be ghastly."

"They should be getting nearer now, Sir."

"Hallo, Thistle Green One. Rescue boats are not many miles to your South-west. Keep a sharp look out for aircraft escorting them."

Green One did not answer.

"Hallo, Thistle Red One. Green Section is over the dinghy not many miles to your North-east. Report when you can see them."

"O.K."

"How are things going?" Group asked Placket.

"We're doing our best, Sir. We're still over the dinghy and its one occupant, and the boats are beating up fairly close."

"It's a grand show," said Group. "Pity about the one occupant. The other poor fellows must have gone. Green and Red have been up a good time. What are you going to do?"

"I'll have to relieve them, Sir. The difficulty is to get the succeeding sections over the right spots."

"I know," said the Group Controller sympathetically. "Keep it up. You're doing very well."

"I thought this was going to be a quiet morning," Placket groaned to Ops. B. "I haven't had to concentrate so hard for months."

CHAPTER TWO

The sentry at the main gate saluted smartly as Roger turned on to the chief road leading to the Station. On his left lay the Guardroom, and outside it was a glass case containing souvenirs from the last war—pieces of Zeppelin, cartridge cases, scraps of anti-aircraft shell and one or two parts of German aircraft which had been displayed there for many years; for even in that first war the Station had been an aerodrome, and Roger had landed on it many times to take tea or other refreshment with the pilots of those days. Few people ever looked at the souvenirs; occasionally a new recruit might be seen bending over them and trying with a vacant eye and unreceptive face to read some story in them.

Beyond the Guardroom side-roads and buildings stretched to the left, the roads leading to the Station parade-ground, and the buildings housing airmen or gas-equipment stores, or various of the other activities now crowded on to a Station originally designed for many less than those at present employed. To the right of the main road were other roads leading to transport, equipment stores, armoury and workshops.

Roger continued on his way, and turned in at a doorway marked "Intelligence Block". Knocking on an inside door, he went into a large room where the Station Intelligence Officer was seated in his usual attitude with a telephone to his ear. Looking very intent and continuing a rapid conversation, the I.O. produced a cigarette case, held it towards Roger, by some process of sleight of hand flicked a matchbox into view and pointed to a cup of tea on a tray. Then with a more embracing movement he waved towards a chair. Roger sat down, sipped his tea, lit his cigarette, and looked round.

The walls were covered with maps. One vast map was decorated with many coloured pins, flags and strands of coloured wool. It purported to show every sort of detail that could possibly be wanted: the position of aerodromes, balloon barrages, gun sites, searchlight sites, and the thousand items of information concerning that area of the countryside at war.

On another wall a huge mosaic of photographs laboriously pieced together gave a pilot's eye view of a large section of enemy-occupied territory. On yet another wall were diagrams and photographs of many types of aircraft, and dotted about on tables stood ingenious coloured models of aircraft made to scale.

The Intelligence Officer finished his conversation and lit a cigarette of his own.

"Well, Sir," he said, turning to Roger, "this is a very welcome visit. And what can we do for you?"

"You've done it," said Roger, pointing to the cup of tea. "What's the gen?"

The Intelligence Officer looked a little startled. "I've never heard you use R.A.F. slang before," he said.

"That's why I use it," Roger answered. "Where does 'gen' come from? I mean what's it derivation?"

The Intelligence Officer's hand instinctively strayed towards a file, and then, realising that this was a question not card-indexed, cross-referenced and filed in triplicate, he pulled thoughtfully at his cigarette.

"Gen," he repeated. "What about 'intelli-gence', with the accent on the last syllable?"

"I suppose that's good enough," Roger answered; "but what's the news, anyhow, since I came off duty?"

"Nothing, except an air-sea rescue going on. There doesn't seem to be much chance of anything unless the weather lifts. Then I suppose they'll be mounting another show."

"What'll be the number of the next one?" Roger asked.

"Let's see," said the Intelligence Officer, his hands straying yet again for a file which this time yielded him immediate information. "The one the other day was operation order number one two two, so we're due for number one two three any time now. Were you controlling during the last one, Sir?"

"No," said Roger. "I was off camp that day. I heard very few details."

"Ah!" said the Intelligence Officer, grabbing yet another file. "I have all the Combat Reports here, if you'd like to read them."

"No," said Roger. "We didn't lose anyone, did we?"

"No, thank God. We were close escort to the bombers, and

they and our lads all got back intact."

"Anything happen to the high cover and the supporting wings?"

"I haven't had the Group summary yet," the Intelligence Officer replied. "But I think for once it was a fairly uneventful outing. The Huns just didn't want to play."

"Was the Group Captain leading?"

"No, he had to attend a conference, so the Wing Commander took them."

"And we didn't get anything?"

"No, we had very few squirts."

"Funny," mused Roger, "to look back to 1940, when the air above us was full of the hum of machines and the burst of anti-aircraft shells and screaming dives and machine-gun fire, when the public could look up and see what was going on and feel that they were getting their pennyworth. Now I don't suppose many of them know anything about what the fighters are doing. The noise and the fury have passed out of their sky, and all they see is a pretty pattern of squadrons in wing formation, and then, some two hours later, aircraft coming home again. Except for the larger numbers, it might be the conditions of peace-time flying once more."

"I suppose that's true," the Intelligence Officer replied. "People often say to me, when I'm off the Station, 'What are the fighters doing these days? We don't see much of them or read much about them.' "

"And yet," Roger said, "we've lost some of the finest pilots the world has ever seen. Do you remember how we used to say last year that our losses must inevitably be greater than the enemy's once we went over his side of the line to fight?"

"Yes," the Intelligence Officer replied, "I suppose we all anticipated a much higher proportion of losses to ourselves than to the enemy. Yet"—and here he reached for another file—"the figures speak for themselves. We still bring them down in the proportion of two or three to one of our own."

"I like your mosiac," Roger said, nodding at the photographic map.

"It's really the fighter-sweep country, so that they can 'pinpoint' themselves when they get over there."

Roger strolled over and looked at it, and even at a glance he could recognise the one stretch over which he had flown so often and so long. But now the earth was not scarred with the confused and interminable lines of trenches. One spot after another he rediscovered and recognised. There the La Bassée Canal, there the slag-heaps near Lens, and the regular patterns of all the little houses of the miners. Maybe in that very spot today they had an anti-aircraft battery, the father of which had fired at Roger. He stood thoughtfully for a long while, mentally winging over the territory photographed on the wall. His mind shuttlecocked between the young faces of today and the young faces of 1916. They were the same faces, with the same look in the eye, the same smile round the lips, the same carriage of the body, the same outlook, very nearly the same jargon, and the same courtesy that was almost humiliating to those older than themselves.

The Intelligence Officer was back at his telephone again, and Roger slipped out of the door. He turned in to the next building up the highroad of the Station. A cheerful Colonel had waved his hand from a ground-floor office, and Roger had saluted back. The Colonel was wearing his snappy little coloured forage cap. It was interesting, thought Roger, how most of the Army always wore their caps in offices, and he wondered vaguely at the psychological reasons for the decision to enliven khaki with little coloured caps. Even if they had something to do with the old school tie, the old school tie must have had an original reason behind it somewhere. Pity, thought Roger as he went up some stone stairs, that we ever gave up sprigged waistcoats and ruffles and cravats, and then we might not have heard so much about the old school tie.

He knocked on a door, and hearing a cheerful "Come in", he entered the Accountant Officer's room. That individual was seated confronting yards of paper. He was a volatile and emphatic man, ready to demonstrate at an instant's notice, and with the apt quotation of countless authorities, that nobody was entitled to anything they thought they should have; and then, having surveyed the crestfallen enquirer with triumph, he would quote many other authorities to show him how the thing should be done properly. Seeing Roger, he picked up a heavy, rounded ruler and beat a sharp rat-tat-tat on the wall alongside him. A W.A.A.F. appeared like a genie out of a lamp.

"Tea for the Squadron Leader," he said.

"God!" growled Roger. "I poisoned my stomach twenty years ago, and I'm doing it again."

"Then don't have it," snapped the Accountant Officer.

"I want it," said Roger.

"Get it!" said the Accountant Officer, and the W.A.A.F. vanished. "Anything?" asked the Accountant Officer.

"A friendly visit," Roger answered.

"Well, Sir," the Accountant Officer replied, "if you've nothing to do, I've plenty." But he opened his cigarette case and proffered it. The W.A.A.F. brought two cups of tea, and the Accountant Officer sat back and smiled.

"Do you really mean to say, Sir," he asked, "that you haven't come in about any travel claims, monthly allowances, pay queries or income-tax problems?"

"No," said Roger. "I'm respectably bankrupt, and money doesn't worry me any more."

"It still seems a worry to plenty of people outside," the Accountant Officer replied.

"Perhaps that's why I'm glad I'm out of it all," Roger told him. "There's a feeling of peace in knowing precisely where you stand in a community of men who have only one aim."

"Meaning?" the Accountant Officer queried.

"The struggle to withstand the common enemy," Roger said, "instead of the individual hand-to-hand struggle for existence as everything seemed to be in peace-time. Do you regret giving up your business and coming into the Service?"

"No," the Accountant Officer said thoughtfully. "No. One has moments of being pretty thoroughly galled by one's ex-associates, whose chief motive still seems to be profit. But I agree with you—I'd sooner be with an outfit where that motive is absent and only the job itself is worth the doing. But I wish to God," the Accountant Officer went on, picking up a ruler as if to flay somebody with it, "that everybody felt that way."

"What's annoying you?" Roger asked him.

"All this pap to persuade people to work. 'Good evening, dear Public. This is Uncle Treacle speaking. I want to talk to you for a moment or two about the War effort—your War effort. Don't think for one moment that I am complaining, for you are simply magnificent, one and all of you. But if our enemies are going to be beaten, I am sure you will agree with me that we will possibly have to make up our minds to work almost as hard as they do. Don't be frightened at the word "work". It is not so bad, really. There are nice high wages and lots of fun and games—dances, concert parties, social gatherings—girls meet boys, and vice versa—and those that are doing it are really quite enjoying it. I know times are hard for you and you can't have everything you want, but there still seem to be so many people—may I say it?—not pulling their weight to the fullest extent. We all may have to eat a little less, use the car a little less—in fact, go without to a teeny weeny degree. So, dear people, would you just think it over? You girls, for example. Why not try on the uniform of one of your friends in the Forces? I am sure you will be delighted with the attractiveness of your appearance. And you boys awaiting call-up—work a little harder and earn lots of lovely money which, remember, you will be able to take with you when you have the proud distinction of wearing khaki or blue.' Pah!" said the Accountant Officer, smashing the ruler on the desk. "Yes, I agree, it's better to be out of it all." He swallowed his tea at a gulp. Then he frowned at Roger. "You are taking up my time, Sir."

So Roger rose to his feet, and as he emerged from the room, the ruler beat a loud rat-tat-tat on the wall again.

Still filled with the spirit of a parish visitor, Roger had knocked at yet another door.

"Come in," said a voice, and confronting him in the formality of their uniforms with their stiff collars and black ties, with their caps severely straight and their hair essentially feminine, sat the two W.A.A.F. Officers who controlled the fate of the assorted womanhood of the Station.

Roger saluted with even more than usual gravity. A Flight Officer, the senior of the two, with an uncontrollable motion put her hand up to feel her hair in case any loose strands should be dangling unbecomingly.

"Good morning, Sir," she said. "How nice to see you! We were just going out, but let's have a cup of tea."

"No," said Roger, and there was almost ferocity in his voice. And then in an apologetic tone he said: "My inside's swimming with it, but if you're going out I'll call again another day."

"Rather not," said the Flight Officer. "Sit down. Have a cigarette."

"Are you just off to inspect your drabs?" Roger asked, removing his cap in the presence of ladies.

"We are not," said the Flight Officer with firmness. "We are about to inspect some of the quarters of the W.A.A.F. personnel."

"That's what I said," Roger confirmed. "You're off to see your drabs."

The second W.A.A.F. Officer, who did not know Roger very well, was looking pained.

"Don't mind him," the Flight Officer said to her. "He's got a poor opinion of W.A.A.F.s."

"I have not," Roger answered, this time seriously, "and you ought to know I haven't. How long have we been here together, Betty?"

Betty smiled in a friendly way at him.

"Long enough," she said, "to have seen many things happen. You see"—and she turned in explanation to the other W.A.A.F. Officer—"Roger is one of those men who want it to be assumed that they are confirmed misogynists because they have really got a very soft spot for us."

"At the same time," Roger said, becoming argumentative, "I'll never get used to the swinging of arms and the stamping of feet and the throwing out of chests and the general pageant of military behaviour from creatures in skirts."

"But," the second officer broke in, "we must have some standard of discipline and some code of behaviour."

"Then why," asked Roger, putting his face forward belligerently, "have you had to borrow it from men? I'd always hoped that women had a standard and a code right above us, but now I half expect your Sergeants to start growing moustaches."

The second W.A.A.F. Officer—she was very young—continued to look shocked. Betty interrupted them.

"Roger," she said, "you know you're only talking for your own amusement. You know as well as I do that at this stage of the war we've got all sorts here. There's got to be control, and as they're working with and amongst the men, it's better and easier all round that the system should basically be the same."

"But any decent girl," Roger broke in, "must simply hate it"

"Does any decent man," asked Betty, "simply hate it when he goes into the ranks?"

"But it's different with men," Roger argued.

"Rubbish, Roger! You're just plain plumb old-fashioned."

"Oh, Lord!" groaned Roger. "This emancipation of women!"

"But seriously, Roger, there are slack, untidy, feckless creatures amongst women just as there are amongst men. Would you have them without discipline?"

"I'd have them without stamping their feet."

"But surely, Roger, it's a compliment to the men that we've borrowed their system."

"I'm sunk," said Roger. "I'd always been brought up to believe that I should borrow my standards from women, and not from men."

"Poor Roger!" said Betty. "How you must have suffered!"

Roger looked at her with a cold eye. "That's my business," he answered.

"Have you still got a saluting complex, Roger?" Betty asked after a moment, and she turned to the other and explained. "Roger has told me that he generally turns up any side street handy when he sees a W.A.A.F. coming towards him."

"No," said Roger, "I've cured myself up to a point. But I don't know whether it's my masculine sense of gallantry that is offended, or the perfectly frightful salutes that so many of them give."

"What do you mean?" said the second Officer with great earnestness, already visualising a Special Parade for Practice Saluting.

"I generally avoid the problem by saluting first. It helps me to overcome my embarrassment as a male, and then I can look away quickly before having to notice their extraordinary contortions."

"And yet," said Betty, "don't you also notice it, Roger, if some brass-faced creature advances straight towards you looking rather challenging and hostile and pays no attention to you?"

"I don't know," Roger answered. "I just assume that she

hasn't much sense of humour, and as I've saluted her first in any case, I leave the matter at that. It's got to be, I suppose," he said after a pause; "we're all in the thing together, and until we're through with it, we must have rules and stick to them."

The second W.A.A.F. Officer looked relieved.

"How's Ops.?" Betty asked.

"You must ask Havana about that."

"But in your view, Roger? How do the girls of today compare with the earlier ones?"

Roger looked thoughtfully out of the window.

"I used to think," he said, "that those earlier days had produced some of the finest young women I could ever imagine. When they went off to get their commissions, it seemed they could never be replaced. But"—and he was rubbing his chin as he still gazed out of the window—"I look down sometimes from the dais in Ops. at the heads clustered round the plotting table, and there is no real difference. The faces may be different, the colourings different, but there is the same look, the same attitude, the same feeling of trust, the same sort of integrity of purpose."

"Then why," burst in the second Officer, who must have been smouldering for some minutes, "do you refer to them as drabs?"

"She's awfully young, isn't she?" Roger said to Betty.

The second W.A.A.F. Officer glared at Roger for a moment, her eager young face thrust forward beyond the constriction of her collar. And then she smiled.

"It's all right," said Betty, who had been watching the two of them. "You'll get to know him in time."

"Oh, well," said Roger, getting to his feet, "I'm keeping you from the W.A.A.F. personnel."

"We'll walk to the gate with you," Betty answered, "if you're going that way."

"That's a new one," Roger remarked, as a very small aircraft-woman went by.

"Do you mean to say," Betty said in a shocked voice, "that you know them all?"

"No, I don't mean that," Roger replied hastily; "I mean, that was a new salute. She tickled her right ear and looked smartly away from us in the opposite direction."

But the gate was reached without further incident, and the two young women passed on down the road to the buildings which housed the W.A.A.F.s, a forbidden territory that no one else could enter.

It was difficult for the average R.A.F. Officer on a Station to imagine the kind of life that these girls were leading; until many more had come to join the ranks of those older ones, they had been housed in the peace-time married quarters and in the houses once provided for Warrant Officers, and, with the first primal instinct of woman, they had immediately set about making their nests. Those earlier ones had been lucky, for they had been able to sort themselves out, to share sleeping-quarters amiably and to have little sitting-rooms. Here, when off duty, they followed their feminine pursuits, laundering, gardening, knitting or sewing—some sleeping and some rising as the revolving hands of the clock bade them to their various duties.

"Hallo, Tartan, Thistle Blue One calling. I can see other aircraft."

"Hallo, Thistle Blue One. It must be Yellow Section with the boats. . . . Hallo, Thistle Yellow One. Can you see Blue Section?"

In the pause before Yellow One's reply Placket could hear Yellow Two speaking to his leader.

"Hallo, Yellow One, Yellow Two calling. I can see them —half a mile away. Ten o'clock now."

"I see them," called out Yellow One.

Placket broke in.

"Hallo, Blue and Yellow One. Please keep in sight of one another. Yellow One, endeavour to guide the boats." He dabbed his forehead with his handkerchief. He was still standing, and seemed to have been doing so for hours.

"We're nearly there, Sir," he said to the Group Controller. "The two sections have spotted one another. They were about half a mile apart."

"That's excellent. I'm afraid we'll have to ask you to keep the patrol going over the boats as they come back. They'll be heading straight into the wind, and it will take them a long time."

"The boys won't mind that, Sir," Placket said, "particularly if they know some good has come out of it."

"Hallo, Tartan, Blue One calling. Boats coming up now" . . . and two minutes later, "Hallo, Tartan, Blue One calling. Boats alongside. All aboard. All aboard."

The rescue was effected. The bomber pilot was in the cabin. They had stripped him of his clothes, rubbed him vigorously, wrapped him up in woollen blankets and given him a hot drink. Up above, the circling aircraft dipped and rose; and slowly the little cavalcade turned round for the six-hour fight with the elements until the friendly port was reached.

Various cars and vans had deposited their occupants at the Mess when Roger arrived back, and he found the pre-lunch activity swirling within. The vestibule inside the swing doors was full of people taking off caps and respirators, coming and going to the telephone, or standing, as some of them always did, in the most congested passage-way, sipping cans of beer, and in imminent danger of having the can knocked out of their hands by each hurrying passer-by. Others were looking at the letter-rack near the entrance to the dining-room, or reading the rather tattered notices on the board beside it.

"What's this about a Mess meeting?" one of them said, hurrying up to the board.

"It's tonight at seven o'clock, or rather, I should say, nineteen hundred hours."

"What a bind! Do we have to be there?"

"Rather. It's an order."

"I say. Good Lord! What a bind!"

Inside the anteroom all the leather chairs and settees were occupied. A group stood in front of the fireplace, although no fire burned, with their cans on the mantelpiece above it. Others were standing by the long table at one side of the wall, on which the weekly papers were carefully arranged each morning at eight o'clock, and completely disarranged by a quarter past. More were clustered round the wireless cabinet. The principle appeared to be that those who wanted to listen to the wireless turned it on louder to drown the noise of talk, and those who were talking shouted louder to drown the noise of the wireless, so that the anteroom was a vast confused sound; and yet in the midst of it there could usually be found at least one individual, legs stuck out straight in front of him, head lolling on the arm of the chair, and fast asleep.

Such was Teddy Ryan at this moment; his black hair had come adrift and his dark, humorous, friendly eyes were closed. He was possibly dreaming of horses, for they were his passion, and on his aircraft was painted a racehorse with a diminutive jockey seated on it, raising his whip for the last burst to the winning-post.

Standing near him was the Gauleiter. He had a long, thin face, hair that grew far back on his forehead, and an earnestness of speech and demeanour that was misleading, for his nickname had come from an aptitude, when feeling relaxed, of bursting into torrents of near-German, when he would leap on a table or anything else handy and deliver himself of an impassioned oration that could have shaken Munich to its bedrock. Then he would descend and look very earnest again.

A little, fair fellow named Humber was standing in R.A.F. battledress near the Gauleiter's elbow. At first glance he looked rather like a white mouse, but it was the eyes that caught the attention. Always the eyes of these fighter pilots. He had been a Sergeant Pilot, and was one of the new members of the Officers' Mess.

Leaning his elbow on a corner of the mantelpiece unoccupied by a half-tankard, Bill Graves, the Canadian, surveyed the room with his steady, almost cynical look. He, too, was fair; he had a wide, sensitive mouth, a slow way of speech, and a D.F.C. ribbon.

And looking out of the window was the big, heavy figure of Max, the Dutchman. It was a Rembrandtesque face, except that it always smiled. In repose, the mouth was a little open, and the face might have appeared stolid; but it was very seldom in repose, for everybody liked Max, and so he always smiled. He was like a great, dependable dog with unfailing good temper to all the others yapping round its legs.

Havering, the grandfather of "Ops. B", was sitting in a wicker chair. He had "gone bald early", so he told Roger. Perhaps it had been the result of the bullet on the Somme, or his crash in Egypt, or the hours of desert flying after the retreating Turk. He sat in his wicker chair gazing in front of him. It seemed as if mental equilibrium had been achieved by him, and that the passionate clamour of the dozens of telephone keys that confronted him on duty no longer had power to upset his balance. He and Placket had been the first two Volunteer Reservists to arrive at the Station just before the war, and whereas Placket was now a Controller with Havana and Roger, Havering had been content to achieve his Flight Lieutenancy and to remain at that end of the room where the telephones buzzed their insistence every moment of his hours of duty.

All these and many others were collected there when Roger went in; but the noise daunted him, and he decided on lunch before a mass instinct drove the others there. He took his place in the small queue formed up at the hotplate, and found himself just behind James Glebe.

"Are you lunching with anybody, James?"

"No, Roger; I shall be honoured."

They were helped to their meat and took their vegetables, sought for their napkins in the numbered pigeon-holes, and sat down at the end of one of the refectory tables. On special occasions the tables were bare, and the last Station Commander had laid in a stock of candles and wooden candleholders for meals on those evenings when the band played. But by day the tables had their white tablecloths, and people came and went as their mood and hunger urged them.

"The weather's breaking a little, I think," James said, as he cocked his eye at the window. "Maybe something doing soon," and he rubbed his hands vigorously together before picking up his knife and fork.

"You really love it, don't you, James?" Roger asked him.

"Love it?" James repeated. "Don't be so emotional, Roger. I like flying very much, thank you."

"When are you going to get your squadron?"

"I may be lucky before long; but after all, Roger, I've only been operational for five months now."

"Yes; but James, when you were in charge of Operations, you managed to get in plenty of flying."

"Maybe, but it was only when I could beg or borrow a machine and go up for a joy-ride. The others had a long start on me, you know."

"How's the dog, James?"

"Very well, thank you, Roger. I have a photograph of him here, if you'd care to see."

Roger studied the snapshot of James' disciple and friend and handed it back. "Why don't you have him with you now, James?"

"He's quite happy at home. Besides, there are no rabbits and squirrels to amuse him here."

The Group Captain and the Wing Commander had sat down at the other end of the table.

"Little brutes!" Roger heard the Group Captain say.

Evidently somebody had done something wrong. He was sitting in his chair as Roger had seen him sitting in his cockpit, head forward from his body, chin depressed, and his glance, as always, resting momentarily on everything, and on nothing for more than a moment. His decorations were almost unnoticeable, for they seemed to blend with the man. It would have been more noticeable if he had been without them. Constantly the pugnacity of the jaw was cancelled by the crinkling laughter round the nose and eyes, and the set of the wide mouth was relieved by its preliminary opening before a head-tossed shout of laughter.

Teddy Ryan stumbled in, rubbing his eyes from his recent awakening, and attached himself to the queue which now stretched from the hotplate to the servery door.

James and Roger were joined by the Padre. He was full of anxiety concerning a kindly tea-urn provided by a well-wisher for circulation round Dispersal Points.

"What am I to do with it?" he asked James.

"Use it for its proper purpose," James answered.

"But nobody will give me any tea! The Sergeants' Mess say they haven't enough, and the Officers' Mess say they haven't enough, and the Messing Officer says that tea at Dispersals isn't his province, and it seems such a shame to the people that gave it to us."

"I should keep goldfish in it, Padre," James suggested.

The Padre regarded James gravely through his spectacles.

"You were much more sober-minded, James," he said, "when you were Operations Officer. I should have thought you would have been only too eager for the provision of tea for your pilots now that you're a Flight Commander."

"If anybody mentions tea again," Roger said, "I shall take

to cocoa for the rest of my life. Tea, tea, tea; wherever you go at any hour of the day, or night—it's tea. 'Where's the tea? Who's making some tea?' "

"A very wholesome beverage," said the Padre, assuming his best parsonical voice.

"Do you make it for your choirs?" James asked him.

"By Jove, I would," the Padre answered, "if they'd turn up to practice."

"Well, there you are!" said Roger. "Let them know it's tea and buns, and you'll have no difficulty."

"Falcon Squadron to readiness. Falcon Squadron to readiness. Operations calling Falcon Squadron to readiness."

It was Placket's voice broadcasting from Operations Room through the loudspeakers on the camp. As always when the voice came from the loudspeaker above the dining-room door, there was a sudden silence, and then, hastily pushing back their chairs, figures rose and made for the exit. Amongst them was James Glebe.

"I told you the weather was breaking, Roger," he said as he went. "Maybe something doing after all"—and his step as he went was springy.

The Group Captain called down the table to Roger: "Find out what that's in aid of, Roger, will you?"

"Yes, Sir," said Roger, departing for the vestibule and the telephone to Operations Room. He came back a moment later and stood beside the Group Captain. "Nothing of immediate importance, Sir; but the weather's lifting and Group want another squadron at readiness in case of need."

"It's about time we had another show," the Group Captain said. "We'll be getting slack."

Roger went back to his biscuits and cheese, and contemplated how he would spend the afternoon. He was not due on duty until five o'clock. Placket would be coming off watch in a few minutes and Havana taking his place. Perhaps he could persuade Placket to continue wandering round the aerodrome with him, for Roger was in one of the moods that every so often sent him from one department to another, chatting and learning, and realising yet again the many activities that made it possible for that call "Falcon Squadron to readiness" to be obeyed on the instant. He went to draw himself a cup of coffee from the urn opposite the letter-rack to await Placket's arrival.

George Cardew passed by as Roger was waiting.

"Don't forget the half-can that's on me tonight, Sir," he said as he went into the anteroom.

And then Placket appeared from Operations. He was looking tired.

"What's been happening?" Roger asked him.

"Air-sea rescue to that dinghy."

"Did they get him?"

"Yes."

"That's grand. It must have been a struggle."

"I don't know how Thistle Squadron did it. They stuck to the dinghy like glue. God knows how they found it in the first instance. It was one of the things that makes one feel our job's worth while." He walked towards the dining-room.

"Are you doing anything this afternoon?" Roger called.

"Not particularly. Why?"

"I thought of wandering about the Station a bit."

"Haven't you seen enough of it?"

"I'm a bit restless, I suppose. I wondered if you'd like to come."

"Right," said Placket. "By the time I've had lunch I expect I'll feel a bit better. I'm due to play squash at half-past three, but I'll come with you till then."

Roger, remembering a query about his laundry, went down the passage beside the bar to the Mess Office. The Mess Secretary, a big man with the last war's ribbons, was seated in earnest conversation with the Sergeant Steward and the Book-keeper, a bespectacled and studious L.A.C. They stopped talking as Roger came in, but he urged them to finish their business.

"It looks like a Board Meeting," he said.

"It's the Accountant Officer," the Mess Secretary groaned. "He's got some bee in his bonnet about the stock books in the bar not being properly kept."

"As I was saying, Sir," the Sergeant broke in, "the books are easy enough to keep for anyone trained to that job, but as the bar staff are drawn from the available batmen, it's not often you can find any that know the first thing about book-keeping."

"Then what are we going to do?" said the Mess Secretary,

looking appealingly at the L.A.C. The L.A.C. swallowed apprehensively.

"Yes, what are we going to do?" the Sergeant said, also looking at the L.A.C.

"Well, of course," said the L.A.C. hesitantly, "I suppose I could—"

"Good!" said the Mess Secretary, "that's settled. You'll keep the books in the bar."

"It makes rather a lot of work," said the L.A.C., "what with all the other books to keep."

"Nonsense!" said the Mess Secretary. "That's what we're all here for. Work— Very good, Sergeant."

The Sergeant, a gentle man for all his stripes, as he went out gave a pitying glance at the L.A.C. who had sat down beside his littered table, and was gazing vacantly out to the garages at the back of the Mess.

"Now, Sir," said the Mess Secretary, happy to have disposed of yet another problem.

"It's about my washing," Roger began.

"What's wrong, Sir?"

They went into the trouble about Roger's laundry. The Mess Secretary made copious notes. The L.A.C. continued to look out of the window in dull despair. The investigation into Roger's problem was protracted, for the door opened and shut with irritating regularity as one Officer after another arrived to cash cheques.

"They treat me like a bank clerk!" the Mess Secretary said. "I wish I was back in the Black and Tans."

As Roger rose to go, the Squadron Leader Administration came in.

"The C.O. doesn't like the blackout in the dining-room. There's a window broken at the end of the passage in the east wing. One of the bulbs is gone in the light in an upstairs bathroom. The bar waiters aren't as alert as they might be. See to these things, will you?"

"Certainly, Sir," the Mess Secretary answered sombrely.

Roger and the Squadron Leader Administration went down the passage together.

"Got to keep them up to it, you know," the Squadron Leader Admin. said.

"Up to what?" Roger asked.

The Squadron Leader Admin, gave him a cold stare.

"Everything," he said.

People were standing now in the Mess porch, or on the pathway outside, drinking their after-lunch coffee. The pall of grey cloud above had lightened in colour, and on the horizon a faint orange glow had relieved the morning's sombre aspect.

Cygnet and Falcon Squadrons were at readiness away over the aerodrome at their Dispersal Points, and it was most of Heron Squadron that was now collected in the garden. Their two Flight Commanders stood a little apart, talking to a third pilot, who had been shot down and wounded in the late summer of 1940 and who had now rejoined his squadron.

Collie Dalrymple, one of the Flight Commanders, was tall, with the weatherbeaten face of an outdoor life, and very slow in speech. It was not that he could not think fast and act fast, but he seemed to have a natural diffidence in expressing any opinion. One of his outstanding qualities was the astonishing quickness with which he could see and identify specks in the sky, long before anyone else flying with him was even aware that anything at all might be there. Time and again his unemotional voice had been heard on the R.T. giving warning to his Flight and describing the lurking dangers they could not see.

The other Flight Commander was also tall, and dark as Collie was fair, and althought Collie wasted very few words in speech, there was a deep bond between these two. When their two Flights were operating, monosyllables sufficed between them for each to have a perfect understanding of the other, and only when the operation was over would Bob Halliwell betray the slightest sign of personal interest. As they streamed back high over the cliffs of Dover, Bob's voice would say:

"Are you all right, Collie?"

And from somewhere out of the surrounding ether, Collie's voice would answer: "I'm all right. Are you all right, Bob?"

"I'm all right," Bob would answer, and each would say "good"—and they had reverted to their monosyllables again.

McBain, the third of this gathering, was protesting vigorously.

"Of course I'm operational," he was saying.

"You're not," said Collie.

"But if I was fit enough to fly in the Battle of Britain, I'm fit enough to fly now."

"We know you're fit enough to fly, or you wouldn't be here, but you've a long way to go to catch up on Operations."

"Rubbish!" said McBain. "I'll talk to the Squadron Leader."

"You won't get any change out of him," Bob Halliwell told him.

"What am I going to do?" McBain complained.

"You're a supernumerary Flight Lieutenant," Collie said to him, "and there are plenty of new pilots you can do a bit of training with."

"But I was flying with you fellows long before the new pilots had ever been heard of!"

"Maybe," said Collie, "but Bob and I aren't going to have the whole of the battle ruined by hanging on your tail seeing that no harm comes to you."

"Hell!" said McBain, kicking at a poppy. He wandered away with his hands in his pockets. Bob and Collie smiled at one another, and silently resumed their wordless companionship.

The Squadron Leader of the Herons was talking to the Group Captain and the Wing Commander. In ordinary times one would not have been surprised to see him sitting in the Café Royal dressed in corduroy trousers, suède shoes and some pastel-shaded shirt. That is to say, one might not have been surprised at first glance at his face; for it was long and delicate and artistic. But one would have been wrong, for though this may have been the face of an artist, he had none of the pseudo-artist's self-advertising little manners. A deep, rich "ho-ho!" would come over the air if he were in a particularly tight corner, and as with Collie Dalrymple and Bob Halliwell, he and Squadron Leader David of the Falcons worked with tacit understanding.

"Don't let them hang about too long, Charles," the Group Captain said to him. "Push them up in the air and get on with training."

"I may go up with you," the Wing Commander said, "if there's nothing else doing. They might let one of the two squadrons now at readiness relax a bit, Sir, sometime this afternoon," he turned to the Group Captain, "so I could take the two of them up."

"I'll go and speak to Group," the Group Captain answered, and walked away. In a few minutes he was back. "They can't promise anything," he said to the Wing Commander and Squadron Leader waiting for him. "They're still waiting for weather reports before they make up their minds whether to mount a show."

Placket called to Roger from the Mess entrance.

"Ready!" he said. "Where do we go first?"

"What about the Link?" Roger suggested.

"O.K."—and they set off down the camp's main road till they came to the building of the Armoury and inside it a room with the squat, foreshortened mechanical device called the Link trainer. This miniature aeroplane, with its wings, ailerons, elevator and rudder, stood in one corner of the room, mounted on a pedestal, inside which all the complicated mechanism, when set in motion, imparted to the Link the motions of flying. Its cockpit contained a control column, a throttle, and various instruments on the board facing the pilot. It could be flown either with the hood open, in which case the pilot could judge his alignment by sky and landscape painted on the surrounding walls, or if the hood were shut, he was completely cut off from outside view and had to control the Link entirely by the instruments. It was very delicate on the controls, and of extreme value for precision flying. Covering a table in another corner of the room was a large map, and over it could move the "Crab", an instrument rather like the planchette board that summons supernatural messages. And there seemed something supernatural about the Crab also, for, leaving a fine ink-trace behind it, it responded to every movement of the Link, so that the instructor sitting by it could check the exactitude of the courses given to the pilot in the cockpit, where he sat with headphones over his ears and his eyes registering the movement of his instruments. Link training was supposed to be part of the pilots' duty, subject to operations. But it was not always popular with those who felt that to descend from a Spitfire to an earth-bound Link was an insult to their flying intelligence. Yet even the most competent fighter pilot might grow careless, and Link training proved a very necessary exercise in concentration.

Roger and Placket found the disgruntled McBain in the room with a Sergeant instructor.

"I think I heard the Wing Commander saying he'd go up with your squadron for a practice flight."

"Good!" said McBain. "That lets me out of this contraption," and he hurried off more cheerfully.

"Would either of you gentlemen care to do a run?" the Sergeant instructor asked.

Roger and Placket looked at one another, each wondering who should be the first to make a fool of himself.

"We'll toss," Placket suggested.

Roger lost, and for the next twenty minutes he concentrated on the vagaries of the delicate Link. The Sergeant instructor's voice spoke through the headphones to him and he tried to follow its orders. It was when he failed to look at the airspeed indicator, went into a spin and with the aid of long-distant experience, straightened the Link out again, that he called through his microphone that he had had enough. He raised the hood and climbed out feeling exhausted. The Crab had crawled about the map in a bewildering maze.

"Hardly operational yet," Placket said to him.

"You get into the thing and do better."

Apart from forgetting to climb and therefore steering a subterranean course through the bowels of the earth, Placket was steady. The two of them came out of the Link well pleased with themselves.

"I shouldn't be surprised," Roger said, "if we could fly again quite easily."

They were both a little inebriated by the flattery of the Sergeant instructor, who was now rubbing out the track-marks on the map and shaking his head sadly.

In the main building of the Armoury men were oiling and assembling rifles, for most of the work on the Spitfires' machine-guns and cannons was done in the squadrons' own workshops.

"I know," said Placket, as they hesitated outside, "what about some camera-gun films?"

They went into the photographic building, where the Sergeant in charge and his assistant were working. In a few minutes the projector was throwing on to the small screen in front of them the films taken by the camera guns whose mechanism came into action as the pilot opened fire with his real guns. There was no sham about these films—none of the production of a film studio. The light for the most part was dim, the action at times jerky, and an audience of filmgoers seated in their cushioned chairs might have felt cheated of their ninepences; but to Placket and Roger no price of admission could have paid for the stabbing, rushing scenes flickering before their eyes. Each separate event lasted only some four or five seconds. It was preceded by a caption, "Spitfire versus Heinkel 111", or "Spitfire versus Me. 109", or "Attack on Shipping", in each case followed by the date and the pilot's name. There, in the bareness of this room, leaning forward on a hard bench, the two of them fought with Bo'sun Spritt and saw, as he had seen, the wavering of the German bomber in front of them, the smoke-streaks of tracer bullets, the lumps of metal flying off the target, and then the billowing smoke as fire raged round it.

It was noticeable that the Bo'sun films brought them to such short range that involuntarily they sat back to withstand what appeared to be a certain collision. Other scenes were over almost before they had begun—perhaps the scene of a cloud, and into it a little ghostly something diving for security as a Spitfire brought its guns to bear as it vanished from view.

And then there were Squadron Leader Whelan's amazing attacks: a placid, rippling sea below, a ship upon it, and suddenly splashes and gouts of water as his cannon and machine-guns found the range, with answering puffs and streaks from the ship vainly trying to protect itself from these swooping, screaming, spitting angels of fury; and the ship approaching nearer, nearer, as the puffs and streaks coming from it ceased and its gunners fled for the safety of any shelter that could save them from this storm of death descending on them. Roger and Placket gripped their fingernails into the palms of their hands as Whelan's Hurricane fell from the sky on these ships, for they grew twice, three times as large, their funnels, masts, their whole solid structure, leaping to huge proportions as the attacker swept over them within inches of collision. The little caption read: "Hurricane: Shipping Attack: Squadron Leader Whelan"—and the date.

One after another of these Whelan films were shown, with others taken from the Hurricanes of his squadron. The two watchers reacted in unison. Forward and forward they bent, and then back suddenly, as the film blacked out mercifully at what seemed the very moment of impact.

They came out very quiet. They looked at one another and smiled a little—not with amusement, but with nervous apprehension to cover their feelings.

"What a squadron!" said Roger.

"What a squadron!" echoed Placket.

Roger was to remember those films very soon afterwards, for in the minds of those controlling the destiny of war in the air, operation order number one two three was taking shape.

CHAPTER THREE

HAVANA WAS sitting on the dais in Operations Room. Around and below him were the many people who made up its activities. In the early days of the war the figures had been uniformly masculine, but early in 1940 the feminine intrusion had begun, and now, except in essential key positions, the room was largely staffed by women—even the key positions were falling to their all-embracing aptitude.

Behind him in the Radio cabins, girls sat with headphones and with log-books in front of them, ready to record all the messages spoken from ground to air and from air to ground, and between the aircraft themselves. They kept a listening watch, but their ambition was to be able to break into speech themselves and to get an answering message. Only on one occasion had such a breach of etiquette occurred. The Gauleiter had been flying; he called to Controller: "Hallo, Tartan, Falcon Red One calling. Are you receiving?"

And before the Controller could operate his switches, a sweet feminine voice cooed into the air: "Hallo, Falcon Red One, Tartan answering. Receiving you loud and clear. Are you receiving me?"

The Controller leapt from his chair. He beat with furious fists against the window of the Radio cabin. The startled R.T. Operator looked up to see a face grimacing like a savage at a tribal feast. The Controller then leapt back for his own keys.

"Hallo, Falcon Red One, Tartan calling," he said. "I apologise for that interlude."

Falcon Red One replied: "Hallo, Tartan. I thought it was charming. Let the good work go on."

Fortunately the Controller did not turn round in time to see the look of beatific triumph which shone from the face of the R.T. Operator.

But, even so, their work was interesting, for sooner or later some distant voice might call which nobody else had heard, and though they were silent participants in this drama of Ops., they were present on the stage all the time.

On Havana's right was the Army staff with its great array of telephone keys. George, its oldest war-time member, sat on duty with maps, coloured pencils, signals, rulers, and all his aids for the collection and dissemination of information. Alongside him were his Signallers—quiet men, who crept about somewhat surprisingly in sandshoes. "Quiet!" Havana had roared at the top of his voice when a considerable clatter had indicated that a pair of Army fieldboots had fallen downstairs. From that time, George had put his Signallers into sandshoes, so that they stubbed their toes at least noiselessly.

In these lengthening years of war George had developed a considerable tact. His main preoccupation was to obtain aircraft for gun or searchlight co-operation. This was willingly forthcoming on most occasions, but after hard spells of flying or in unpleasant weather, it was sometimes difficult to persuade tired people to do it with alacrity. George had therefore introduced a negative form of technique. He did not ask for what he wanted, he suggested that what he wanted was not possible, and thus by putting everyone on his mettle, the matter was concluded with satisfaction all round. In the days gone by, George would have come to Havana and said at this hour: "What about some anti-aircraft co-operation?"

"Nonsense," Havana would have replied, and George would have slunk back to his chair and pushed a few telephone keys mournfully. But now, while Havana was thoughtfully scratching the offside of his neck with his nearside hand, George's raised voice could be heard speaking to some battery.

"No," he said, "not a hope, I should say. Conditions definitely against it."

He came over to Havana with a solemnity that was always belied by a watchful twinkle in his eye. "I am assuming," he said, "that gun co-operation is quite out of the question."

"Why?" said Havana.

"Weather," said George.

"Who told you?" said Havana.

"Well, I mean," George answered, "it speaks for itself."

"Wait a minute," Havana told him, "it may not be impossible. Let's ask one of the squadrons. . . . T.B., ask

Dispersals what about ack-ack co-op.," he called to a Pilot Officer sitting farther down the dais on his left. He, too, worked a multitude of keys like so many diminutive beer-handles. Telephone calls on the important lines he always took himself, but beside him a W.A.A.F. Corporal sat to assist him with the other calls, and on his other side was the W.A.A.F. in touch with Observer centres. Templeton-Browning was a red-faced individual with a complete and unruffled good humour, who bore all the outward look of a country life and who discoursed with unclouded enthusiasm on fish and foxes, deer and ducks—particularly ducks. He telephoned Falcon Squadron's Dispersed Pilots' Rest Room.

"Can I speak to a pilot?" A moment later he called over to Havana: "Gauleiter on the 'phone, Sir."

"Hallo, Gauleiter," Havana called him. "What's it like?"

"What do you mean, Sir?" the Gauleiter replied.

"I suppose it's not possible for some co-operation with the guns?"

"Wait a moment, Sir; I'll go outside and have a look." His voice returned a minute later. "It's definitely better than it was. Shall I go up for a weather test?"

"O.K.," said Havana, "and if it's fit, would you like to carry on without landing? I'll know it's fit if you ask for a course."

"Right," replied the Gauleiter.

"Details are as follows—" and Havana gave him the heights, distances and details for assistance to the guns. Havana turned to George. "We'll have a shot at it," he said.

"Oh! thank you, Sir," George replied, with his eyes twinkling even more suspiciously. "I shouldn't have thought it was possible."

"It's not for you to judge." Havana gazed at him severely.

"No, Sir," said George, outrageously dropping a little curtsey.

"Floor Supervisor," Havana called to the room below. "Get everything ready. Aircraft about to take off."

The W.A.A.F. at the Observer Corps lines was reacting to her routine business. "Hallo, hallo. One Spitfire flying such-and-such course, such-and-such height, taking off five minutes' time. O.K.? O.K.!"

The Floor Supervisor was superintending his crew. More

W.A.A.F.s than men were grouped round the great plotting-table, with the section of map whose lines had burned themselves into the eyes and brains of those who had pored over them so long. The counters and discs and plaques, with numerals and lettering and little holders for carrying them, were stacked in neat rows adjacent. The plotters, with long wands like billiard cues, pushed these holders and counters about the table according to the information which came to them from the headphones which they wore. At a different table, people stood with coloured chalks and rulers and mathematical instruments, and round the room on blackboards and on maps pinned to the walls, the varied information necessary to Operations was displayed—weather conditions over a wide area, states of squadrons, numbers of aircraft and pilots available, searchlight and gun batteries—and in large books were pasted the hundreds of instructions, warnings and details that might affect the conduct of any flight.

A fair-haired Sergeant with an irrepressible sense of humour took up his place on one side of Havana, and a very large Corporal sat down on the other side. They, too, each had their radio-telephone instruments beside them, so that they could be deputed to get in touch with aircraft by the Controller, harassed with other immediate problems.

"Everything ready, Sir," the Floor Supervisor had appeared at Havana's side to report.

The voice of the Lookout perched in a high position on the aerodrome spoke through the loudspeaker: "One Spitfire, Falcon Squadron, taxi-ing out. One Spitfire, Falcon Squadron, about to take off. One Spitfire, Falcon Squadron, now airborne."

Havana and the Gauleiter exchanged normal messages, and a few minutes later the Gauleiter's voice said: "Hallo, Tartan, Falcon Red One calling. Give me a course, please."

"It's all right," Havana said to George; "he can do it."

"Grand, Sir!" said George, beaming, and told the good news to the batteries as if he were a headmaster granting the school an unexpected half-holiday.

"Pilot Officer Ryan for you, Sir."

Havana abstractedly picked up the telephone.

"Controller here."

"Hallo, Sir," said Teddy's eager voice. "What about a sortie?"

"What sort of a sortie?" Havana asked.

"Well, Max and Humber and Sergeant Bush and I wondered if we could go over in two sections and have a crack at anything we could find. Do you know what the weather's like generally, Sir?"

"Wait a moment," Havana said. "Have you got Squadron Leader David's permission?"

"Rather, Sir," said Teddy, self-righteously.

"And where do you want to go?"

Teddy mentioned a variety of places.

"What do you think you're going to find there?"

"Enough to keep us amused, Sir, and to make the Hun damned angry, I hope."

"All right," Havana said to him. "I'll do what I can."

A moment or two later he had spoken to the Group Captain to obtain his approval, and was waiting for the meteorological department to produce details of the anticipated weather on the route of the four restless pilots. Within a few minutes the details were put in front of him written on a sheet of paper. He telephoned Teddy Ryan at his dispersal hut.

"Here's the weather, Teddy," and he gave him the particulars of cloud in its various layers and heights and thicknesses, wind speeds and directions and the visibility from different altitudes.

"Sounds just ideal to me," Teddy said. "When can we get cracking, Sir?"

"I'll talk to Group."

The voice of the Group Controller sounded dubious, but with a little persuasion on the part of Havana permission was forthcoming.

"Now," said Havana to Teddy when he had contacted him again. "Let's have the full details. When are you taking off? What are your call signs to be? Where are you going to cross the English coast? What area will you cover? Where do you intend to come out again, and where do you intend to cross in home?"

Teddy, interrupting his conversation with Havana for

frequent consultations with Max, whose slow, good-natured voice Havana couuld hear in the background finally supplied the particulars.

"Max is taking Sergeant Bush as Yellow Section, and I'm going with Humber as Red Section."

"All right," said Havana. "Enjoy yourselves."

"We shall!" said Teddy with conviction.

For the next ten minutes Teddy and Max pored over a map, arguing fiercely their respective targets, neither willing to concede a likely objective to the other. Humber and Sergeant Bush stood by silent and smiling, content to be led wherever they might be taken; but at last an agreement was reached.

Teddy and Humber would proceed on a left-hand sweep North of a chosen point; Max and Sergeant Bush would make a right-hand sweep South of that point. They arranged their times of exit from the enemy coast, and agreed to look for one another on a converging course as they came over the sea. And then, chuckling with suppressed excitement, they put on their flying clothes and, all four chattering in unison, they made for their aircraft.

A dark cloud hung over the aerodrome as they took off, and Teddy called to Havana.

"Hallo, Tartan, Falcon Red One calling. Are you receiving? Over."

"Hallo, Falcon Red One, Tartan answering. Loud and clear. Over."

"Hallo, Tartan, Falcon Red One answering. You also. Listening out."

And from then, as far as Havana was concerned, there was silence. The four pilots set their course below the cloud. From time to time they were enveloped in lower banks of misty cumulus, and they put their aircraft lower until they could see the damp English countryside once more below them.

Then in a moment they were over the cliffs and out to sea. The clouds were higher here. There was a comfortable ceiling for them at two thousand feet, and through breaks in it they could see the succeeding layers above. They revelled in the sight of them for the infinite opportunities they gave for dodging up and down and playing hide and seek. Visibility underneath the lowest cloud was excellent. Nothing stirred upon the waters, and even the big waves looked motionless, except for the caps of white foam that broke and dispersed.

The four Spitfires rose and fell as if they were sailing on an invisible sea above the ocean. So clear was the air that they saw the opposite coastline from miles away. Teddy stared hard to find recognisable landmarks and, with a cheerful shout to Max, picked up his position and steered for the enemy coast.

Before they were within range of the watchful anti-aircraft, the Spitfires had risen into the cloud, and for the next five or six miles they were sailing contentedly and sufficiently securely between two layers.

"O.K., Max," called Teddy. "Break away now. See you later." And he and Humber swung away to the left.

"O.K.," said Max, as he and the Sergeant at the same time swung to the right.

Sergeant Bush was an Australian. The war to him was one great adventure that seemed to have been brought about by a kindly fate especially for his benefit. He had heard those older Australians of an earlier war talk of their world travels in defence of an Empire; but riding round the sheep station at Bourke, he could only imagine the coloured countries of the Middle East and of Europe as his seniors had tried to describe them to him. And now he had exchanged the saddle of his horse for the cockpit of a Spitfire, and the arid leagues of New South Wales for the crazy quilt of Europe's varied fields.

He was very little and lean, with a head narrow and long from crown to jaw, and the hair on top of it stuck up like rusty wire when he removed his flying helmet. And here, suspended between the layers of cloud, he watched the floating shape of Max's aircraft and waited for its nose to dip to the first attack.

They were going down. At one moment they had been sandwiched between two layers of cloud, the one above them being broken and showing layer after layer above, with momentary hints of blue sky on top of it all. The next moment a grey vapour was all round them—a cold and eerie world removed from space and time. But it was only momentary, for they had broken cloud again, and the muddy fields of Belgium's interminable vegetable-growing presented their drab picture, with dykes and long pavé roads intersecting them.

Max seemed to know his position, for he did not waver on his course. He bore left a little, flying parallel with but some distance from the clearly defined road. The height of the two aircraft was just under two thousand feet. The road was very deserted, but in the fields scattered labourers ceased their hoeing and looked up. Some few continued to present their patient, bended backs, as if to them this idiocy of war was no justification to cease tending the young things growing in the ground. One fellow in a blue blouse took off his cap and waved it frenziedly.

Some further distance along the road a group of grey-green uniformed figures sprang to their feet and ran for rifles, but Max and Bush were almost out of sight before a shot was fired.

Then Max found his first target. It was a small goods yard with sidings adjacent to a busy little factory. From some distance he had seen dirty smoke drifting from a stationary engine drawn up there.

" 'allo, Yellow Two," he called to Bush. "You take the power-house. I take the engine."

They put their noses down into a shallow dive. The engine-driver had been leaning out of his cabin and, looking up, saw the two shapes approaching. He sensed what to expect. Unfortunate Belgian that he was, he knew that he took his life in his hands every time he drove the railway engine that drew munitions for the enemy. He leaped from his cabin and fell at the foot of an embankment. He was just in time, for the cannon-shells from Max's guns had hit his engine with the first burst. There was a sound of steam trying to escape under colossal pressure, and then a loud explosion, for the boiler could stand it no longer, and the engine was a mess of jagged metal. Max climbed a little and turned to see the result of his attack and to watch what Bush was doing.

The latter had come in behind Max, and had found some difficulty in identifying the power-house.

"It is that building," Max called to him—"on the right-hand side of the smoke stack. I come in with you."

The two Spitfires had completed their turn, and began a shallow dive again. Startled people had rushed from some of the buildings when the engine had exploded.

"God help them," thought Bush; "working for the Hun. Hope I don't hit any."

The power-house was an easy target. They both decided to give it a good long burst. Its arched windows registered the accuracy of their aim, for they fell inwards. One of the pilots then shot a little high, for tiles flew off the roof and holes gaped. Not knowing which of them it was, they both aimed lower, and then, as the building assumed an alarming size in front of them, they pulled up and over its roof.

It seemed to be unprotected. At least, they were aware of nothing fired at them, so Max decided to turn again, and they circled once to see what had happened. It was very gratifying. A cloud of steam and smoke hung over the power-house and was drifting round the factory buildings. As the wind blew it to one side, they could see that the power-house roof no longer existed and that much of the wall had caved in. They had been lucky. The cannon-shells had hit a vital spot. The factory would not work again for many a long day.

Max looked at his compass. "Going up," he said to Bush, and they ascended once more into the friendly cloud that was acting so comfortingly as their screen.

For three more minutes they flew on, and once again Max prepared to descend. The country was the same as previously. They might, indeed, have emerged precisely where they did before. The monotony of Belgium spread all around them. It seemed this time as if Max were a little off his course, for he bore right and then left again, nosing to pick up something recognisable.

The visibility here was worse, and still there was so little sign of any human activity. He edged closer to the straight road on his right. He could not be sure which one it was. Still pondering his exact position and looking out in front, he gave a shout to Bush.

"In front," he yelled. "Going down." For, lumbering along the road between the sodden fields, and spaced at intervals, were twenty German army lorries in convoy. Perhaps they had no windscreen wipers. Possibly the sound of their own massive engines had drowned the noise of the engines up above, because the first lorry had received a cannon-shell through its screen, had swerved violently across the road and overturned on the grass verge at the side before the rest of the convoy had any idea of what was happening.

The whole of the little action was over in a matter of seconds. Brakes had screeched, lorries had cannoned into one another from behind, the crews had sprung flying from their cabins, one shot dead in mid-air as he jumped. The stretch of quiet road was now a tangle of bent and twisted metal, flapping canvas and motionless bodies, with others crawling painfully to escape this fiendish death-trap into which they had run their heads.

As Max and Bush came back down the line of this destruction, one of a lorry crew had managed to man his machine-gun. He did his best to bring it to bear. The last Bush saw of him was staggering in the arc of a circle and bending forward with his hands pressed to his eyes.

"O.K.," said Max. "Going up." He looked at his compass again. It was time for home.

Meanwhile Teddy and Humber had pursued very much the same preliminary tactics. Teddy had a hunch. He did not know on what wave of insight it had been brought to him, but there was one spot he wanted to have a look at. A few weeks ago he had seen some wooden huts there where none had been before. It was just an ordinary village, with its one long street with small red-brick or white-washed houses—drab, dejected, with its mairie, a few estaminets, the uncompromising-looking school, the dirty back yards—but the newly-built huts had intrigued him.

"We're about there," he said to Humber. "Keep close." And they were through cloud and in sight of the land below. His dead reckoning had been perfect. There was the village slightly to port.

"God Almighty!" shrieked Teddy. "Look at it!" For the long, straight road was packed from end to end with motor transport, horse transport and uniformed figures swarming like an invading army in the constricted space.

Teddy's sensation afterwards was as if he had been reaping a macabre corn-field. The two of them came down the village street about two hundred feet high. They desolated it from end to end. Horses reared, twisted in their traces, kicked their vehicles to pieces or fell in bloody heaps beside them. Lorries crashed and jammed. Figures fell headlong and were crushed by driverless wheels or flying hooves. Absolute and demoniac chaos raged. The orderly semblance of a brigade on the march was now a scene of pulverised flesh and splintered vehicles.

The two of them turned to resume the attack, but the reception on their next run was staggering. Every form of explosive burst in variegated colours around them—red and brown and orange; dirty black and billowing white; snaking tracer shells and bullets. They were in a ring of fire. It had to be passed through if escape were to be made. There was no time to see any more. They both tore upwards. As they reached the cloud they could both feel jarring reverberations from the screaming hate let loose about them.

In the clear air above they found respite. They flew together, silent, for a moment or two. The magnitude of the destruction they had caused had left them without words. At last Humber found his voice.

"Pretty hot, eh?" he said.

"Wizard!" Teddy replied.

"What do we do now?"

"Steer course for home, I think. But we might have one little dekko as we go out."

In front of them bursts of anti-aircraft shell showed that a battery was trying to range on their unseen presence. Teddy turned away a few degrees.

"One final look," he sang out to Humber, and down they went again. There was nothing of interest to be seen. The appalling flatness of the country stretched to the sea-coast some miles away. Teddy could not recognise the spot. He turned farther to his port side until he could see, far away, the outline of a coast town he thought he knew.

"We'll go out North of the town," he said to Humber, "to avoid flak." They had crossed a main road leading to the town in the distance when Teddy turned back.

"Where are you going?" Humber asked him.

"Thought I saw something," was the reply, and Humber obediently followed.

"Do you see what I see?" Teddy called, with a note of excitement in his voice. For travelling down the road in front of them was a large military staff car.

"I see it," Humber answered.

"Let's give it the works."

They were both too excited with their first bursts, for they missed the car. It wavered for a hundred yards or so and then skidding violently came to a sudden stop. They had passed over it, and they turned outwards to come back. At their next view they could see one figure, obviously the driver, running for his life for a heap of stones, but what delighted them was the spectacle that had been disgorged from the back. Four exceedingly agitated German Officers were darting about like dragon-flies, none of them knowing where to go.

"Machine-guns," Teddy called, and they fired.

A splatter of dust and chipped stones rippled over the ground just short of the demented figures. Like a lightning shower of rain it licked forward. It seemed to pause for an instant around the group before it passed on, and the two Spitfires had screamed into the distance down the road.

"One more go," Teddy shouted.

But there was no need for it. The four figures were lying still when they saw them next. The beautiful uniforms were stained with the mud of the road; the jaunty caps had fallen off. General Müller's eye-sockets were full of the smashed glass of his pince-nez, although he was past feeling any pain, and the trembling chauffeur had scrabbled stones over himself and was moaning a little as he heard the Spitfires pass into the distance.

They were up above the cloud again. They were out at sea. Rising and falling, two specks were visible on their port beam. They steered a converging course. The two specks became two Spitfires.

"Hallo, Yellow One, Red One calling. Are you receiving?"

" 'Allo, Red One, Yellow One answering. Loud and clear. Is that you near me?"

"Here we are, Max. Just behind."

" 'Allo, Teddy. Did you have success?"

"So-so, Max. Pretty so-so. What about you?"

"Oh! So and so also."

"Then," said Teddy, "a good time was had by all."

The exercise between the guns and the Gauleiter proceeded, but there was nothing more of any vital interest. As the cloud lifted and the wind changed direction, other aircraft began to take the air. But the enemy, over that strip of water, seemed quiet. Perhaps his preoccupations with the Mediterranean and his plans to eliminate Soviet Russia had reduced his strength. Perhaps he at last needed to conserve that precious oil without which he would be beaten. Perhaps his pilots sitting there were not of the same vintage as those whose bones lay under the quiet English turf, or were bleached still whiter by the tides of Britain's sea.

Roger and Placket had visited the dinghy and parachute shop and seen their marvels. The Sergeant had opened a dinghy container the size of an attaché case, which hung suspended with the envelope of the parachute. As he opened it, the rubber dinghy sprang out, and within seconds it was there on the floor, large enough to accommodate a man lying with his knees up, and dangling from it were its rubber baling cup and its little sea anchor.

"Mr. Cardew doesn't like them," the Sergeant said.

"Why not?" Placket asked.

"Says he's got enough lumber in the cockpit without this."

"He may need it some day."

"He seems to prefer his Mae West," the Sergeant replied, beginning to pack up the dinghy again.

A W.A.A.F. and an Aircraft-hand were folding the long beauty of a parachute. Its lovely white silk, its multitude of silken cords and the little pilot parachute that hopped out first and opened like a mechanical parasol to bring the main parachute after it, were stowed away with meticulous care into the case which dangled below the pilot's back when he put on his heavy webbed harness. And accounted in his parachute and dinghy on top of his flying suit and Mae West, with his heavy flying-boots and his flying-gloves and his leather flying-helmet, he looked, as he lumbered towards his aircraft, like some misshapen diver.

From the Watch Office window, Bywaters, the aerodrome Control Officer, looked out.

"Anything doing?" Roger asked, as they stopped to greet him.

"Some of the Falcons have been up. Looks as if they can get on with some practice flying."

"What's that collection?" Placket pointed to a group at

the entrance to a hangar.

Bywaters leaned farther out of the window. "Those are some of the A.T.C. boys. They come up periodically, when their work permits, and spend a day on the aerodrome."

"Are they keen?"

"Keen?" Bywaters echoed. "You almost have to tie the Spitfires down for fear they pinch one."

Roger and Placket moved off towards the group. In its centre was a little genial man whose forage cap sat jauntily on his few remaining hairs, and whose A.T.C. uniform bore wings and a D.S.O. and an A.F.C. and the ribbons of the old battles. Roger peered at him for a moment or two.

"What's your name?" he asked, almost rudely.

"Dowie," said the A.T.C. Officer.

"Good God," said Roger suddenly, "the last time I saw you, you had been flying from this very place, and your squadron and mine had dinner at the Café Royal."

Dowie smiled from ear to ear, and drew himself up to a salute, while his lads stood round and watched with interest.

A Spitfire was standing there on the tarmac, the long barrels of its cannon thrust out from the wings, the hood of its cockpit pushed back, and an absorbed boy standing on the wing where it joined the main fuselage, while a Sergeant pilot in the cockpit talked to the pilot yet to be. A Sergeant mechanic had been lecturing the main body grouped round, and after a moment or two, Dowie and Roger and Placket wandered away inside the hangar, sharing old recollections and all talking at once.

Intent figures stood on trestle ladders peering, with the aid of inspection lamps, at the engines stripped of their cowlings. Everything was in good order and the floor of the hangar was surprisingly clean. The economical lines of the Spitfires looked very beautiful in the half-light, illuminated by the orange splashes of the lamps. Massive engines, charged with hundreds of horsepower, stood on carriers awaiting overhaul or final assembly into machines. There was little noise, and a raised voice sounded hollowly as it echoed round this steel-built structure. In one corner armourers were at work on the long, snaky belts of ammunition that would soon be pouring towards the enemy. In an inner workshop other armourers cleaned and oiled and overhauled cannons and machine-guns.

Everyone seemed quietly absorbed in his own specialist work.

"It's a great experience," said Dowie, as they stood in the hangar looking round them, "to be allowed to see the modern R.A.F. at work."

"How often have you been up here?" Roger asked him.

"Only twice before. My Cadet Squadron was affiliated to this Station a short time ago."

"What do you notice most?" Placket asked him.

Dowie paused for a moment. His face nearly always wore a smile, but something about the erectness of his figure and the way he wore his uniform showed the early military training that most of the R.F.C., the forerunner of the R.A.F., had had.

"I think maybe," he said, "it's the difference in discipline."

"It's what struck me first when I first came back," Roger told him. "How do you feel about it?"

"I think," Dowie answered, "we have to realise it's changed a good deal since our day. It seems to be ridden with a looser rein. I suppose that so many of the men are highly skilled technicians and craftsmen in fact, with detailed and expert work which only they can perform, that the modern discipline of this Service comes more from within than without. The men are proud of their pilots, proud of the machines that carry them, and proud of the work they themselves do to keep them serviceable. And that being so, there is perhaps an easier spirit of camaraderie and a greater readiness to trust individual intelligence than there used to be."

"I think things tend to get a bit slack," Placket broke in, with his blue eyes attempting to look stern, and his cap set at a most correct angle.

"He's a bit sour at times," Roger explained to Dowie. "He does like his cup of tea, and he can't always get it in Ops. when he wants it."

At one side of the hangar were doors to Squadron Offices, and the whole impression was that of a mechanised cathedral nave. They went through one of the doors which led them to the outside of the hangar, and they found themselves once more near the Watch Office, and here Dowie, saluting again with perfect decorum, left them to rejoin his lads.

A terrific shattering rattle from a firing-butt broke the air round them into a thousand pieces as the guns of a Spitfire were tested, and jets and clouds of sand rose from the piercing concentration of the bullets.

High up above from an eminence, Lookout gazed over the aerodrome and into the surrounding sky—Lookout, the voice that spoke so often in Operations Room, the accent and the intonation changing as each watcher succeeded each, but whose personality remained a mystery, high up there with his machine-guns and his field-glasses and his telephone. Echoes of past Lookouts' voices still whispered silently round the walls of Ops. "Ack-ack fire in the south-east—many enemy aircraft approaching—twelve, twenty, thirty, fifty enemy bombers approaching from the south-east—ack-ack fire ceased —Spitfires approaching enemy—they're bombing, Sir—bombs on the aerodrome, Sir—six, seven, eight, nine, ten, exploding all round, Sir—nothing much hit yet, Sir"—never betraying excitement, never varying his tone, steadily the voice used to come from the square box in the room: "Dog fight, Sir—two enemy bombers in flames—Spitfire coming in to land, in trouble, Sir—ambulance started up, Sir"—so the voice of the Lookouts not so very long ago. There he was now, up above, outlined against the sky, only head and shoulders visible from where they stood, revolving as if on a turn-table, scanning sky and country all around.

The two of them walked away along the perimeter road. About it and beyond it, at irregular intervals, were the rest-rooms of the pilots at Dispersal, Flight by Flight. Looking round in a wide sweep, the dark figures of the Spitfires emerged one by one, propellers at rest, silent guns and engines pointing inwards to the landing ground. Here, then, was this vast arena—hangars and buildings grouped on one side—huts dotted about in the distance—and in them the actors waiting to make themselves as one with the lovely metal shapes whose beauty flashed across the sky.

In the hut of B Flight, Falcon Squadron, a game of poker was just finishing when Roger and Placket came in. James Glebe was playing for unexciting stakes with two Sergeants and a Pilot Officer.

They were sitting in easy-chairs, their Mae Wests over their tunics, and everything ready for the first call to action, when they would leap for their parachute harness and be off to their machines. The walls were covered with a variety of decoration: diagrams for the recognition of aircraft, charts, coloured pictures cut from weekly papers—invariably including some of feminine creatures with astonishingly elongated limbs—caricatures and cartoons by the squadron's own artists, and boards with details of names and aircraft. Iron bedsteads were ranged round the walls, and more often than not there would be a figure asleep on one of them despite the shouts from a game of cards, the noise of the wireless on a table, and the roar of engines outside. There was an air of uncanny peace in a pilots' Rest Room, for always there hung over it the knowledge that instant alertness might be demanded at any moment.

The card game broke up, and the players pushed back their easy-chairs. One of the Sergeant pilots, looking out of the window, jumped from his seat and ran for the door. A Y.M.C.A. van had appeared, and as its wheels ceased revolving, a cluster of figures appeared round it, men in stained and oily overalls carrying spanners or screwdrivers, and pilots and airmen mixed up with them. The van lowered its counter to serve its customers with tea and coffee and slabs of apple pasty, and clear gums to suck, and cigarettes and slices of cake.

"This is a bit boring," Glebe said, producing his pipe and tobacco; "time we had some action. Curse this weather."

Placket and Roger knew that feeling as if, deprived of the wings of an aircraft, one had lost a physical sense. To the flying man of flying age, nothing equalled the sensation of being in the air, and to be cut off from it, even for a short time, was like losing a limb, or aching from a hunger.

"Jerry doesn't seem to like us as he used to," Glebe mused. "Now we've got to go and persuade him to play."

"His tactics seem to be very much those of our war," Placket remarked. "Never attack unless you have the position and numbers to make as certain of success as possible. That's what he did in our day."

"It's generally so," Glebe agreed. "Usually he tries to nip off any straggler, some idiot who can't keep formation," and he seemed to address his remarks to the Pilot Officer sitting near him. "But sometimes, though it's rare, I admit, he'll go bull-headed for a sweep."

"Is it the bombers he's always after?" Roger asked him.

"I suppose so," Glebe answered. "But if he's feeling like it, he'll try to draw away the fighter escort first."

The young Pilot Officer to whom he appeared to have spoken his warning about keeping formation was plucking contentedly at a little fair moustache. His first appearance at this aerodrome had been in the early days of 1940. Roger remembered him then; he was very pink and well-mannered with little to say, and when he had damaged two aircraft in his first attempts to fly with his squadron, there had been even less said to him. It was not that there was a conscious decision to ostracise him, but the younger pilots were at a loss to know what to talk about to a man who in their eyes had made such an unfortunate ass of himself. He wandered about the Mess very quietly for some days, and then completed his shame by landing a slow training machine in an inaccessible spot from which it could not be extricated. Roger had tried to talk to him, but although his face showed friendliness, he was either too sunk in the enormity of his actions, or he was blandly unaware of them; it was impossible to determine which was the case. A few days later he had departed to some humdrum occupation where he could not be a danger to other pilots or to valuable machines. But here he was again, fifteen months later, as imperturbable as before, and as pink and as fair.

"How long have you been back with us, Wishart?" Roger asked him.

He ceased pulling his moustache and turned his bland eyes in Roger's direction.

"Only three days, Sir."

"Have you been on a show yet?"

"No, Sir."

"He's coming on the next one," Glebe growled, "and he'd better keep formation."

Roger looked at Wishart again. Nothing seemed to affect him. He had no shell of vanity, no assumption of carelessness, but it seemed as if there were something missing from his make-up as a fighter pilot. The unruffled calm of his pink face hid neither a perfect assurance nor any nervous care. Perhaps, deep down in his soul, he was pleased to have come back. Perhaps the expressionless eyes were already seeing countless enemy that would fall to his guns, or perhaps there was just nothing there at all. Roger could not tell. The remaining Sergeant pilot, a humorous-looking, stocky man, smiled at Glebe.

"We'll look after him, Sir," he said.

Wishart's moustache still seemed to be his only interest. He might not even have heard.

"What are you two doing?" Glebe said to Roger.

"Paying friendly visits."

"What's the weather like?" the impatient Glebe said, getting to his feet and going to the door.

It was still improving. The full loveliness of a British summer was now not far off. Already all the colours seemed to be changing and brightening. The grass and trees, the drab of the hangars, the red brick of the buildings, even the barbed wire and the gun emplacements were taking the first shine of the lustre of the evening to come. Glebe stood looking out over the aerodrome which had been his home since he was little more than a boy. All its activities were known to him, and his memories of it embraced those that the others could never share. Here he had done his peace-time flying, with that giant of the sky, Bo'sun Spritt. In the air above it, he could recall the improving types of aircraft that had led to the marvel standing on its wheels not many paces from him.

An aircraft circled to land; its undercarriage dropped like the unfolding legs of a gull, then its flaps descended, and, gliding in over their heads, the Gauleiter returned from his exercise with the gunners. His wheels and the tail wheel all touched the ground together, and, his landing complete, he swung his aircraft round to taxi towards Falcon Squadron's other Dispersal hut.

"Good-bye, James," said Roger, and when, after some two hundred paces, he turned round to look, James was still standing there, the yellow of his Mae West caught up now in the livening colours of the background, while contented figures munched at the Y.M.C.A. van, and shimmering light dispersed the brooding of that long day's sullenness.

"Will there be time this evening?" Roger asked.

"What for?" said Placket.

"The next show."

Placket turned his eyes upward to the sky, and then looked round the horizon. "Hardly, I should think."

"Tomorrow, then," said Roger, "for certain."

Placket suddenly stopped and looked at his watch.

"Good Lord!" he said, turning quickly in the opposite direction.

"What's the matter?" Roger called after him.

"My game of squash," Placket answered as he began to run.

"Who are you playing?" Roger went on shouting.

"Don't keep talking to me. I want all my breath for the game."

As Roger went on towards the next Dispersal, watching the riggers and fitters tinkering about with the machines standing on the grass, a practice dog-fight developed up above. The crescendo of the whines of aircraft diving and climbing one after the other first drew his attention to them, and he paused to look. He could see other figures outside the huts looking upwards, and they were joined by yet more, to whom this spectacle was not new, but who had been attracted by the sound of its nearness. One Spitfire was doing its best to keep on the tail of the other despite all the aerobatics which the target could do to try to throw its pursuer off its tail. It dived with dizzying speed and then climbed almost vertically into the sky again, turning on to its back at the top of the climb as if to perform a loop, and then rolling right way up again and diving once more. But always the pursuer seemed to anticipate each movement and to be in position to bring his gunsight to bear. The heights of the practice combat changed momentarily: now the aircraft were through the cloudbank overhead and the sound of their engines came only faintly, and then, screaming through the cloud, they would dive earthwards, still the one behind the other. Roger shook his head and walked on. He joined David, the Squadron Leader of Falcon Squadron, outside A Flight Dispersal hut. David was muttering to himself.

"Damn fools," he said, over and over again.

"Bit stupid," Roger said, as he stood beside him.

"Stupid! It's suicidal. They've no right to dog-fight at that height. They can get all the practice they want at a respectable distance from the ground, and save this nonsense for the Hun when they meet him."

The two machines had disappeared into the cloud again,

then one of them emerged, spinning in the vertical downward corkscrew motion that meant an aircraft voluntarily or involuntarily out of control. Out of the cloud came the other aircraft. The machine that was spinning checked its motion and immediately span in the opposite direction; and then, checking this, it came out in a steep dive. The dive ended as the pilot pulled back his control stick, but even as the nose of the aircraft pointed upwards, its body still sank towards the ground before the strength of the engine pulled all of it up once more. It cleared the ground by some fifty feet.

"Lunacy," said David at the top of his voice. Some of the other pilots collected round him, looking at him apprehensively.

"Look out!" he shouted, as if hoping that his voice might reach the pilot of the aircraft following that which had spun, but it was too late. Intent on trying to keep his target in such a position that he still had the advantage, the second pilot dived and never checked his dive. And beyond the barbed wire at the perimeter's edge and out in the fields of summer vegetables, the Spitfire buried its nose feet deep in the earth.

"Who is it?" Roger asked David.

"I don't know," he said. "It's not my squadron. My God, the other fellow's for it."

"How?"

"Playing the idiot like that. They've no business to be fighting at that height. He'll have a lot of explaining to do when it comes to be investigated."

Men had run through gaps in the barbed wire, the ambulance was crossing the aerodrome at full speed, down in the Watch Office Bywaters had already telephoned Sick Quarters, and Lookout had spoken his unhappy message to Operations Room. The silent group outside A Flight turned back into their hut, David's face still cloudy with anger.

"There are some of them that think that sort of thing's clever," he said, "and that's the result—a good machine gone and a pilot broken his neck for nothing." For there was no hope when the ambulance reached the wreckage in the field. It was there a long time, and then figures came slowly back through the barbed wire, and the breakdown party went out to salvage what remained.

"Which squadron was it?" Roger asked the Gauleiter, who was standing by the table, writing down details of his co-operation flight.

"I didn't see," he answered. "It may have been Heron. They've got a bunch of new lads, and perhaps it was two of them."

The other of the two mock combatants had been circling for some time as if loth to land. He must have seen the crash in the field, and the dawning realisation of his share in the responsibility was giving him much to think about. Presently, however, the wheels of his undercarriage came down and he glided in, landed, and ran slowly to the opposite side of the aerodrome.

"He'll be lucky," said the Gauleiter, who had been watching through the window, "to get away without a court martial."

"For an accident?" queried Roger.

"For an avoidable accident," the Gauleiter amended. "If orders had been obeyed, it couldn't have happened."

Squadron Leader David had a broad face, a pug nose, a cannon-ball shaped head, and a pipe drooping constantly from his mouth. He was laconic at most times, and the Falcons listened to his words with respect, for there were so few of them. He sat now in a wicker chair, sucking his pipe, which was empty, and thinking of the feelings of the Leader of the dead pilot's squadron. He knew what anger and bitterness the other would feel at this wretched waste, and the slur he would resent which had been brought upon his squadron. He tapped his pipe needlessly against the iron stove in the middle of the room, and "Damn fool", he kept on muttering.

It was no place to sit and gossip, and Roger went outside, followed by the Gauleiter.

"David seems to be very down on the other pilot," Roger said.

"It's an outrageously unnecessary risk," the Gauleiter replied forcefully.

"But I think," Roger went on, "that every pilot sooner or later gives way to the thrill of low flying."

"Low flying, perhaps," the Gauleiter said. "Every now and then you've got to get it out of your system; and, besides, it can be useful practice under sensible conditions, but not dog-fighting like a maniac near the ground. The kindest thing we can suppose is that they were both so concentrating on their fight that they just didn't know how low they were."

Roger looked at him. His face was rather white, and there was dark shading below his eyes.

"You don't look terribly well," he said.

"I'm fine," the Gauleiter replied shortly, but he was shivering slightly.

"When did you last have leave?"

"It's not leave I want; it's action."

"No point in flying," Roger said to him, "if you're not fit."

"No point in anything," the Gauleiter answered, "if I can't fly."

They smiled at one another as Roger turned back along the roadway. It was nearly tea-time, and he had one more visit to pay before he went to Mess, and then to duty.

As he left the perimeter road four Spitfires circled to land. They were Teddy and Humber and Max and Sergeant Bush. Two by two they landed and trundled away to the other side of the aerodrome.

CHAPTER FOUR

At the forward aerodrome, not so many miles away, from which the escort for the morning's rescue had been supplied, Squadron Leader Whelan and his Tower of Babel were getting impatient. His squadron consisted of a very mixed bag of Frenchmen, Czechs, Norwegians, Australians, Canadians, and a massive and imperturbable Dutch South African. Any break for the better in weather conditions was a signal for Whelan to telephone Operations: "We must *do* something."

"I'll speak to Group," the Controller would answer.

"Right, but get a move on. Three attacks a day is my aim, and it's no use letting the enemy get complacent."

If Group could not find a target, Whelan and his fighters would obtain permission to go and look for one for themselves. They were the terror of all enemy shipping plying up and down its own coastline. At any moment the anti-aircraft guard-ships surrounding the fat merchantmen whose protection it was their duty to ensure, would be savagely attacked by these venomous cannon-fighters coming in at low level to silence the guns. Roaring in behind them came Hurricane bombers to assault the merchantmen, and higher up still in the sky, a squadron of Spitfires kept watch for any air attack that might develop on these deadly avengers below.

If, however, Whelan was not given the organisation of a large force, he would set out with five other pilots to rove the sea stretches and to terrify and to destroy any likely target he could find.

He was tall and sandy, with a freckled face, a small moustache, and very deep-set eyes, buried behind cushions of high cheekbones. His nose was small and aquiline; his appearance was that of a mettlesome hawk, and his voice was nervously rapid. In contrast to him, his Dutch South African Flight Lieutenant, Holsteyn, was broad and square and calm. And his other Flight Lieutenant, a Frenchman, Maréchal, was dark and pale-faced, and, unlike the conventional Gallic fighter, as quiet and unruffled as Holsteyn.

On this aerodrome the Hurricane cannon-fighters and the Hurricane bombers messed together and worked out their tactics one with the other. Once they were in the air, few words were ever heard from them. Whelan's voice saying "Line astern—go" was the only signal to the outside world that the battle had been joined, and some thirty minutes later, his voice again would say "Land by Sections, Red Section first", and his laughing voice, with a catch of excitement in it, would tell Controller the total of three or four minutes' astonishing events.

Here at this forward aerodrome, with very little outside distraction, the Hurricanes talked, ate and slept flying, and if any enemy aircraft were so foolish as to approach within miles of their lair, the Hurricanes charged into the sky almost as quickly as they were told of the imminent danger. Nothing satisfied Whelan and his international brigand brigade unless they were in the air and seeking the enemy. And if the weather was too bad for them to hunt as a pack, ones and twos set out, if only to find, shoot, maim, and destroy some water-borne slinking German motor craft.

"Tell Group we must *do* something," he said to Havana.

"I've told them," Havana replied.

"Well, what about it?" said Whelan with his voice rising to a screech.

"You've got to hold your horses. They say there's something being planned."

"Yes, but while they're planning, we could do plenty and still be ready for their plans."

"I'm sorry, Whelan, but they won't play."

"Is it any use if I speak to them?"

"Not a bit. You can't have a private war of your own just now."

"We must harass the enemy!" Whelan shouted. "It's what we're here for."

"It's what you're doing," Havana answered. "It's no good, Whelan; Group has got something up its sleeve, and we can't go on pestering them under the circumstances."

"Oh! Lord," said Whelan, with a groan of disappointment. "All right; but we're all here, ready."

Three minutes later he was back on the telephone. "Can we go and do some practice firing?"

"Where?" said Havana, suspiciously.

"Just a few miles out. There are one or two wrecks we can poop at."

"No going over the other side," Havana warned him.

"Goodness, no—wouldn't dream of it."

And ten minutes later this band of enthusiasts for offence were diving and roaring over the skeleton ships offshore, flaying their useless hulks and the water round them with streams of cannon-shell.

The Hurricane bombers were equally inspired to action.

"Can we go out practice bombing?"—and off they leapt to drop their bombs at little more than mast-height on the targets which their imagination built into tankers and merchantmen, whose destruction was all their hope and joy.

This huge forward flying ground was indeed a thorn in the flesh of the enemy, and however much he had tried to pick it out, it had buried itself with greater venom into his sprawling limb.

Down there too at this hour, Flight Lieutenant Hereward was asleep in his bed, with the blinds drawn and nothing but the ticking of his clock and the rustle of the curtains to destroy his quiet. Maybe he was dreaming of the figures in the photograph on the chest of drawers. They were of a woman and two children, and there was nothing left of them to him but dreams, for one night a bomb had fallen, and only the photograph and his memories remained. He was asleep now, waiting for the fall of night, for the time when he would step out of the building and his clear blue eyes would look into the darkness with a vision that was almost unique. His solitary figure would walk towards the black Hurricane waiting for him, and in the darkness he would sit, waiting, waiting always for his chance. Night after night he ascended; he was never talkative, he never wanted much assistance.

"Anything doing?"

"Not yet."

Half an hour might elapse.

"Enemy aircraft some miles to your south."

"Tell the guns to give them hell."

A harassed Army Officer would approach the Controller. "There's a friendly fighter in the middle of the ack-ack bursts."

"That's all right. He likes it. It lets him know where the enemy is."

As long as the enemy was destroyed, Hereward did not mind who caused the kill. It was one more bomber and its crew dead—dead and smashed and obliterated. Hereward continued his nightly vigil long after other aircraft had come down for lack of fuel or because weather conditions were thickening. He never lost himself; for long periods nobody knew his position.

"Anything doing?"

"Not a sausage."

"What a pity!" And he would land.

Now he was dreaming.

Roger had visited Sick Quarters. This miniature hospital, with its wards, operating theatre, consulting-rooms, and dentist's surgery, stood at one corner of the parade-ground. A few dejected aircraftmen were sitting in the waiting-room, each with a look as if he were about to be tortured or otherwise shamefully misused.

The Dentist, a cherubic little man with dark curly hair, was drilling away contentedly, while his W.A.A.F. Orderly stood by waiting to hand him instruments or to mix up amalgam for his stoppings, Roger opened his door to say good afternoon to him, and the Dentist turned round cheerfully while the drill whizzed in his hand and glugs of discomfort came from his victim. "Do you want me?" he asked.

"No. Sorry I intruded."

"Not at all," said the very polite Dentist. "Delighted to see you at any time." And he returned to his excavation.

"Are you free?" Roger asked, knocking on and entering the opposite door. The Doctor, smoking his pipe, nodded.

"What is it?" he said. "Inoculation? Medical inspection? Old age?"

"Colour test," Roger said.

"Oh! Yes," the Doctor replied; "you're about due for one, aren't you? I want you to read the figures you see on the pages I'm going to show you."

He opened a book and turned over page by page, roundels made up of little coloured circles of every different shade.

Each large circle was therefore composed of countless little ones, the whole forming a blur of kaleidoscopic colour. Woven into each large circle was the pattern of a numeral, and at a glance the reader to be tested mentioned the numeral which was immediately apparent to him. The Doctor turned the pages, and Roger recorded glibly.

"Let's do it again," the Doctor said.

"It was as plain as a pikestaff."

"Yes, I'm sure; but let's do it again."

Roger rattled off the figures without hesitation.

The Doctor, outwardly a lugubrious man, but inwardly the soul of undisturbed cheerfulness, blew sad bubbling noises on his pipestem.

"Colour defective unsafe," he said.

"What on earth do you mean?"

"You didn't get one of them right."

"Suppose you read them," Roger said.

The Doctor turned over the pages, mentioning figures entirely different.

"That's what you ought to have seen," he said to Roger. "You're colour blind."

"But," Roger persisted, "are the figures I see in fact there?"

"Yes," said the Doctor.

"And you don't see them?"

"No."

"Then you're colour blind. It's outrageous to tell me I'm colour blind when I can see things that actually exist that you don't see."

"The point is," said the Doctor, "that about ninety per cent of people see what I see, and only ten per cent see what you see. Therefore you're colour blind."

"Thank you," said Roger. "What does it mean? A bowler hat?"

"I shouldn't take it too much to heart," the Doctor comforted him. "Your flying days are over, or you might have been dangerous."

"Pity they didn't discover it in the last war," Roger answered. "I must have shot at an awful lot of our own side thinking they were the enemy."

He retired on to the parade-ground rather crestfallen. He looked at the brighter weather, and really wondered if it were any brighter or merely the hallucination of blind eyes. He examined the intensity of an a W.A.A.F.'s red hair with such concentration tha girl took fright, turned away, and nearly broke int

"I suppose it must be green," Roger said to h

At tea he sat down next to Squadron Leade George Cardew was sitting on his other side.

"I thought you were at readiness," Roger said, as brought him a buttered teacake.

"We left them out there," Ogilvie answered, "an back with George hoping to find a bit of spare cake."

"Nothing as childish as that, Sir," George sa Mother promised me a pint tankard."

"I hear you don't like dinghies, George," Roger s

"Give me corns, Sir."

"What on earth do you mean?"

"Where I sit down, Sir."

"What nonsense, George! You know perfectly w thing was designed for comfort as well as utility."

"Sorry, Sir, I disagree. I like my old cockpit se without that contraption plonked on top of it."

"Are you a good swimmer, George?" Ogilvie aske

"Wizard, Sir. My breast-stroke was the pride of th baths."

"Nevertheless," Ogilvie said more seriously, "carry dinghy, George."

"Yes, Sir," and George winked at Roger.

Dalrymple and Halliwell were having their tea tog They both gazed in front of them and exchanged not a v And here and there other pilots of Heron Squadron eating their scones, or cutting into slabs of chocolate c At a far table was a group of new pilots allotted to the t squadrons, but not yet sufficiently absorbed in them to c to mix freely. Therefore they still held together, look rather self-conscious and a little defiant, but pleased to h McBain amongst them, who, finding that there was to be practice formation flying for him, had returned disgrunt to the Mess.

At a quarter to five Roger rose, and accompanied Havering to act as Operations "B" Officer, he left the M and its garden, and turned towards Operations Room.

The change-over of the watch did not take long.

"Nothing doing now," Havana told Roger. "The Gauleiter's been up for ack-ack co-operation; four of the Falcons had a sortie and enjoyed themselves; there's been some practice flying, and a Spitfire crashed—pilot killed."

"I saw that," Roger told him.

"Seems to have been asking for trouble," Havana said. "Whelan as usual is howling for action, but they and the Hurricane bombers are letting off steam practising. Otherwise all quiet.

At the other end of the room Havering was taking over from Templeton-Browning, and soon the latter and Havana had left. The crew did not change; their watches had been left to be arranged by themselves as best suited the majority, and they had decided that each crew should work with breaks during duty in their rest-room, for three watches totalling twenty-four hours out of forty-three, and then to have an extended break of twenty-nine hours. The present crew had come on duty at one o'clock and would remain until eight in the evening. Next morning they would return from eight until one o'clock, and at night they would work from eight o'clock until eight the next morning. From time to time members of the crew would relieve one another, and during the night a few hours' sleep could be obtained if there were not excessive activity. It would not be called a hard life on actual hours of working, but people grew progressively more tired without understanding why. The broken rhythm of their lives, the subconscious air of tension, the extreme concentration necessary when work was to be performed, and this constant necessity to be alert at any hour of the day or night in a confined atmosphere under hard electric lights, could be enervating to those who did not use their rest periods to the full advantage for recuperation and healthy relaxation.

The humorous Sergeant and the big Corporal were sitting on either side of Roger, and a plotting exercise was in progress on the floor below. From distant points the courses and positions of supposed aircraft were being told to the plotters, who were placing the details on the map, and all departments were working as if actual flying were in fact taking place. As Roger began to make his opening entries in the Controller's log-book, the exercise came to an end, and the W.A.A.F.s took out their knitting, or their sewing, and the men their books and papers. The great map was cleared of its counters and plaques, and the only tokens of life on its large surface were the indications of convoys crawling round the coast. Hour by hour their positions changed as news was flashed from Navy to Air Force.

"Group for you," Havering called.

Roger took up his telephone and switched over a key.

"Controller here."

"What's the weather like with you?"

"Improving all the time, Sir."

"Can you manage a convoy patrol?"

"I think so, Sir. I'll make sure from one of the Squadron Leaders."

"What squadron will you use?"

"We've got Falcon and Cygnet at readiness, Sir."

"I see. Well, use whichever you like, and a little later on we might be able to relax the state of one of them."

Roger called to Havering: "See if Squadron Leader Ogilvie has returned to Cygnet's Dispersal. He was having tea with me, but he may have gone back.... No," he said, "I'll do that myself. Ask Group details of the convoy so that I can describe it to Ogilvie when I'm speaking to him." He pushed over the key to Cygnet Squadron. "Is the Squadron Leader there? Ask him to speak to me. Oh, hallo, Ogilvie. Is it fit for your boys to do a convoy patrol? ... All right, I'll wait."

Ogilvie had gone outside to look at the weather.

"Good," Roger said to him when he came back. "Four aircraft. Wait a minute; I think Ops. B has got the details now." Havering had handed him a slip of paper on which was written the latest position, the number of ships, the direction and the escort of the convoy. "Here it is.... Who will you send? Red and Yellow? What, is George deigning to fly on his birthday? All right, I'll tell Group and ring back your Dispersal to give the O.K." He turned towards Havering again. "Tell Group it can be done, and if they'll pass the order, we'll crack off immediately."

A minute or two later a W.A.A.F. sitting below Havering's telephone keyboard handed up a piece of paper containing the official order from Group passed to her on another telephone line. Havering spoke to Cygnet Dispersal Point: "Convoy patrol ordered off. Let me know when they are airborne."

The light from the late afternoon sun was streaming into the room illuminating the map, and reflections of it came from the metal of the headbands which held the telephones to the ears of the plotters sitting round the table; the clatter of a teleprinter sounded from a nearby cabinet, messages passed backwards and forwards between Operations Room and Observer centres and other aerodromes; the Army's soft-footed telephonists breathed quietly into their mouthpieces to give information to forward gun and searchlight sites. There was little sign of activity on the plotting map: a few friendly fighters showed at various places over land or across the coastline, but there was nothing to stir the pulse or to require close concentration.

The Lookout called: "Four aircraft, Cygnet Squadron, lining up to take off," and after a short pause, "Four aircraft, Cygnet Squadron, now airborne."

At the same time the Dispersal hut telephoned and Havering confirmed to Roger: "Cygnets are off."

Roger picked up his hand microphone, and beside him the Sergeant and Corporal picked up theirs. The rush of atmospherical disturbance sounded in their ears, not too uncomfortably, but like the sound of water gushing from an active kitchen tap. Suddenly it ceased, and "Hallo, Tartan, Cygnet Red Leader calling. Are you receiving? Over"—called George's voice, with its buoyant note.

"Hallo, Cygnet Red One, Tartan answering. Loud and clear. Are you receiving me? Over."

"Hallo, Tartan. Loud and clear also. Any special instructions?"

"Hallo, Cygnet Red One, Tartan answering. Did you receive your orders?"

"Yes, Tartan, yes. Proceeding on patrol."

Roger permitted himself a breach of proper procedure. "Hallo, George. Got a comfortable seat?"

"Like a feather bed, Sir," came the happy reply.

The reported positions of the four Spitfires showed them making a steady course for the convoy, and Roger put down the telephone receiver. "Listen out for them, Sergeant," he said to his Deputy Controller.

"What shall I do, Sir?" asked the Corporal, crestfallen at being left out of it.

"You can take over any local flying."

The Sergeant and the Corporal pressed their receivers to their ears with such firmness that it looked as if they were trying to press them through their heads and out the other side. There was something excessively thrilling about the radio control of aircraft, but something that needed to be controlled in itself. The glow of importance on the faces of those having their first opportunity for this work, gave the impression that they imagined themselves minor Nelsons, ordering the dispositions for the Battle of Trafalgar. But they soon settled down, realising that while it was their information and clear speech and anticipation which helped the pilot in the air, it was the man in the aircraft who fired the guns and who had them fired at him. Sitting on the ground thousands of feet below that lonely fighter, the Controller had little to worry about except to keep his wits clear, his mentality alert, and his demeanour unruffled and assured. Roger when controlling could go into a trance-like state. Sitting on this dais overlooking the map, was to him as if he were flying over that portion of country at a vast height. He could see the winding threads of road and river, the sharp outline of the coast, and the myriad irregular patterns of field and forest. He could watch the enormous bastions of cloud, remembering how, when he himself used to dive into them, he had so often shrunk involuntarily in his cockpit, expecting their solidity to be real. He could see, as he approached the side of a cloud, the illuminated circle of rainbow-coloured lights with the silhouette of his aircraft outlined in the centre. He could remember the sense of soaring power and freedom as he ascended from a grey world below, up through the wet mistiness to illimitable sunlight spread over the solid sea of cloud-top beneath him. Always these mental pictures flashed their film over the screen of his mind when he sat controlling. But now, because the convoy was a routine matter, he sat back and relaxed while the Corporal and the Sergeant assumed their most martial looks.

Standing behind him was a young Czech Flight Lieutenant, a man with soft brown eyes and a sensitive, intelligent face.

"Hallo, Horval," Roger said to him. "What are you doing

here?"

"Oh," the Czech answered him, "I come down to watch for a little."

"When are they going to let you fly again?"

The Czech smiled and shrugged his shoulders. "Who know?" he said.

Roger rose to stretch himself. "How long have you been in this country?"

"Since May, 1940."

"It was the Battle of Britain, Horval, wasn't it, when you got hit?"

"It was," Horval replied, "but maybe they let me fly very soon again now."

"How long had you been at it before?"

"Please?"

"You had been a pilot for how long?"

"Oh, five—six years."

"In Czechoslovakia?"

"Yes." Horval's face clouded. "In Czechoslovakia."

Roger looked at him curiously. "What did you feel in September 1938, after the Munich Agreement?"

Horval smiled with a wry mouth. "Do I have to remember?" he asked. He was silent for a moment. "I was Duty Officer on my aerodrome in 1939 when the Germans marched in. It was my duty to hand over to the Germans."

"What happened to you when war broke out?"

"Some good friends and I," Horval said, speaking slowly, "just before the war, had managed to escape over the border into Poland. We had no passports, no papers, and then the Germans pressed into Poland, and very soon afterwards came the Russians in the other direction. What were we to do?"

"What did you do, Horval?"

"Oh, I must not say in detail, but eventually we got away."

"Where to?"

"To France."

"But how?"

"By Roumania and Turkey and Syria and North Africa."

"Did you fly in France?"

"But of course we flew in France."

"And then you escaped here?"

"Yes, some of us escaped here."

"Did you find it hard, Horval?"

"Not so very. I go back to my country some day." The soft brown eyes were looking a long distance off. "Besides," he said, "I am still young man. I wish to see much more of the world. It is harder for some of my older compatriots. It was hard for a while for a great friend of mine, who is a Wing Commander now."

"What happened to him?"

"He escaped with me, but he leave his wife behind in Prague. She was expecting baby. When we arrive in France at last, he ask permission of French authorities to admit his wife if he can make contact with her. He had managed in many secret ways to hear news of her through friends in Yugoslavia. That was, you remember, before Yugoslavia was attacked. She had by then had the baby. But you know what French authorities were like, first this delay, then that delay, and before they could make up their minds, France had fallen. So he come to England, and he ask English authorities for permission to send for his wife, which they give. One day, therefore, his wife leave Prague, and she leave the baby behind with her parents. She have no money and she have no papers, but she walk, and she walk from Prague through Hungary and Roumania, until she come to Yugoslavia. All the time she have no money and she must avoid questions, with no papers. In Yugoslavia some good friends help her a little, and she manage to go through Turkey and Syria and Palestine till she come to Egypt. It is from there she can send message to her husband. He tell her that the British authorities give permission for her, and will help her to reach England, so she take a boat, and it goes round the east coast of Africa and to Cape Town, and here she take another boat, and where do you think that take her?"

"Where?" asked Roger.

"To New York, and from New York she take a boat, and at last she join her husband."

"How long ago was that?"

"About three months. They are very happy couple now, but it was a long journey."

"And the baby?"

"It is in Prague. Perhaps they see it some day."

"There's an enemy plot, Sir," the Sergeant said to Roger.

"Excuse me, Horval." Roger studied the big map, and the latest information it showed. Then he picked up the telephone.

"Hallo, Cygnet Red One, Tartan calling. There's a bandit a long way from you to the North-east. Keep a sharp look out."

"O.K., O.K.," came George's voice.

"Group for you," Havering said.

The Group Controller's voice spoke in Roger's ear.

"You see that hostile plot? You'll watch it, won't you? We've got something from another aerodrome going to try to take care of it, so don't let your boys leave the convoy."

"All right, Sir."

The enemy seemed to be hugging the coastline as in the morning, using the clouds as his cover, into which he could escape and from which he could emerge again to scan the seas for ships and targets.

"Hallo, Tartan, Cygnet Red One calling. Any information for us?"

"Hallo, Cygnet Red One. He is still a long way from you. Maintain your patrol. . . . Can your fellows help?" Roger said to the Army Officer seated on his right.

"I've warned all coast batteries already, Sir. They may be able to spot him and give us a height soon."

"Ask Group," Roger said to Havering, "if they've any idea what it is."

A moment later Havering rang off from Group. "They think it's a Dornier," he said. "It's come over in cloud."

Cardew and his three others toured up and down the line of ships, which were seeking their safe harbour at the end of another vital journey. Dirty and caked, they steamed their slow way through the perils of the night and day, and their destroyers fussed round them as shepherds bringing the flock to rest at eventide. Round and round the shores of Britain these craft plied, near the minefields, watching and waiting for motor torpedo-boat attack, and listening always for the heavy drone of aircraft that might sink them from above. But over them, appearing at one end and disappearing down the long column of steaming ships, were the four Spitfires, eyes watching the distance, ears listening for the message, fingers on their gun-controls, waiting for the menace from the North-east. For the enemy had turned South-west towards them.

"Hallo, Cygnet Red One, Tartan calling. Bandit has turned towards you. Still some miles away."

The Army Officer had come up and put a slip of paper in front of Roger's eyes. He read it aloud into the telephone. "Reported height, two thousand. Using cloud cover."

"Hallo, Tartan, Red One answering. That won't help him much if he comes near us." George's voice was still gay, but quite firm.

The Dornier turned inland as if to swing away.

"Any information?" called George.

"Hallo, Red One, he's turned away a little."

"Blast!" said George.

The plots seemed to show a German pilot hesitating to make up his mind. Perhaps he thought he had done enough for one day; perhaps, having found no target, it was time to go home and report that the English shipping seemed to be too frightened to have put to sea; perhaps he looked at his petrol gauge and decided to make one further course to the South—for his plots turned again.

"Hallo, Red One, bandit has turned towards you again. Maybe making for your patrol."

"O.K.," said George. Then he spoke to his other pilots. "Hallo, Yellow One, Red One here. Are you receiving? Over."

"Loud and clear. Over," Yellow One replied.

"If we spot the bandit, you and Yellow Two try to get above cloud. Red Two and I will remain below cloud. If we drive him up, you send him back to us."

"Received and understood," Yellow One answered.

Roger was calling again: "Hallo, Red One, Tartan calling. He's still approaching—coming towards you fairly fast—" Roger paused and watched the plots. "Hallo, Red One, he should be approaching you now, now. Over."

"Hallo, Tartan, Red One answering. Message received. Hallo, Yellow One, échelon starboard. Hallo, Red Two, are you behind me?"

"Here I am," sang out Red Two.

"O.K. Stick by me."

Yellow One's voice rang out: "One o'clock, one o'clock

just under cloud."

"I see him," said George. "Up you go, Yellow One. Tally-ho, Tartan, tally-ho!"

The crackle of the atmospherics in Roger's ears seemed to him the rattle of machine-guns.

"He's into cloud, Yellow One. He's coming up."

"Hallo, Red One, we've broken cloud. What course are you steering?"

"Hallo, Yellow One, ninety degrees, ninety degrees."

"O.K., O.K. Turning on ninety now."

Again a silence.

"He's through!" from Yellow One. "Tally-ho, Tartan!"

Then again the atmospherics.

"He's into cloud, Red One. I'm on a hundred and fifty."

"Tally-ho!" yelled George from below the cloud, with a roar that nearly split Roger's ear.

After that there was a long pause. At last Yellow One could contain himself no longer.

"What's happening? Red One, what's happening?"

"Shut up," said George. "I'm finishing the blighter off... Zonk!" said George, "that's another of them in the drink."

"Hallo, Red One, Tartan calling. Did any of them bale out?"

"Didn't have a chance," George replied.

"Anything to be seen, Red One?"

"Nice lot of bubbles, Tartan."

"Resume patrol, Red One."

"O.K.," said George. "Can you join Yellow Section up on me again?"

The operation was concluded. The four of them re-assembled, and up and down the lane of ships they pursued their steady beat.

"What's that flashing?" Roger heard Yellow One call to George.

"Somebody's signalling from a ship," George answered. "My morse isn't too hot. Can anybody read it?"

Red Two spoke up. "T... H... A..." he spelt slowly. "I think they're saying 'thank you, Fighters'."

The patrols kept on their steady courses, one succeeding the other, and there was to be no more operational excitement before night fell; so the room resumed its routine business, Havering organising the continuous relief of the patrols, the Liaison telephonist warning wide stretches of the country of the passage of aircraft, and the Sergeant and the Corporal taking and passing formal messages on the radio. From time to time the Signals Officer came into the room to see that all went smoothly, and one of the Flight Sergeants in that Section, who could nose out faults in communications as a terrier noses a rat, was busy on the floor below with a screw-driver and pliers. At intervals other members of the crew relieved those whose heads ached from their headbands and whose ears drummed with countless messages.

At seven o'clock in the evening the Group Controller rang through to Roger.

"You can relax one of the squadrons. Which is it to be?"

"Cygnet have been doing most of the work, Sir. I think we might stand them down and let Falcon carry on till the end of the day."

"Very good. Signal me when it's done."

"Hallo, Sir," said Roger, detaining him on the line, "there's a general Mess meeting at nineteen hundred hours. We'd be grateful to let as many attend it as possible."

"Oh," said the Group Controller, "a really serious matter, eh? Perhaps the enemy will condescend to leave you alone during it. I'll let you know."

"Tell them in the Mess," Roger said to Havering, "to hold the Mess meeting up for a little while. Cygnet Squadron will be coming down from Dispersal, and perhaps we can get some of Falcon there too."

Group did not keep him waiting long. "As long as you keep the convoy patrol going, you can let the other pilots go down to the Mess."

"Thank you, Sir."

Roger made contact with Squadron Leader David and explained the situation.

"O.K.," he said. "I've nothing to say at the Mess meeting, so I'll send Glebe off on the next patrol, and take the one after that myself, which should be just about the last."

Down at the Mess the Steward and the Mess Secretary had arranged all available seating accommodation in the ante-room in rows facing a table with chairs round it for the

Mess Committee; Group Captain Faversham had indicated that he intended to be present only as a member of the Mess. Easy-chairs for him and the Wing Commander were prominently placed in front of those of the ordinary members. At seven o'clock there was much coming and going as people struggled into the anteroom and fought their way out of it, trying to obtain their tankards of beer before the opening of the Mess meeting forced abstinence on them. The delay announced for the arrival of the pilots from Dispersal was received with delight, and the busy Bar waiters breathed a little more easily. The Mess Secretary was solemnly arranging minute books, accounts, agenda, and Mess rules on the table. The Messing Officer was nerving himself to defend any attacks on the quality of the food and cooking, and the Bar Officer was prepared to justify his choice of beer. The Mess President was still in the Secretary's office trying, at this eleventh hour, to equip himself with the answers to possible questions.

The anteroom was full of smoke and chatter. The windows to the garden stood wide open, but it was insufferably hot inside. Such a meeting was, on the whole, typical of democratic government. The officials in charge were there to render account for the last four months, to explain and to answer. The citizens of that community were there to assess, to question, and to judge; but the great body of them were only too eager to get to their supper, and felt that this intrusion on their time was tiresome. Only some few among them were ready to be interested, one or two for the good of the common cause, one or two from motives of self-interest, and a few more entirely for the sake of self-importance. But there was one advantage over the ordinary workings of democracy; attendance at a Mess meeting, unlike attendance at an election, was a compulsory matter, and however disinterested a member might be, he was forced to be present and to give his vote. Thus the long-winded gentleman whose aim was self-interest or self-importance had little patience shown to him, for the great body of lazy, but sane, public opinion could soon judge the value of his words, and, having let him exhibit his ego, relegate him to the sphere of forgotten things.

Squadron Leader Ogilvie and George Cardew led the influx of fresh pilots from the aerodrome. George bellowed for a half tankard as he came in.

"Come along, George," the Group Captain said to him; "we've no time for that. People want their supper."

George looked crestfallen. The Group Captain turned away, but stopped.

"Wait a minute. You got a Dornier, didn't you, George?"

"Number Two and I got one," George said, and with a twinkle in his eye, "It's my birthday too, Sir."

The Group Captain smiled at him. "Very well, George; but pour it down your neck in one and get a move on."

"Half can for Cardew," George shouted at the back of a retreating waiter.

The anteroom was settling down. People took their places, and at last, with the Group Captain and Wing Commander Romilly seated in front, the Mess Committee was able to begin.

The Mess President rose: "I call upon the Secretary to read the minutes of the last meeting," he said, and sat down.

The Mess Secretary, tall, burly, an expert in tommy-guns, gas, and all forms of offence, began to read shakily. The polite looks of boredom on the faces of the members indicated that they were paying no attention at all.

"The minutes of the previous meeting having been read, it is put to this meeting that these be passed. Those in favour?"

A forest of hands shot up, for the sooner the votes were taken, the sooner it would all be over.

"If I might ask, Mr. President," said a voice from the back, "and arising out of the last minutes, what has been done about the provision of a rest for the long billiard cue?"

"We'll come to that," said the Mess President, frowning on the interrupter, "when we get to the heading 'Other Business' on the agenda."

"Yes, but," the enquirer went on, "the last minutes specifically said that a long rest would be provided."

"Climb on the table," called a voice.

"Come, come," the Bar Officer said, "we can't have people climbing on the table. We've only just had it re-covered."

"That wouldn't be necessary if we had a long rest," the original interrupter persisted.

The President hammered. "The matter can be raised later in the meeting. Are there any against the passing of the minutes?"

The interrupter's hand shot up.

"Minutes passed unanimously," growled the President to the Secretary.

"But," the Secretary pointed out, "Pilot Officer Jukes has voted against."

"Damn Jukes!" said the President. "Forget him. We now come," he declared, raising his voice, "to the consideration of the balance sheet for the last four months. This has been audited by the Audit Committee and it has been published on the Mess notice-board for the last seven days. Are there any questions before I put it to the meeting that the balance sheet be adopted?"

Pilot Officer Jukes leapt to his feet.

"Has a reserve been made for the purchase of a rest for the long billiard cue?"

"A reserve?" said the Mess President. "Why a reserve?"

"Because as shown by the minutes of the previous meeting, it was decided that such a rest should be bought. If it has not been bought already, then a reserve should have been made in the accounts."

"What's he talking about?" the President said to the Secretary.

The Secretary was gazing stonily at the agenda sheet in front of him. "I haven't the faintest idea."

"We will come to that, as I said before," the President remarked, "under the heading of 'Other Business'."

"But," Pilot Officer Jukes told him, "the reserve is a matter for the accounts."

There was a long pause while the Mess Committee looked bewildered. Despairingly the President sought the eye of the Accountant Officer, who rose with alacrity.

"No purchase having been made and no commitments to enter into a purchase having been made either, there is no necessity to create a reserve for a non-existent creditor."

The Mess President fixed Pilot Officer Jukes with his eye, and Jukes subsided.

"Do you think," the Group Captain said from his easy-chair, "you could explain the accounts in detail to the meeting? Not many of them really understand a balance sheet."

The President rose unhappily, but taking heart from the thought that only the Accountant Officer had the knowledge to criticise him, he plunged into an astonishing discourse of explanation. It meant very little to most of his hearers whose attention had wandered long ago.

The business of the meeting proceeded. There was difficulty in disposing of each item on the agenda, for the self-important and the self-interested chose each vote to thrust themselves forward, and very often the original resolution was lost in a tangle of suggestions, amendments, and irrelevant details. But by the time the hands of the clock had reached a quarter to eight there were distinct signs that the main body of the meeting was growing restive, and it did not need the Mess President to deal with obstructionists, for their fellow members were by now using very firm methods.

"The meeting is concluded," the President said hoarsely, through the billowing clouds of tobacco smoke. Everyone stood up, and the Group Captain and the Wing Commander went out. The stampede for supper had begun.

At eight o'clock the crews in Operations Room changed watch. The last convoy patrol under Squadron Leader David had taken off. There was five minutes' bustle as the relief picked up the threads of its duties, but Roger and Havering were to continue to occupy the dais until ten o'clock, for their watches differed from those of the crews. On the floor below a young W.A.A.F. Sergeant was arranging details for the night, specifying those who should rest and how they should share the twelve hours till the morning. The tea-maker went off to attend to her boiling water; blankets and pillows were carried to the rest-room, and because the weather was warmer and the room would soon be confined within its blacked-out windows, permission was given for tunics to be taken off. Sitting in their blue shirts with their sleeves rolled up, the W.A.A.F.s now looked like office girls at work; the rigidity of uniform had gone, and the collars and ties appeared less formal. In fact, they seemed to suit most women, who were now at least spared the problem of whether to wear high necks or low necks, brooches, ear-rings or beads. As the sun sank, the electric lights beat a harder glow over the room, and the figures of the intent plotters round the table stood out more sharply. Darkness was spreading from the east as

David left the convoy.

"Is the flare-path all ready?" Roger asked Havering, who telephoned Bywaters in the Watch Office.

"Everything ready," he replied. "Do you want obstruction lights on?"

"Yes, please."

"Aerodrome obstruction lights now on," Lookout called.

All the sky had cleared. It was the beginning of a gentle summer night. A thin new moon had come to life, and there was no haze. Roger had been standing at the door, sniffing the air outside, and gazing upwards.

"Might be busy tonight," he said to Havering when he came back. "Poor old Placket won't get much sleep."

"There go ours," Havering answered, pointing down to the map. Already the British bombers were taking off. One after the other their tracks showed as they set off, each on his solitary course for the enemy objective. The Whitleys and Wellingtons and Hampdens, the Manchesters and Stirlings, were starting their day. Roger tried to picture them as they turned their backs on the last light in the West, and climbed towards Europe and their targets.

Soon the four Falcon Spitfires were circling overhead with their navigation lights on. One after another they came down, with the Squadron Leader last of all. The obstruction lights were put out, the squadron was released; night had fallen, and the aerodrome was very quiet.

The dining-room was quite empty when David and Glebe came in for their supper, and except for those who were playing billiards, or table tennis, or bridge in the card-room, the remainder had disappeared off the camp to favourite places in the vicinity.

The Group Captain had gone back to Station Headquarters, and the Wing Commander had joined some of the pilots elsewhere.

Flight Lieutenant Hereward had wakened; at the forward aerodrome he was sitting in a deck chair outside the Dispersal hut, with his black-painted Hurricane not many yards from him. He was equipped for instant flying and he was accustoming his eyes to the surrounding darkness. At last he called into the hut, without entering it himself: "Tell Controller I'm going up to stooge about, and he can let me know if anything happens."

"Hereward's going to take off," Havering told Roger.

"There's nothing doing yet."

"No, but you know what he is. He'll just hang around in case anything does happen."

There was no sign of the enemy yet, and after a preliminary call from Hereward which Roger answered, the pilot disappeared into the blackness and to his own loneliness. Every twenty or thirty minutes he called to Roger: "Any news yet?"

"Nothing yet."

The tracks of the British bombers had disappeared, but those of other night fighters practising, or on patrol, were weaving over the table. Others had gone across the water to search out enemy aerodromes and to make still more unpalatable the hazards of any night raiders who might come from them.

Roger was reading. During the night watches he had taken to books again, after long years during which he had found no time for them. Book after book he read, of commentary, biography, and incident of the past ten or fifteen years. Each time he finished one he swore that he would not choose another of these histories of futility for they made him morbid, but he sought them as he might have sought a drug, and he could not stop. It was as if he were patiently trying to discern in all these millions of words what had brought the world to this chaos since the days he had re-entered it from the last war, so ready to believe then that all would be well again. He could not read novels, and his only relief from the painful analyses of past misdeeds was to explore some unknown country with the voyager who had written about it. But even these were unsatisfying, for there was no escape to the jungles and the deserts, each now itself threatened with the all-embracing tide of world upheaval. And yet there was some comfort in knowing there was no escape, in facing facts, however grim and terrible, and in finding again the simplicity of existence shorn of all its dazzling trappings. This one common cause made life so much less complicated—even so, he could not stop reading of the passions and perversions, the lies and greeds and follies of the past.

The Sergeant beside him interrupted his absorption.

"Something coming down from the North, Sir."

An enemy plot had appeared. The plotter, seeing Roger look at it, called up to him: "Observer Corps say there's another, Sir, some miles behind."

"Hallo, Silver One Five," Roger called to Hereward, "there's a bandit a long way North. Are you near your base? Over."

"Hallo, Tartan, Silver One Five answering. Approaching base now. What height is he?"

"Reported twelve thousand."

"I'll hang around, Tartan."

"What are you going to do with Hereward?" the Army Liaison Officer asked Roger.

"If the bandit comes within range, Hereward can have a look for him."

"But what about the guns?"

"They can go on cracking. They act as a pointer to Hereward."

"Yes, but he may get hit himself."

"That doesn't worry him. The more gun-fire you can give him, the better he'll be pleased."

The Army Officer shook his head dubiously. "Well, if you say so," he said, "but I don't like it."

"Hereward will be furious if your guns don't fire."

"What about searchlights?"

"He hates them."

"All I can say is," the Army Officer remarked, walking away to telephone his batteries, "it's all very peculiar."

"Hallo, Silver One Five. Bandit still coming down from the North. There is another one behind him."

"Fine. Give me a course. Over."

"Hallo, Silver One Five. Steer three-three-zero degrees. Over."

"Hallo, Tartan. Your three-three-zero degrees received. Listening out."

The black Hurriçane streaked through the night. The thin curve of the moon gave little radiance, and the darkened houses below heard the heavy beat of a bomber's engines. Some of the dwellers had made for shelters, others sat inured to many raids, but still with that sense new to man—of destruction descending at vast speed on his person, and on his alone. The enemy aircraft were not part of a big attack; they were lone marauders with little object in view but to spread terror to those beneath.

"Hallo, Silver One Five. Twenty degrees port, twenty degrees port; bandit still coming towards you."

"What height?"

"Reported still the same—twelve thousand."

"They're coming into a heavily defended gun area," the Army Officer said apprehensively.

"All the better," Roger told him. "Hallo, Silver One Five, Tartan calling. There may be fireworks round you soon."

"That's what I want, Tartan."

In the North reverberations sounded, the noises sharpening as the raider came nearer. Gigantic crackles and the upward diminishing rush of shells filled all the air round Operations Room.

"Hallo, Silver One Five, Tartan calling. You're closing in on him now. He should be on your port side turning South-east."

"Hallo, Tartan. He can't be far away. There's plenty of stuff bursting near me."

The cracks and detonations reached a peak of furious intensity, and the noise of them passed over and along the course of the enemy's flight.

A W.A.A.F. Liaison telephonist looked over excitedly to Roger. "Observer Corps say there's an aircraft falling in flames."

Roger grabbed his telephone: "Hallo, Silver One Five. Are you all right?"

"Hallo, Tartan," came Hereward's placid voice. "I'm all right, but the Hun isn't."

"Did you get him?"

"No, the gunners got him first."

"Bad luck."

"Bad luck nothing. It doesn't matter who gets him, does it?"

"There's another one about ten miles behind."

"Right. I'll look for that. Tell the guns to keep going."

Again the noise of explosions rose in a crescendo as they travelled over from the North.

"Hallo, Silver One Five. Bandit has turned East."

"O.K."

The bursting shells flashed their pin-points of light against the velvet sky. A tremendous concentration of them winked for several minutes.

"Hallo, Tartan, Silver One Five calling. I've picked him up. Stand by."

"He's on to him," Roger said for the benefit of everybody.

"Shall I tell the guns to cease fire now?" the Army Officer asked.

"No, man, no. Pump up everything they've got."

The Liaison telephonist spoke again. Her cheeks were flushed and her eyes were shining. "Observers say they can hear an engagement. Machine-gun and cannon fire."

"Hereward will get him," Roger said.

"How many has he got already?" Havering asked.

"Fourteen."

"All at night?"

"Yes, all at night. Twice he's had two on one night."

The W.A.A.F. telephonist was giving all her attention once more to her instrument. "Observers say, Sir," she said, "an enemy aircraft has just crashed on the beach. It burst into flames on the ground."

Roger grunted. "Hallo, Silver One Five, Tartan calling. Bandit confirmed destroyed." There was no reply. "Hallo, Silver One Five, Silver One Five, Tartan calling. I say again, bandit is confirmed as destroyed."

He waited for what seemed a long time.

"Hallo, Tartan, Silver One Five calling. Were you calling me?"

Roger repeated his message.

"Hallo, Tartan, Silver One Five answering. Sorry I didn't reply before. I must have been dreaming. Thanks for the message. Good."

CHAPTER FIVE

TEDDY RYAN, Max and Humber had gone to the big city. Teddy had suggested it; he was feeling restless, and he was always at his most wakeful at night. The three of them walked the half-mile to the station, Teddy dark and small, and Humber fair and small, on either side of Max's big geniality. As always, they discussed the tactics of fighting, but Max was more interested in the possibilities of his departure to the Dutch East Indies. They had no set plan for the evening, except that Teddy had a vague hope that he might find some of his friends in that world of horses which had been his before the war. The electric railway with its glim-lighted carriage carried them through the disembowelled districts. It was too dark to see, but they knew the views on either side—the piles of rubble and bricks, the skeletons of beam and after, the houses blasted open, and the lonely air of desolation. If, indeed, the enemy had been aiming for the railway, their bomb-sights needed adjustment, for they had so conspicuously missed it.

"This is your East End we go through, eh?" Max asked Teddy.

"Yes."

"Why do you have an East End?"

"Because it is the east end, you fathead—north, south, east, west. The East End is in the east."

"No," said Max affably, "I do not mean that; for you do not speak of the North End or the South End, you only speak of East End and West End."

"What do you mean, why do we have it?"

"Why, in this rich country of yours, do you have something so horrible as the East End?"

"I'm not from these parts," Humber broke in, "but it's the same with all big cities."

"Why?" asked Max.

"Just happens, I suppose," Humber replied.

"But why," Max persisted, "does it allow to happen?"

Teddy started to sing.: "There'll always be an England," he carolled unmusically.

"Maybe it's a good thing," Humber said, "that it's been blasted wide open."

"Was that the best way?" Max asked.

"That's the worst of all you blooming people from the Continent," Teddy said to him, "you always start getting political."

"But there's nothing political in asking why you have an East End, and then by contrast a West End."

"Maybe that's what we're supposed to be fighting for," Humber said.

"What?" asked Max, astonished, "the East End and the West End?"

"No, to blast them both away."

"East is east and west is west," recited Teddy.

Max, still in perfect good humour, looked at him.

"Do you know why you fight, Teddy?"

Teddy's cheerful brown eyes looked at him. "I've a vague idea."

"What?"

"To get back to my horses and to train Derby winners."

"It is so hopeless with you British," Max said; "you are never serious about what matters."

"But I am serious," Teddy stressed. "I want to get back to what I like best. That's what I'm fighting for, I suppose."

"Is the East End what the people who live in it like best?"

"Here, Max, what are you, a blooming Red?"

"What is it, this 'Red' you mean?"

"This is a nice way to begin an evening," Teddy said to Humber. "We'll end up at the Church Army."

Humber, ex-Sergeant pilot, looking very fresh and new in his Pilot Officer's uniform, sat silent for a little while.

"I come from a different world from horses," he remarked at last—"a world of back streets and getting up early in the morning and marge on the bread—"

"Full of vitamin D, old boy," Teddy broke in.

Humber disregarded him. "There's always smoke about, and even on the sunniest day the light looks sort of powdery and only half shines. Nobody's very happy, and nobody's very sad. They get some fun out of the dogs and the local football match and filling up their coupons for the Pools, and the women go to the cinema and have a good cry or a good laugh. But most of the time it's a struggle, and if I say it's a hopeless struggle. I mean it's a struggle without real hope of better things. Everybody knows he'll remain just as he is unless he's worse off by being unemployed; everybody knows that if he lives long enough, he's got the Old Age Pension to look forward to, and any help the kids can give him. I don't think I'm fighting for that."

"You know, then," Max asked him, "what you are fighting for?"

Humber took off his forage cap, and scratched his beautifully brushed hair. "Yes," he said, "quite definitely I do. You see, I broke away; I got into the Service. It seemed tough at first, discipline, and having to do what you were told, and no Union to back you up, and all that; but I found that the discipline wasn't so bad if you didn't kick against it. I found I had a job to do that interested me. I wanted to be a pilot; I got the chance. I didn't take a commission because I thought I was better than the folk I had come from, I took it because it seemed to me wrong to refuse. But it would have made me more class-conscious if I had refused it. I've been lucky, but I'm fighting for a state of things that doesn't depend on luck, that gives all the lads in those back alleys, and the lasses too, the same sort of chance that I've had."

Max beamed with gratification. "What a speech from an Englishman!" he said.

"That's why you get nothing out of me," Teddy told him. "I'm Irish."

At their destination they came up into the dark night.

Teddy leapt into the middle of the road, and disregarding all danger from passing vehicles, yelled, at five-second intervals, "Taxi!" at the top of his voice, waving his arms and dancing about to attract attention. Max and Humber, more discreetly, stood on the pavement. Nothing paid any attention to Teddy; he came back to the other two.

"It's only about ten minutes' walk," he said.

"Where do we go?" Max asked him.

"The Elysée Palace."

"What do we do when we get there?"

"Oh, have a drink and see if any of my friends are there."

"And if they are?"

"Have another drink, maybe a dance, and then come home."

Three abreast, they walked up the rise from the station, but the commotion they caused to people coming in the opposite direction made Humber fall back behind the other two. He did not really know why he had joined them this evening, for this was a world of which he knew nothing and in which there was little he could recognise. Yet he wanted to see something of the way in which that other and infinitely smaller world lived—the world that to him seemed to have postured and prinked and set the standard of fashion and behaviour for so long.

The streets were not excessively dark, for that same thin moon cast a greyish tingle across the buildings and down the long streets. There seemed to be many people about; doors swung open, and chinks of light emerged with shouts of laughter and the heavy smell of food and enclosed humanity. Solitary female figures drifted slowly by, most of them murmuring "Good evening, dear", as they passed. One such figure detached itself from under a doorway and advanced towards little Humber, who was now some paces behind the others.

" 'Allo, *chéri*," it murmured. "You are nice boy. *Gentil*, yes?"

"No, thank you," said Humber politely.

"Ah, *chéri*, you are Air Force boy; I make you 'appy."

"No, thank you," said Humber, still more definitely, and quickening his pace, for a heavy stench of cheap scent was sickening him.

"I like Air Force boy very much. I am always good to Air Force boy.'

Humber felt a prickling sensation in his neck. "Please go away," he said.

"All right, you dirty little rat," said the accoster, now in her coarsest English accent; "don't give a poor girl a chance. 'Oo d'you think you are?" She followed it with a stream of blasphemy that caused Humber to trot up to the other two.

"Enjoying yourself?" Teddy asked him.

"Worse than an ack-ack barrage," Humber said.

"I suppose," Teddy said to Max, "you're used to it in your country?"

"I beg your pardon?" Max said solemnly.

"You Continentals, I mean, it's nothing new to you."

"Indeed it is," said Max. "We exercise a little more control over such professions. You English, as I learn, prefer to pretend that they do not exist."

They came to the Elysée Palace. They left their hats at the cloakroom, and Humber alone of the three retained his respirator. "I'm taking no chances," he said.

They descended the stairs into the vast lounge. There were not many people about. The concealed electric lights cast an even glow over the walnut tables and the small armchairs. Waiters, each with a look of supreme and bored contempt for the clientèle they served, stood against the walls or wandered noiselessly over the thick carpet, flicking the tables for imaginary dust.

"Bit of a morgue," Teddy said. "I'll wander round and see if there's anyone about I know." He lit a cigarette and strolled towards the restaurant.

Most of the tables were unoccupied and he stood looking from one to the other. The same heavy odour that oozed into the streets thickened the air. A dance band played on a raised platform. Its members all looked the same: they were young, their hair was black and greased, their faces sallow and lean, and they wore pencil-lines of moustaches on their upper lips. Only the leader wore no moustache, and his high cheekbones, sunken face and thin figure gave him the appearance of a skeleton in evening dress. The head waiter, in the overlong tails of his uniform of servitude, came up to Teddy, appraising his value with a cold stare that was ready to change to a false smile of welcome.

"It's all right," Teddy told him. "I'm looking for some friends."

The head waiter wordlessly swept by.

But there was no one that Teddy knew, and standing there with no companions to set light to his good spirits, he felt a shiver pass over him, and he walked out.

"There's no one here," he told the other two, when he rejoined them. "I suppose we'd better have a drink." He snapped his fingers. "What's yours, Max?"

"Beer," said Max.

"No, dash it," Teddy said, "you can't drink beer here."

"But it's what I want," persisted Max.

"You can't have it," Teddy told him. "What about you, Humber?"

"I'd have liked beer too."

"What a party!" groaned Teddy. He turned to the waiter. "Isn't there some law that says that every inn must serve beer and bread and cheese to the travellers that ask for it?"

"But we are not an inn, Sir."

"You're only a glorified edition of one. Ask the manager to speak to me, will you?"

"I think, Sir," the waiter said after a moment's hesitation, "it can be managed if I bring it in a glass jug."

"What, no tankards?" asked Max.

The waiter shook his head, and went away.

"Another thing we fight for, friend Humber. The right to drink beer out of a tankard when we will, and where we will."

A fat man paused at their table. He was in a dinner-jacket and a soft white shirt and collar. The folds of the shirt looked somehow revolting as they spread across the breadth of his body. His face was red, the eyes unwinking, and the mouth small and thick. Beside him stood a woman, her little hat poised like an exotic flower on top of hair that might have been manufactured from some plastic material set hard. The thickness of her fur cape was wound round a slender body, and her hard, brilliant eyes seemed the only live feature in the immobility of her doctored face.

"Mind if we join you?" said the fat man, pulling up two chairs without waiting for a reply. "Always glad to see the Air Force boys, aren't we, Dolly? Had something to do with it in the last war. It was called the R.F.C. then. Too old for this one, unfortunately, though you mightn't think so."

His gold cigarette case flashed, and he offered the contents round.

"What squadron were you in?" Teddy asked him.

"Squadron?" said the fat man. "I wasn't in a squadron, I was making small tools for aeroplane factories. I daresay there wouldn't of been many squadrons if it hadn't of been for people like me. What are you boys drinking?"

"Beer," said Teddy and added, "Sir."

"Beer? What nonsense!"

"But we like beer," Max told him gravely.

"Not when you come up for a night out," the fat man said. "Waiter! Now what would you really like?"

"Beer," said Max.

"Beer," said Humber.

"And you?" he turned to Teddy.

"Well," said Teddy, "a rye and dry, perhaps," and after another pause, "Sir."

"You, Dolly, the usual?"

She nodded.

The fat man leant back in the chair, and it creaked under his weight.

"Well, what are you boys? Bombers? Fighters?"

"Fighters," Humber answered him.

"Ah, that's the life! I was talking to one of my friends, an Air Vice Marshal, yesterday. I was only saying to him, 'Give me my time over again and I'd be a fighter boy,' wasn't I, Dolly?"

The glittering eyes flicked an acquiescence.

"And what, Sir," said Teddy, "if it isn't rude, do you make of this war?"

"Stupidity!" the fat man cried. "I've something to do with supplies, you know. The mismanagement is criminal. You wouldn't believe the disorganisation. God knows, some of us want to do our best, especially for boys like you, but will they let us? No. And do you boys realise the drag on production that taxation is?"

"How?" Humber asked him.

"Well, for example, I've a lot to do with tin mines. Do you realise that I'm only allowed to make a certain profit, and that one hundred per cent of any profit over that figure is taken in tax? Do you realise that a tin mine is a wasting asset? And that all the profit that should be put aside for the wastage of that asset is being taken away? Think how production would go up if we got something worth having for our efforts."

Humber's eyes were fixed on the broad expanse of shirt-front. "What is a wasting asset?" he asked.

"Why, an asset that you are using up and can't replace."

"Like life," said Humber.

"Eh?" said the fat man.

"Nothing," Humber said, and finished his beer.

"Would you boys care to join us in a little party? Dolly and I have got an apartment here, and there are some friends coming round in about an hour's time. We'll be sure of a good time—make you feel the war's worth while."

The other two looked mutely at Teddy.

"It's awfully good of you," he began, and after the same imperceptible pause, "Sir—but we only called in to leave a message for some friends, and we've got to be getting along now."

"Sure, boy? You'll be welcome. Dolly likes a bit of a change from me, don't you, Dolly?"

Dolly's eyes flicked again. The diamonds on her ears and on her fingers flashed no more hardly than those eyes.

"Thank you," said Teddy, but he rose. "Another time, Sir. It'll be great fun."

"Good night, boys," said the fat man, waving a dimpled hand. "Keep on shooting 'em down."

They sought their caps in silence. They were in the dark street again. "What would you like to do?" Teddy said.

"Anything you suggest," Humber answered.

"What about going back to camp?"

"Yes," said the other two in chorus, and their voices rang with a deep conviction.

The teleprinter was clattering in the cabinet which housed it Roger looked at the clock. It would not be long before Placket relieved him.

"Hereward on the line for you."

"Hallo, Hereward. You want me?"

"Yes. I feel like going the other side. Would you ask Group?"

"Haven't you had enough for one night? What do you want to do?"

"See what I can find round some of their own aerodromes. They're sure to be active on a night like this, even if it's only practice flying."

"But haven't you had enough?"

"I've never had enough."

"Very well, I'll ring you back."

The Group Controller was not too happy about the request. But after a few minutes' delay, he gave permission.

"That's in order, Hereward," Roger said to the pilot at the forward aerodrome. "When are you going to push off?"

"A bit later on. I'll let you know."

"All right. There'll be a new Controller by then, but I suppose you want to be left to yourself."

"I'll call if I need any help."

The clattering in the cabinet had ceased, and an arm was thrust from it with sheets of paper. They were put in front of the W.A.A.F. telephonist. She picked them up and brought them to Roger.

"Target," he read, "aeroplane factory at Proyelles, for twelve Stirling bombers. Rendezvous 1000 hours at 15,000 feet.

"Close escort, three Spitfire Squadrons, W Aerodrome.

"Second escort, three Spitfire Squadrons, X Aerodrome.

"High cover, three Spitfire Squadrons, Y Aerodrome.

"Second cover, three Spitfire Squadrons, Z Aerodrome.

"There will also be an attack on shipping, which may be located off the enemy coast. For this purpose, Shamrock Squadron will act as Bomber Hurricanes, Thistle Squadron will act as anti-flak Hurricanes, and one squadron Spitfires as close escort from Q Aerodrome.

"There will also be a further attack made on the shell-filling factory at Derdrier. Rendezvous time, 1000 hours. This will be conducted by another Group, and details will be signalled later."

Roger read the Operation Order carefully. He turned to see Placket's smiling face.

"Anything doing, Roger?"

"Yes. Havering, get the Group Captain, please."

He sat with the telephone to his ear. Already his eye was roving over the map of France to locate the targets for the morning.

"Yes?" the Group Captain said.

"Orders for tomorrow, Sir."

"Yes?"

Roger read them through. "I have a copy for you, Sir, and

one for the Wing Commander. I'm just coming off duty. Shall I bring them to the Mess?"

"Yes. Where are the pilots?"

"I expect some of them are out, Sir."

"Do you know where?"

"Not exactly, Sir, but I'm sure we can find out."

"Right. You say you're just being relieved?"

"Yes, Sir, Placket's here."

"Tell him to find the pilots and get them home to bed."

"Right, Sir."

"I don't want any woolly heads in the morning. Get them all back at once."

"Right, Sir."

"Conference at nine o'clock."

"Right, Sir. Will you be leading?"

"Yes, I'll be leading. Good night."

"Good night, Sir."

"Which one is it?" said Placket, picking up one of the sheets of paper.

The teleprinter had printed in spaced capitals at the head of the sheet of details: "OPERATION ORDER NUMBER ONE HUNDRED AND TWENTY-THREE."

CHAPTER SIX

When Roger came into the Mess, the Group Captain was standing in the vestibule talking to James Glebe.

"Here's the Operation Order, Sir," Roger said, handing it to him. "I've got a copy for the Wing Commander. Shall I give it to you, or hand it to him later when I see him?"

"I'll take it," the Group Captain answered. He looked at his own copy. "A decent job for us," he told Glebe. "Second escort. There's a good wing above us as high cover, so there ought to be some chance of action. We'll see if we can make the blighters stand and fight for a change."

There was a slight smile on Glebe's face. In the dim light of the vestibule he looked like an eagle, poised, ready to strike.

Roger turned away and, after a quick glance at the empty pigeon-hole bearing his name in the letter-rack, he went in to his supper. He could hear chatter from the anteroom, for some of the pilots had already returned from their evening's outing, and word had passed round. "There's a show tomorrow." "There's a show tomorrow." It seemed to echo in the passages, round the card-room, in the billiard-room, and to steal into the night air outside, for as pilots returned from elsewhere and came in to hang up their caps, their first words were: "I hear there's a show tomorrow."

The dining-room was empty except for Roger and the waiter who had remained to attend to his wants. He ate his fishcakes and potatoes, his cheese and biscuits, while he sat in this room of white-clothed tables, ready laid for the morning's breakfast. Only a few of the many electric lights shone, and now that Roger's meal was nearly ended, the waiter had silently retired through the servery door and into the kitchen.

Nothing very profound was in Roger's mind; but sitting there alone in the big, half-lit room, people and voices filled the empty spaces with their disembodied presences. If the surrounding ether were indeed surcharged with the imperishable waves of speech that had been voiced there, a magician's sound recorder could have captured, held and reproduced so many of those voices as when their owners had sat in this room, laughing, talking, and arguing. Bo'sun Spritt, most fearless leader of them all, with the clean-hewn power of his jaw, the pugnacious turn of his head, and his constant reiteration of air discipline. "Silly little so-and-so! Why didn't you keep close behind me? When I say close, I mean close, not your pansy attempt at formation, milling about somewhere out of sight. I'll take you up tomorrow, and God help you if you can't fly when I've finished with you." Bo'sun Spritt, head thrust forward, finger on gun-button, closer, closer, never firing till he was certain, never caring for what was fired at him, always closer, till his eight guns split the startled sky, and lumps of metal fell from the quarry in front, before, in smoke and flames, it hurtled to the ground.

Flying Officer Rorke, gay, with the scar on his face, and the d'Artagnan moustache, lithe like a fencer, quick-smiling and with an assumed carelessness. "Got another Hun today. Frightful fun. Saw the rear gunner holding his stomach. Must have given him a bellyful."

Bill Sharp, fair, curly hair, boxer of renown, quick of speech and argumentative, taking each astounding thing that happened to him as yet another personal grudge against the enemy; blown up by bombs just as his aircraft was taking off, ramming a Messerschmitt, crash landing in an aircraft on fire because his hood had stuck and he could not jump in his parachute, baling out after another aircraft had run into him, shot down over Dunkirk in the morning and back in the Mess in the evening; Bill Sharp, after each event, spluttering with rage: "God! Let me get at them."

Larry Cartmell, with his disintegrated Australian uniform—Stubby, nearly as broad as he was long—the fighters of 1940, the fighters who had eaten their food in that room, and laughed and joked, and turned out helter-skelter to their aircraft, and fought and fought again. They were gone now, many of them to responsible positions elsewhere, others of them in enemy hands, and some to join the pilots of their own age who had ceased to be in Roger's war.

With a cup of coffee in his hand, Roger went into the anteroom. Placket had done his best on the telephone, for most of the pilots were back at camp. The Group Captain was standing talking to the Wing Commander, but his conversation soon ended and he turned for the door. He paused when he reached it.

"I'm not being grandmotherly," he said in a louder voice, and the room fell silent, "but don't be late, boys—we've a job to do in the morning. See you all at nine o'clock. Good night."

"Good night, Sir," the chorus of voices answered, as the various figures rose to their feet. A number of them followed the Group Captain out of the room. They clustered round a sheet of paper in the hall, putting down their names and the numbers of their rooms, so that the early morning waiter might know when to call them. He was hovering expectantly on the edge of the throng, waiting for any particular and personal instructions. He was a bald-headed man with a fringe of woolly hair round the bald patch, and his main interest appeared to be the invention of efficacious methods for rousing reluctant sleepers. The newcomer to the Station would be startled and nonplussed to waken and find him sitting on the foot of the bed, producing a newspaper and beginning, in a firm voice, to read the various headlines. Or he would drift about the room, picking up personal articles and commenting on them, until the sleeper, now awake and infuriated, asked him to go out.

Roger sat down in a chair with an illustrated paper in front of him. The occupants of the room were Wing Commander Romilly, James Glebe, Wishart—still pulling at his moustache and looking at the wall—the Padre, and the Intelligence Officer.

"It's a bit difficult," James Glebe said after a silence, "to know where to escape to, if you come down the other side. There's scarcely anywhere left to go that isn't infested with Jerries."

"Down through France, I should think," the Wing Commander said.

"And try to get through Spain?" Glebe queried.

"That's what some of them have managed to do."

"Poor old Arkwright wasn't so lucky."

"Why?" Roger asked. "I remember his voice saying 'Give my regards to the squadron' as he was going down."

"Didn't you know what happened to him?" the Wing Commander went on. "He landed somewhere in France, managed to destroy his aircraft and got clean away. He found his way down into Unoccupied France, and it looked as if it was going to be a fairly quick job. He met another Squadron Leader who was bound for Spain, but unfortunately a neutral journalist got hold of their story. Arkwright, if you remember, was rather well known, and pretty rich too. The neutral newspapers immediately carried a story about him dodging through France, and the result was that the Germans instructed the Vichy Government that he was to be produced. Poor old Arkwright got as far as the Franco-Spanish border, where they greeted him with great joy, and more or less sewed him up in a bag and gleefully handed him over to the Germans."

"I wonder how the neutral journalist feels about it."

"I don't suppose he minds," the Intelligence Officer said, "as long as he got his story."

"You were a prisoner, Roger, weren't you?" the Wing Commander asked.

"Yes, Sir."

"Did you ever try to escape?"

"I only made one abortive attempt, but that was soon after my capture. It was quite futile."

"What happened?"

"Oh, in a railway carriage during the night. I said I wanted to go to the lavatory. A big fat sentry accompanied me, but remained outside the door. I'd managed to get half-way through the window, when he opened the door, which had no lock on it, and hauled me back. It was all very ignominious."

"What had you hoped to do?"

"I had a vague idea that I'd make for Switzerland, about a hundred miles away. The train was doing about forty miles an hour, and I'd have travelled very far, if I had got out of the window."

"I wonder," the Padre broke in, "if many of the Germans escape from here."

"Bit difficult for them, I should think," the Wing Commander answered. "Not like the last war, when they could hope to find a lot of neutral shipping plying backwards and forwards between our ports."

"It reminds me of a friend of mine," the Intelligence Officer began. "Before the last war he had been a very keen rugger player. The three-quarter who played outside to him was a German, a very popular fellow. They played many matches together and spent many evenings together after the game. Sometime in 1916 my friend, who was a despatch rider, was pottering along on his motor-bike down one of those long, straight French roads. It was some distance behind the lines, and everything was very deserted. He saw an aeroplane losing height, and was rather shaken when he could see Maltese crosses on its wings. It was obviously in trouble, and it came down behind some trees, across the fields. He left his motor-bike and dashed over to see what had happened. When he reached the German machine, he found it was a single seater, and the pilot had just got out, unhurt. His engine must have been hit, and he had had to force-land. When he got to the pilot, he discovered it was his friend, the rugger player of before the war. It must have been an extraordinary meeting. He produced a cigarette and they sat down to have a chat about old times.

"Suddenly a Sergeant appeared. He too had seen the aeroplane come down, and he'd come across to investigate. He was a bit astonished when he saw a British despatch rider sitting on the grass with a German pilot, chatting with him as if they were the oldest of friends. In fact he was so astonished that he put the man I know under arrest at once. For the next three months my friend, who was court martialled, had the utmost difficulty in persuading the authorities of the truth of this coincidence.

"It wasn't until 1936 that he met the German again in London, and they checked up on their mutual experiences since the day they had sat smoking by the damaged aircraft. The German, too, had been put through a whole series of interrogations. I suppose the powers that be thought he had very likely been trying to land to collect messages from my friend. However, that's not really the point of the story. The German had then escaped from his prison camp in England, and when he escaped, he had memorised a series of names and addresses. He came right across England, handed from one enemy agent to another, till he got to an east coast town.

There he was put up for a few days by the last of the agents, and one morning he was carefully packed inside a crate, with a flask of water and some biscuits, and told to keep quiet. The crate was labelled 'Boots and Shoes'. He noticed that when the crate was handled, it was always kept the right way up, and when they knocked it open again, it was to let him step ashore at Rotterdam."

"Do you think that sort of thing is going on today?" the Padre asked with a startled look.

"You may be one of them," Glebe said, looking at him piercingly.

"One of what?"

"The enemy agents."

"Good gracious," the Padre said, and his spectacles slid forward on his nose. 'You can't mean that seriously?"

"I should hate to think it of you, Padre; but after all, this intensive choir practice of yours is very suspicious."

"What do you mean?"

"Well, for all we know, you've got a nice little pocket transmitting set, and under cover of the horrible noise your choir is making, you broadcast the most frightful secrets to Germany."

"No, I mean," the Padre protested, "a joke's a joke, but you shouldn't say things like that."

The door opened, and Teddy Ryan, Max and Humber came in.

"Hear there's a show on," said Teddy.

"Where have you been?" the Wing Commander asked him.

"I took these two deadbeats up to town, Sir. It was more like a funeral than a party."

"What brought you back?"

"Oh, I don't know, Sir. The place got us down. When you meet some of the types up there, it makes you wonder."

"Wonder what?" the Doctor, who had just entered, asked him.

Teddy paused for a moment. "Oh, I don't know, Sir, it doesn't matter"—and he swung round and went out.

"Aren't you two going to bed?" the Wing Commander said to Max and Humber.

"Are you hinting at me, Sir?" Max grinned at him.

"No, you big bear. I'm ordering at you."

"Good night, Sir," said Max and Humber simultaneously.

"Good night," answered the Wing Commander. "We'll be meeting in the morning."

"Will you let Group know that I'm pushing off now?" Hereward asked Placket in Operations Room.

"What do you want to do?"

"I've already told MacMurray. If the weather's cleared over there as it has here they're sure to be flying, and it might be interesting."

"Hereward will be starting to patrol round one or two of the aerodromes on the other side at any moment now," Placket told Group.

"Very well," Group answered. "Let me know when he takes off." And so for the second time that night Hereward's black Hurricane went off into the night sky. He called Placket once to establish contact and then he began his sea crossing. Flying over the shrouded world was to him what walking in the noon-day sun was as to ordinary men. On the enemy coastline a burst of anti-aircraft fire met him. He disregarded it and went on.

"Teddy seemed a little downcast," Glebe remarked.

"The outside world does rather get one down," the Wing Commander said.

"What's gone wrong with it? Can you tell us, Padre?"

The Padre's serious eyes looked through his glasses at the floor for a moment.

"It's gone against God," he said.

"It's gone against Nature," the Doctor said.

"It's gone against facts," the Intelligence Officer said.

"Perhaps all three are the same thing," Roger remarked, looking up from his paper. "How has it gone against God, Padre?"

"It's forgotten the faith of its fathers; the discipline of that faith; the rigour of that faith; the unwavering devotion to that faith," the Padre answered.

"But," Glebe broke in, "have you people of the Church really done your stuff properly in the last hundred years?"

"How have we failed?" the Padre asked him.

"I don't think you've kept up with the progress of modern

thought."

"But perhaps we have not agreed very much with modern thought."

"That may be so, Padre, and much of it may have landed us in our present mess. But my complaint is that you have got so far away from the original simplicity of your creed."

"Are you a Christian James?"

"I may be a Christian, Padre, but I'm not a Churchman."

"Why?"

"For the reasons I am trying to tell you. The Sermon on the Mount should have been good enough for people—that and nothing else. But the teaching has become so involved with mysticism, super-naturalism, dogma and pageantry that it's difficult to discern what you really are driving at."

"Then you're a Low Churchman, James?"

"I've just said I'm no Churchman. It would be wrong of me to deny the right to anyone to enjoy candles and incense and gleaming chalices and resplendent vestments, as it would be wrong to deny anyone's right to a hard bench in a white-washed building and a parson who preaches for one hour by the clock. But I feel the main issue has become obscure, both in the pageantry and in the Puritanism."

"What do you consider the main issue, James?"

"Love thy neighbour as thyself. Do unto others, and all the rest of that sort of thing."

"But," said the Padre, "there are many other mysteries."

James broke in with a shout. "Mysteries," he said. "Hang mysteries! What mysteries? That's the whole trouble. There should be no mystery. There is no mystery. But it's you Church people who have shrouded plain simple truths in yards and yards of cotton wool. You're out of date, Padre. You're not in touch with the times. People haven't lost their faith, but you're not giving them the faith they want in the language and the fashion they want it."

The Padre looked a him kindly.

"What is your remedy?"

"Start again, Padre, from the beginning. Forget that you're a shareholder in a big limited company, or, if you like, a privileged member of a very rich club. Stop theorising and embroidering simple statements with masses of words. I'll give you an example," he went off at a tangent. "Why, in

Heaven's name, can't a woman go into a church without covering her head? I know some ultra-modern buildings will allow it, but what's the sense of the rule? All right," he said, stopping the Padre from speaking, "St. Paul laid down the rule. Do you really expect the modern world to have any feeling of reverence for such absolute tommy rot?"

The Padre adjusted his glasses.

"You mentioned, James, that we are members of a Club. Clubs have their rules, and if you wish to avail yourself of the benefits of the Club, you must observe the rules."

"Yes," said James. "But the rules must march in accordance with common sense if you expect new members to replace those who must die."

The others were smoking their pipes and cigarettes, listening and smiling a little. James caught Roger's eye, and seeing the amusement in it, turned to his tankard on the mantelpiece.

Patterned ground lights, flashing colours, the grouping of searchlight beams and the orange glow of bursting shells were what Hereward was watching. He knew his position. He was headed for an aerodrome. He could see signs of faulty black-out down below and he read what he saw as if it were a map. He was prepared to stay a long, long time. He had no cramped feeling of discomfort. These hours were what he lived for, when, alone in the night, he could seek out and destroy what he believed to be evil.

He was quite unemotional. His triumphs caused no raising of the voice or laughter. He grudgingly told of them in the same tone as of his disappointments.

In the distance he saw two coloured lights flare from the sky. "So they're awake and busy," he thought as he steered for the aerodrome that was his objective.

"O.K.," said the Wing Commander. "This is becoming a Debating Society. How have we gone against Nature, Doc.?"

The Doctor growled as he puffed at his pipe.

"I'm not a lecturer," he said. "I'm just a G.P."

"Yes. But you must have meant something."

"Well, we have."

"Have what?"

"Gone against Nature."

"I've been about the world a certain amount," the Wing Commander said, "and from what I've seen of it we seem to have been pretty successful in linking up with Nature—in controlling her and bending her to a rational purpose."

"That isn't quite what I mean," the Doctor replied, "and I've no proof for my views. But although you, Wingco, say we've turned Nature to our purpose, does anybody deny that the last twenty or thirty years have been anything other than restless, unhappy years, with two wars thrown in, in which more destruction of life and property has occurred than ever in the history of man? If we were so darn clever in making use of Nature, why have we turned round and destroyed ourselves?"

The Wing Commander's lynx-like face looked high above the curtained windows.

"Maybe because we human animals haven't mentally evolved or philosophically evolved as fast as our ingenuity. We haven't known what to do with the clever things we've made or the amazing things we've discovered."

"I don't think it's only that," the Doctor told him. "I think that in being so very clever we've got away from our fundamental purpose."

"What's that?"

"The living of life."

"Yes, but don't be silly. Am I standing here living or am I not?"

"Yes. You're living and breathing, but what are you creating?"

"Give me a chance, Doc. When I've finished knocking out Germans I can begin to answer you."

"I think," said the Doctor, "that some of my complaint is very like James' complaint against the Church. We've all got away from fundamental facts. We've tried to dodge them, and they're having back at us now."

"What have we dodged, Doc.?" Roger asked.

"One important thing, for example. Families."

"But wait a moment, Doc.," the Wing Commander said. "What about the economic side?"

"Economic rabbits!" said the Doctor. "In the old days when Mamma told Papa that he might expect another one, he would piously exclaim, sighing deeply nevertheless, 'The Lord will provide.' That was as far as the poor man's mind went. It is what our friend the Padre had taught him to feel. But what he really meant was 'My hat! Here's a go. I must do something about it.' So he went out and worked a bit harder, or thought up a good idea, or made himself so efficient and indispensable to the boss that he got a rise. That's how the Lord provided—because the man damn well went out and provided for himself."

"But hey, Doc. You can't have people running wild and scattering families all over the world. There won't be room to stand."

"That's not quite my point," the Doctor went on. "I don't say that a woman should produce an infant year after year until she's wrecked in body and mind, and until there's such a crowd of ill-nourished deficients calling themselves human beings that they ought to be put in a lethal chamber, but I do say that this avoidance of families—and by families I mean three or four children—has had the most distastrous results."

"But I must insist," the Wing Commander broke in, "on the economic factor. Apart from feeding and clothing them, how do you educate them?"

"If everybody," the Doctor answered, "had a family of three or four, and insisted that they should be given the best chance, your questions would answer themselves, because the great mass of the people would see to it that they should be answered. You see, what I am getting at is that there is no ultimate satisfaction in living for yourself. That's what most people have done for many years. There is no mental satisfaction in thwarting Nature."

"Meaning?" said the Wing Commander.

"Contraceptives," said the Doctor.

Glebe looked at the Padre.

"Are you blushing, Padre?"

"No, James," said the Padre seriously. "It's not often in Mess we can have a sensible discussion. Nothing sensible makes me blush."

"O.K. Go on, Doc."

"Do any of you deny," the Doctor continued, "that you started on your maturer life with a keen and excited interest in sex?" He paused for a moment. "Well, anyway, you'd be hypocrites if you did deny it. Your interest in it— and I know I'm talking platitudes—was given you for the one sole purpose of creating the future generation. I'm not going to discuss whether you, Padre, or the teachers and moralists of this world haven't, by your taboos, laid the most fearfully smutty fingers on the minds of mankind; but the trouble is that we have treated that sex-urge rather in the spirit of going to a nightclub and getting drinks after hours. It's exciting; it's forbidden; and it's stimulating up to a point. But no healthy person of sense or sensitivity is going to prefer a nightclub to the beauties of Nature, whether he be sitting in the moonlight on a river bank, or whether he be sound asleep in a comfortable bed. We all know what happens. He thinks he's having a good time. He gets tight. The next morning his mouth feels like the bottom of a parrot's cage. He's got a hangover for hours. And then the damn fool goes and does it again to try to recover from the first outing. That's what we've done with sex. Because we've avoided the natural outcome of our actions—because we've ruined the whole spiritual set-up that goes with those actions—we've got restless, greedy, dissatisfied, and finally we've set out to bust up the whole state of things. All right," he waved his pipe. "I've nearly finished. But if, instead, we had mated discriminatingly with the right people, and the results of our mating had been the families we did nothing to prevent, and the result of having the families had meant hard but joyous work each for each—you know, the all for one and one for all principle—your women would have been satisfied, your men would have been hard-working and much more honest—because you feel a bit of a swine if you do dirty tricks that your family know about—and the world might have been a better place."

Hereward had arrived at his target just a couple of minutes too late. The aircraft had landed and the flare-path had been switched off. To avoid attracting attention he withdrew for some distance, throttling back his engine to idle at his slowest speed. He could still see lights and signals at different points below. The searchlights had failed to find him and the anti-aircraft fire had temporarily died away.

Placket was getting a little anxious. He knew how Hereward hated to be disturbed and how after many anxious nights he had returned safely to his base, but it was never pleasant to know that an aircraft was far away, and perhaps in difficulties, and to have no contact with it.

Two more coloured lights had dropped. They were what Hereward had been waiting for. He turned in their direction and opened his throttle, diving slightly as he went. He saw that the flare-path had been lighted on the enemy aerodrome. He circled it, losing height, while he peered into the surrounding darkness with his amazing night vision.

Something was flashing from the ground. They were giving a signal to the aircraft above that it was all clear for it to land. Hereward narrowed his circle and increased his dive as he got into position for the glide that the enemy aircraft must make to come in.

There it was, straight in front of him. He could see flickering, stabbing light from its exhaust. He closed rapidly. It was a Dornier 217.

Its crew had relaxed their watchfulness. The pilot was concentrating on the last few seconds before touching down. The navigator and gunners and bomb-aimer had collected their belongings so that they should waste no time in getting to their late supper and to bed. Maps had been folded up, pencils put away, instruments securely stowed. They had no worry about their actual landing, for their pilot was a good one. He was not likely to make a mistake. Had he not bombed Warsaw and Rotterdam, Coventry and London? Had he not flown many hundred hours as a commercial pilot in days of peace, spying out the routes over which he was later to carry his devastation?

Tonight it had been an uneventful trip—a pleasant bombing run to the coast of North-east England. The hazards of it had not been great and the crew had met with no trouble. The undercarriage was down, the engine throttled back. The pilot's practised hand was waiting to ease back the stick when agony struck the Dornier.

Hereward had fired from dead astern at one hundred yards. He had slowed down his speed to accommodate himself to that of the bomber, overhauling it very, very slowly. He could not miss and he did not miss. He ceased firing almost at point-blank range and drew up over the black shape before him.

The navigator was dead, and the pilot had been struck in the middle of his back. He fell forward. The gentle glide became a downward screeching dive. As the flarepath crew ran in all directions, the Dornier hit the ground. It was an inferno of flames immediately. No living thing could get near it. It was not till the morning that they could remove the mess of metal and what was left of its contents.

But the ground defences had sprung to life. As Hereward climbed up with the full power of his engine, great explosions of angry fire were bursting in myriad constellations around him.

"I'm constituting myself," Roger said, "unofficial Chairman. What about you and your facts?" he asked the Intelligence Officer.

"Well," the latter replied, "I was thinking more along the lines of production and the distribution of money. It's becoming a trite remark to point out that it's scandalous to burn thousands of tons of wheat in America while millions of people are starving in China. But although we are supposed to have lived in an age when science and invention have never been more varied, we seem to have been sadly lacking in minds that can grapple with what, in effect, should be the simplest of problems."

"And the chief problem is?" asked Roger.

"The problem of how to get from each according to his capacity and to give to each according to his needs."

"Yes," said the Wing Commander, "but what about money? That's the only really interesting thing that matters." And he jingled some coins in his trouser pocket.

"It's taken this war," the Intelligence Officer said, "to work a revolution that hasn't dawned on most people yet. Do you remember how, once upon a time—and not so long ago—a bank-note was just about the most solid thing you could possess? I mean to say, dash it, a bank-note! If men had only regarded it as a piece of paper not very suitable for lighting a pipe, this country would have fallen in a flat panic. For generations they had been taught to believe that that piece of paper represented gold—the magic word, gold. Well, what about gold? You can't eat it or drink it. It doesn't even make very adequate teaspoons, but people were so bemused by the thought of gold that a bank-note fairly went to their heads. What's happened now, and is going to happen increasingly? Your bank-note can't buy you much unless you produce another bit of paper. In a short time if you want some meat, or some milk, or a suit of clothes you'll have to present a coupon. You can put all the bank-notes in the world on the table of the butcher's shop and it doesn't mean a thing to him if you can't provide a coupon. You get your coupon because you are entitled to it. You become entitled to it, and as the war goes on more people will become entitled to them, by reason of their service. I don't mean uniformed service. I mean by reason of their service as members of the community. But you remember how even our greatest minds predicted that Russia and Germany were bankrupt—that it was impossible for them to carry on. They had no gold. They learned something important by the chance of poverty and chaos, and just because they hadn't any gold. That is the simple fact we've missed in all our history. Money can only be based on the products you get out of the soil you own, the finished article that you have placed on that soil, and the man-power of your community. There can be no other standard. That is the simple fact we've avoided in all those bitter years before. In fact, you might make it even simpler. Money is man-power, for without man-power the soil cannot yield—the finished product cannot be made."

"You're a Socialist," the Wing Commander said.

"I'm not an anything-ist," the Intelligence Officer replied hotly.

"Well, what has the forum decided?" Glebe asked.

"Speaking as independent Chairman," Roger said, "I think it has decided this. First things first. Win the war first. Go to bed, Sir. Go to bed, James."

All the others except Roger and James made for the door. Good nights were said and voices drifted down the passage.

"Aren't you going, James?"

"I'm not sleepy enough yet, Roger."

"What do you want to do?"

James did not answer. He slowly moved across to the

radio-gramophone standing in the corner. He opened the cabinet of records beside it and knelt on one knee while he turned over the contents one by one. Then he stood up and put a record in place.

"What is it, James?" Roger asked.

Glebe turned round and smiled. "A concession to you, Roger, though I can bear with it."

He returned to the mantelpiece and stood with his back against the empty fire-place. He reached for the tankard and found a last mouthful in it.

Roger struck a match and lit his pipe, and the strains of Delius' "On Hearing the First Cuckoo in Spring" softly stole across the room.

The anteroom was empty except for Roger. Glebe had gone to bed, and as he was going they had both become aware that Wishart had detached himself like a shadow from the wall and was silently following Glebe.

"Have you been here all the time?" Glebe said to him.

"Yes."

"You managed to hide yourself very successfully." And they had gone.

The night waiter looked in.

"Early morning call, Sir?"

"Not as early as all that, thank you. My batman will call me."

The waiter began to arrange and tidy the papers.

"Nice lot of gentlemen we have here, Sir."

"Very."

"Gives me quite a thrill to call 'em up in the morning when I know they're going on a show."

"How do you know that tonight?"

"Couldn't help hearing 'em talk about it, Sir."

"Well, don't go and imitate a waiter we had some years ago."

"What was that, Sir?"

"At about two in the morning, when everybody had gone to bed, he would telephone a Press Agency and give them interesting scraps of information."

"Fifth Columnist, Sir?"

"Good gracious no! He only wanted to earn a few bob

for himself. But the silly fellow didn't realise the danger of his stupidity."

"But there must be a lot of Fifth Columnists about, Sir."

"I think," said Roger, "there are more fools than Fifth Columnists, because the Fifth Columnists wouldn't get much information if the fools didn't give it them."

"How do you mean, Sir?"

"Well, there was a case of a Sergeant pilot in a bomber. He had been told his duty for the coming night, so he rang up his home and told them not to expect him, and why, with details. Unfortunately, the news leaked. It was a clear moonlight night and the enemy fighters were waiting exactly over the target. The Sergeant pilot didn't come back. What's worse, nor did his crew and several others."

"Served him right, Sir."

"Yes. But what about the others?"

The night waiter had finished his tidying, and went out, shaking his head.

The phrase "Fifth Columnist" stuck in Roger's head. Why, he thought, these emasculated words? Whatever the faults of the more distant past, its people had at least been virile. Fifth Columnist meant traitor—spy. But we scarcely used these words now. The common talk of years immediately preceding had been of "pansies"—"cissies". The Elizabethans had used a stronger word, and if, indeed, succeeding generations had shunned that word, they at least expressed themselves with dictionary forcefulness.

All this emasculation, thought Roger, this over-rated psychological approach—this pandering to the weaknesses of the mind, instead of counteracting them by slapping them out of the body.

He remembered a story told in the billiard-room a few nights previously. It was an old story, and he had heard it before, but it was apt to his thoughts.

Fond parents took their only little Willie to a toy-shop to buy him a Christmas present. Little Willie despised everything he was shown. A long time passed while little Willie expressed his ego and his rage, and at last the choice lay between a rocking-horse and a model railway; but still little Willie created scenes, heartache and despair. Finally the weary shop-assistant said to the parents:

"Can our Psycho-analyst help?"

The parents expressed surprise.

"We are completely up-to-date," said the assistant, "and we have a Psycho-analyst on the staff for just such cases as this."

The poor parents acquiesced, and little Willie was led away. He was back within three minutes, quite happy, in company with a benign-looking man who led him by the hand.

"He has chosen the rocking-horse," said the Psycho-analyst.

The parents were extremely gratified.

"But this is amazing," said the father. "How have you managed to do in three minutes what we hadn't managed to do in an hour?"

"Very simple," said the Psycho-analyst. "I simply said to him, 'You choose that rocking-horse, you little devil, or I'll take your trousers down and smack the lights out of you'."

Roger stirred restlessly in his chair and went on thinking. What had come over us? The Padre, the Doctor and the Intelligence Officer had all voiced their opinions of the disease, and whenever a group of ordinary people chatted and discussed, Roger believed that there were millions of others chatting and discussing in just the same way. What was to be their focal point? Who was to crystallise it so that all men's tongues could cease and their eyes all turn to the common goal? Phrase-making would not do. Tentative suggestions to put right obvious wrongs would not do. But who was to find a way of life for which all normal men and women would answer suddenly "Yes", having seen a great and simple vision?

George of the Army stealthily put his head round the door.

"Hallo, Roger. What are you doing up?"

"Hallo, George. I've gone a bit broody. Where have you been?"

"Out at one of the searchlight sites. They get a bit lonely sometimes, and fancy nobody's taking much interest in them."

"How did you find them?"

"Pretty cheerful, but it would do them good if they saw a bit more of you people."

"Going to sit down, George?"

"Yes. Have a cigarette?"

"We've been quite a time together, haven't we, George?"

"Yes," George said reflectively. "We've seen a lot of things."

"Somebody else said that this morning," Roger answered. "Funny to think that these boys will be boring their sons in twenty years' time with the stories of this war."

"You're an optimist, Roger."

"How?"

"Their sons may still be fighting the same war," George leaned back and laughed.

"And what will we be doing, if we're still here?"

"Exercising our rheumatism by trying to make two potatoes grow where one did before."

"What you said about the searchlights, George," Roger said, "makes one rather sorry that we don't have more opportunity of getting together. It's the same old thing. The other fellow's difficulties—the other fellow's point of view. It's a pity we can't share it more often. But when we do get together we're all so darned tongue-tied."

"Sometimes," George replied, "it's suggested, isn't it, that we ought to get on better than we do together?"

"Maybe," Roger answered. "Sometimes I feel that the real cause of it isn't far to seek. You remember that in the last war the Royal Flying Corps for the first year or two was composed entirely of people from the Army.

"I joined it from the Infantry, and although I was only a temporary soldier, I carried with me my Army training and my Army outlook. The people who came into the R.F.C. were, I suppose, the most adventurous and restless spirits, to whom that new thing, the air, gave relief from the more formal life of the ground.

"As the war progressed, and when the R.A.F. was formed, people were commissioned straight into the Flying Service. That was only just over twenty years ago, George. When that war ended there weren't many of the earlier ones left, and so the R.A.F. started its separate career with a bunch of grand fellows who only had their short time in the R.A.F. as a background.

"Do you remember that, for a few years after the last war, the R.A.F. wasn't thought too highly of by the other

Services? We decided, apparently, to cut down our Air Force to the minimum, and the other Services, with their hundreds of years' tradition, and their hundreds of years of belief that they alone could fight our battles, took rather a poor view of us. It's only twenty years ago, George. It wasn't until this war that it became apparent that, whether the other Services liked it or not, the R.A.F. had to take a major part. While we stood reeling under the shock of Dunkirk and at long last thought it time to take off our jackets and do something, a handful of fighter boys saved this country. It didn't mean that they were any nobler or finer than other people. It meant that they were so placed that they were the only people who could do it. And if the public have praised them by word and song and story, it isn't really surprising how irritating it may be to others who pray for the same opportunity."

George's round, smiling face turned to Roger.

"Well, I've never ceased to get on with everybody here, particularly with the pilots."

"Yes," Roger echoed, "particularly with the pilots. Sometimes I think that the rest of us who fly no longer, or who have never known and are never likely to, are just a bit too cocky. We preen ourselves and chuck our chests out because the bomber and coastal pilots and air crews and the fighter boys have done a great job of work, and we gather in some of the reflected glory."

"Where's Placket?" said George.

"He's on the night watch. He'll be off at eight in the morning."

"It's a pity he's not here. We could have had some music." And they both smiled, remembering Placket's late night sessions with the gramophone when he had it to himself, undisturbed.

"Anything doing?" George asked Roger.

"Yes. While I was on, Hereward got a night bomber, just after your guns had got one."

"Down at the searchlight site I heard there had been some success. I'm glad it was Hereward. What does that make his total now by night?"

"Fourteen or fifteen, I think."

"Anything else?"

"Yes. There's a sweep on in the morning."

"Is there? Good. We haven't had one for a little while. What's it all about?"

Roger gave George the bare outline.

"Group Captain leading?"

"Yes."

"Has he missed any yet?"

"That's hard to remember, George. I think there was one he missed when he had to go to a conference, and he was pretty mad about it."

"What time will they be taking off?"

"I should think about nine-thirty."

"That being so," George said, getting up, "I think I'll turn in. I go on duty at eight. Will you be controlling, Roger?"

"No. I'm not on till one. Havana will be in charge."

"Good night, Roger."

"Good night, George."

Roger picked up a weekly paper again. He could not bring himself to go to bed, and yet he was tired. Impending events always made his mind active, and he resented the long hours spent in sleep.

But after reading for some minutes, he found his head nodding. He could not stir his limbs to lift him from the chair, and when he raised himself with a start it was to find that the clock on the mantelpiece showed three o'clock, for he had been asleep for nearly three hours.

Very cramped, he stood upright and stretched his arms. He went out of the anteroom and stood in the entrance door, breathing the air of the infant morning. The thin moon had fallen below the horizon, and the scent of Tom's flowers lingered in the still atmosphere. There was no sound of any sort. Yes, there was. A loud grunt came from the Group Captain's pig in the Group Captain's garden.

Roger came in again, and feeling the loneliness of the night, went to the telephone.

"Give me Operations, please. . . . Hullo. Is Placket still awake?"

"Who is that speaking?"

"Squadron Leader MacMurray."

"Yes, Sir. He's here. I'll switch you through."

"Hallo, Placket. Roger here."

"Good Lord! What are you doing up?"

"I fell asleep in the Mess. Anything doing?"

"Well, yes," and Placket's voice grew troubled. "It's about Hereward."

"What about him?"

"He's long overdue, and I can't get anything out of him on the R.T."

"He went over the other side, didn't he?"

"Yes."

"Did you hear from him at all?"

"Yes. I contacted him when I thought it was about time he would be coming back, and he said he was staying on a bit longer."

"And then?"

"Nothing."

"What do you think's happened?"

"I don't like to think."

"Good Lord! Hadn't he done enough for one night?"

"That's the trouble, you see. He's never done enough."

"Do you think there's any hope?"

"Well, he must be down somewhere by now, and I don't think it's this side."

"How sickening!" said Roger. "How absolutely sickening!"

"Why don't you go to bed, Roger?"

"I'm just going. Any other news?"

"No. Nothing else. It'll be readiness time before long."

"All right, old Placket. See you at breakfast."

"So long, Roger."

He put the telephone down and came out into the hall. So that was Hereward gone. Whatever had happened to him, he had paid off his score.

Roger walked down the dimly lighted passage to his bedroom. In the other rooms, right and left, upstairs and downstairs, the pilots lay asleep. George Cardew, starting his second year of adult life. Glebe, dreaming of his aircraft and the dog he had left at home. Wing Commander Romilly, with souvenirs of Egypt and India and America on his mantelpiece round the photograph of his pretty wife. The Gauleiter, tossing in fever and discomfort. Humber, with his new Officer's uniform carefully hung and folded. Bill Graves, the Canadian, his packet of Sweet Caporal beside him for the first cigarette on waking. Max, mouth wide open, and mind in distant Java. Dalrymple and Halliwell perhaps still conducting wordless conversations with one another in their sleep. McBain, now fully operational, floating through the ether in the fastest fighter in the world. Charles and Ogilvie and David, the Squadron Leaders of Heron, Cygnet and Falcon, dreamless and relaxed. Wishart, still with fingers to moustache. Teddy Ryan, jerking in his sleep as his knees gripped the thoroughbred that carried him past the post, two lengths a winner.

And the Group Captain? The Group Captain had just gone to bed. He had read for a while. Then he had switched off the light and walked to the open window to stand by it, looking out into the night. Then he had pulled his curtains to blackout once more, put on the light and sat on the edge of his bed.

A review of the previous day had passed through his mind. The files and files of correspondence. The delinquents brought before him. The constant queries to be settled. Going back and forth, from Defence Post to Armoury, from Dispersal Point to Men's Quarters, from Workshop to Equipment Stores, and finally to his own aircraft, where the fitters and armourers and radio mechanics stood waiting with eagerness to tell him all was well. Then, thoughtfully, he had put out the light, pulled back the blackout and climbed into bed again.

Roger switched out his light too.

CHAPTER SEVEN

THE NIGHT activity in Operations Room had died away. Placket had retired for a short sleep before the first squadron came to readiness for the day, and Havering was left at his telephone keys in charge. Some of the crews were also sleeping in rest-rooms, and Operations Room itself presented a picture of still life.

The Liaison telephonist sat beside her keyboard reading a book. Havering leaned back in his chair with a cigarette between his fingers, while he looked upwards at the slowly spiralling smoke. Placket's chair was unoccupied. Of the two Army Officers, one studied a game of patience and the other was reading an Intelligence summary. The khaki telephonists were silently gazing in front of them.

On the main floor the plotters round the table also were all motionless. There were no plots to put on the map, and this was the dead hour—the last of the night, when all things were still. The electric light filled the room with an even, yellow glow, and it was stuffy with the curtains close-drawn across the windows.

In one of the radio cabins a W.A.A.F. operator was on watch, but she, too, might have been a sculptured form. The teleprinter rattle had ceased, and its W.A.A.F. attendant could be seen through the little window, sitting upright, hands folded on lap and eyes staring into a distance.

The maps that covered the walls had varied with the changing years. Once there had been a great map with little flagged pins marking the Allied positions, which after many months of static waiting had changed so rapidly that it was bewildering each day to trace where the new positions might be.

Then that map of the Continent had been rolled up and put away, and those which had taken its place had depicted the outline and contours in large scale of East and South-east England. Soon the names of every little village and hamlet had been identifiable after a moment's glance.

Next, after a pause for breath while the Luftwaffe sorted its dedraggled pinions and the R.A.F. sharpened its talons afresh, the map had changed again. Now it showed not only East and South-east England, but Holland, Belgium and Northern France; those names so well remembered by the men of the other war, and which had leaped into significance in the early summer of 1940, were being revived again and mentioned increasingly. Lillie, St. Omer, Abbeville, Amiens, Lens—all the old places—the cockpit of Europe, that had seen the thousands battling on its surface and now watched the hundreds battling in its skies.

The German, after his three months' sustained onslaught, had retreated to the old defensive attitude as when the R.F.C. had fought him. He stayed over his own lines. The fighter sweeps had gone out, trailing their smoke-trails as an inducement, but the German had not left the ground. So a few bombers had been added to the fighters to make it uncomfortable for the enemy, and in weather that permitted it, the bombers, with their swarming fighter escort, roamed France and Belgium till the Germans were forced to take action. Thus the large-scale operations were born; and if the cloud conditions did not warrant big activity, roving bands of fighters in twos and threes and fours, such as Teddy and Max and Humber and Bush, would suddenly appear over German gun positions, or columns on the march, or parks of mechanised transport, so that at any moment, from any direction, these lethal wasps might descend to shake the arrogance of the enemy; while over the coast flew Whelan and his men, materialising from rain-clouds or from mist, to rake the shipping crawling round the shores as the fighter-bombers came diving to unload their cargoes on the stricken decks.

And all the time the quiet English counties which, so short a time ago, had heard the whistle and blast of the bombs and the screech and whine of falling aircraft, the rattle and hollow plopping of machine-gun and cannon, and which had seen the twisting patterns in the sky and the white unfolding of parachutes, now went about their business undisturbed. From North and South and West they might see the lovely pattern of squadrons flying, headed East, and in an hour or two's time, smaller and more disjointed patterns returning. But that was all they knew. The drone of aircraft was still a common noise, but the sound of battle had receded.

It was the Frenchman and the Belgian who now looked up, hearts, maybe, filled with a conflict of emotions, and wondering when these battalions of the skies would swarm above the legions in their fields again.

The changing maps on Operations walls had given their own commentary.

The telephone buzzed, and so startled Havering that the hot ash from his cigarette fell on his hand. It was a forward aerodrome.

"Is there any news of Hereward?"

"Nothing at all," Havering replied.

"Does Group know anything?"

"No. They're relying on us. Do you think he could have put down anywhere else?"

"It's unlikely. Conditions have been quite good most of the night, and he's never lost his way. I don't suppose we'll hear much more."

"I'm afraid not," Havering said.

"You'll let us know if you do, won't you?"

"Of course."

The night was fading. The telephone broke the silence more frequently. Those of the crew that had rested came in to relieve those others who needed rest. The W.A.A.F. dispenser of tea passed smilingly round, staggering slightly under the weight of the large tray with cups in rows upon it.

Down in the Mess the night waiter was going from room to room calling those for first readiness. The stillness of the night had gone. First one aircraft engine and then another, and others in their turn, warmed up and opened their gigantic lungs as throttles were pushed forward. Telephones began to ring increasingly.

"Now at readiness, Sir," Havering reported to Group.

The teleprinter rattled again, and the lights in the radio cabins came on. Everybody rang everybody else, testing lines.

Doors opened and the figures of Signalling staff, Meteorological staff, mechanics and engineers, passed in and out. A few plots of early morning aircraft showed on the plotting table, and Placket, rather pink from his short sleep, came in smiling.

"All quiet," Havering reported to him.

"Any news of Hereward?"

"No."

Placket sniffed the atmosphere. "What about the blackout, Corporal?"

"Just going to do it, Sir."

The curtains were drawn back, the shutters taken down, and the blue-green sky showed through the window-panes, with the first pale lemon spreading over it.

"What's the weather report?" Placket asked, turning to a file.

> "Wind 2,000 ft. 200 degrees, ten miles per hour. 5,000 ft. 210 degrees, fifteen miles per hour. 10,000 ft. and upwards 210 degrees, twenty to twenty-five miles per hour.
>
> "Clouds light, broken and dispersing rapidly.
>
> "Weather fine.
>
> "Visibility ten to fifteen miles. These conditions apply particularly to East and South-east England."

He went to the door leading to the outside and opened it. He looked at the sky and along the horizon.

"No question of the weather today," he said to Havering when he came back. "There'll be no cancellation."

"Group want you," Havering told him, a moment or two later.

Placket listened to the Group Controller's orders.

"You know we've got a show on, Sir, this morning?"

"Of course I know, but the rendezvous isn't till ten o'clock. That doesn't prevent you doing a convoy patrol until near that time."

"But they've got to get some breakfast, Sir, and be at the Group Captain's conference at nine o'clock."

"I know, I know. But there's time enough for that."

"As long as we can be relieved, Sir, over the convoy, so that they can get some breakfast."

"Certainly they'll be relieved; but the convoy's got to be done, show or no show."

"Yes, Sir."

"Let me know when they're off."

"Another convoy patrol," Placket told Havering. "Get it off."

A Sergeant had taken his place beside Placket, ready to act as Deputy Controller when called upon. He was a genial man, with a passion for mathematics. Every few months he would produce some new slide-rule or protractor or instrument to aid the calculations affecting wind speed and drift of aircraft at varying heights and varying speeds. He and his chief partner in these pursuits, a tall, lean Sergeant with a dry voice, who looked over the top of his glasses at his crew as if he were surveying a classroom at the beginning of a lecture, would retire to some quiet place with paper and pencil and argue their calculations for hours.

"Look after the convoy patrol," Placket told his Sergeant.

"Very good, Sir."

It was an uneventful routine matter. No enemy aircraft put in an appearance on this fine morning.

The day had developed and the Station was alive with increasing activity. From seven o'clock onwards the dining-room was full of chatter. Pilots and ground staff had risen earlier, for the lovely weather had swept away the slight depression of the previous morning.

Havana and Templeton-Browning were breakfasting together, preliminary to relieving Placket and Havering.

Roger had not yet come in. He was in his bedroom, trying to sew a button on his tunic. He had waved away the proffered assistance of his batman, and was now coping with a tangle of knots and false stitches. But his temper was good, and even in the bedroom he could feel the renewed zest which the sunlight and the warmth had brought. The raised voices in the passage had a gaiety in them. The figures that walked past his window had a spring in their step, and when the button was secured with such firmness that it creaked, he came out cheerfully to breakfast, past the flowers which the cleaners were arranging in the vestibule, and turned into the dining-room to find Placket drawing his first cup of coffee and the Group Captain deliberating his choice between kippers and sausage and bacon.

At a quarter to nine the Mess was empty again. Placket had gone for a bath and shave. The Group Captain, the

Wing Commander and all the pilots had left. The Intelligence Officer of the Station and the Intelligence Officers of each squadron had followed the pilots. The Station Adjutant and the Squadron Adjutants were all in their offices, and the Squadron Leader Administration was sitting in his big room turning over the files that lay in front of him.

The Station Doctor and the Squadron Doctors were in Sick Quarters, and the Dentist's drill had begun to whirr again.

The Accountant Officers were entering and checking and adding up. Defence Officers were visiting gun positions and strong points. Engineer Officers were in the hangars and workshops. The Armaments Officer was verifying lists of new stores. The Equipment Officers were dealing with requisitions and issues.

The Padres were busy in their respective denominational centres, arranging discussions, music programmes and means of filling leisure hours.

The Aerodrome Control Officer sat in the Watch Office looking out over the great flying-field. The Transport Officer went the rounds of his transport yard. The Sports Officer overhauled the stock of boxing-gloves, jerseys, shorts and games equipment. The Messing Officer was having a long discussion with the cooks of the airmen's Mess regarding swill and varied menus. The Education Officer was compiling a list of new technical and scientific books which had recently arrived.

The W.A.A.F. Administrative Officers were in their Orderly Room, and the W.A.A.F. Cypher Officers were de-coding the recent messages.

The Sergeant Steward in the Officers' Mess was arguing on the telephone with the Administrative Warrant Officer. The Disciplinary Warrant Officer was walking round the airmen's quarters, ready to express indignation at any moment. The Flight-Sergeant Instructor of the Link trainer sat at his table with nothing to do, for there would be no pilots to train this morning.

Armourers, fitters, riggers, radio mechanics, busied themselves from aircraft to aircraft, overlooking the guns, giving final adjustments to instruments and controls, and testing the radio systems.

In an office all to himself a Leading Aircraftman sat with a drawing board and his crayons, pens and indian ink, and sketched and drew the cartoons which spread throughout the R.A.F.

Clerks and orderlies passed from building to building. Army infantry and gunners drilled and marched or cleaned their guns. Aircraft-hands with no technical qualifications swept the roadways, trimmed the flower-beds, or carried baskets of rations.

Cooks were already beginning to busy themselves with the midday meal.

Transport drivers cleaned and oiled their tenders and lorries, or drove from point to point with their messages and cargoes.

The Camp Post Office sorted mails. The Guard Room answered questions and inspected passes. Medical orderlies took particulars and filled in forms. Ambulance and Fire-Engine staff sat in their vehicles beside the Watch Office and waited for any call that might summon them.

Petrol tankers lumbered round the perimeter road. Civilian workmen dug, or climbed, or unrolled lengths of wire. Boot-makers, hairdressers and instrument repairers all bent over their professional work, and W.A.A.F. clerks and cooks, drivers and telephonists, waitresses and parachute packers, went about their varied businesses as if the service of war had always been the service of woman and man together.

Here, thus, were all the activities of all the countless people to put thirty-eight fighter pilots in the air to rendezvous at ten o'clock.

Roger had just caught one of the Intelligence Officers starting in his car from the Mess to go to Dispersal.

"Are you going to the conference?" he asked.

"Yes, Sir. Are you coming? Jump in." And a few minutes before nine they got out by the long wooden hut of the Dispersal where all the pilots had collected to await the coming of the Group Captain and the Wing Commander Flying. Most of them stood in the open air, with their Mae Wests on and their short, fleece-lined flying boots. They stood there, hands in their pockets, not talking very much, but looking out towards their aircraft, each with its parachute and harness draped on the left wing and ready for its pilot.

Mechanics were still climbing about the Spitfires, standing on the wings or sitting in the cockpits with their heads lowered over some intricacy.

A shimmer had started over the ground in the middle distance, and the uncompromising line of the hangars was solid against the clear sky.

Sweeping round the perimeter road was a large saloon car, with a W.A.A.F. Corporal at the wheel. It stopped at the Dispersal hut, and the Group Captain and the Wing Commander descended. They wasted no time. The assembly parted to make a lane for them, and they went inside. The pilots and the Intelligence Officers and Roger followed after.

The two leaders had gone to the end of the room, where an orderly sat beside the telephone. Some of the others sat down on those chairs that were available, and the others stood around. The Group Captain waited a moment or two.

"Shut the door," he said, and to the orderly, "Get me the Controller on duty."

Nobody spoke. In a moment the orderly said:

"Duty Controller for you, Sir."

"Hallo. Oh, it's you, Havana. What's the form? No alterations? Right. I'm at the pilots' conference now. If anything happens during the next few minutes you can get me here."

He put the receiver down. He stood looking at the floor for a few seconds, and then he threw his head back and for another few seconds he seemed to take a long look at the thirty-seven men who would be following him into battle.

"The job this morning," he said, "is quite an interesting one. We are providing the second escort to the Spitfire wing which is taking care of twelve Stirlings. The target is the aeroplane factory at Proyelles. It's been working pretty hard for the Germans recently, and it's time that it got a packet.

"We rendezvous at 1000 hours at fifteen thousand feet. The close escort is provided by W Aerodrome. Their job, as you know, is to stick to the bombers and never leave them out of their sight. We are between them and the high cover, a grand wing from Y Aerodrome.

"After the rendezvous we will gain height to our respective positions, and in our wing Cygnet will be on top, Falcon, led by the Wing Commander, will be next, and I shall be leading Heron at the bottom. Heron and I will be out in front, with the other two squadrons stepped up behind me and behind one another.

"The high cover will endeavour to engage the enemy who may be waiting for us. Those that break through the high cover wing or who may attack from a lower altitude will be our cup of tea. It's up to us to mop up anything that is trying to get at the bombers and their escort.

"Don't start getting interested in the bombing. It's nothing to do with you whether the bombers hit the target or not. You have got to keep your eyes skinned for enemy fighters.

"Cygnet Squadron will take off first at 0930 hours, to be followed immediately by Falcon with the Wing Commander, and finally by Heron and myself. We will form up over the aerodrome, and I will then set course with Heron for the rendezvous.

"I do not want a lot of unnecessary chatter in the air. Save your breath for the big stuff.

"If any of you has reason to think that anything is wrong with his aircraft, he is to return immediately and land. A lame duck provides no useful function, for it merely means that others have to take care of him.

"When the rendezvous is effected, I shall set course for the target. We will be flying in close formation. When I say 'Loosen up', you will open out as you have done before. Any sighting reports of the enemy will be given immediately, and I remind you not to forget to give your call signs when you speak. It's no help to be told that there are enemy aircraft two thousand feet above on the starboard, if we don't know where the call is coming from, so I say again, don't forget your call signs.

"I do not want people peeling off to make individual attacks until and unless the situation justifies it. If possible I will let you know when you can break up for that purpose, and should you break into sections, I particularly impress on the Number Two of each section that his job is to watch the tail of Number One.... By the way, Charles. Who are you giving me as Number Two? He'd better be good."

"Humber, Sir."

The Group Captain singled out Humber from the crowd in front of him.

"Does that suit you, Humber?"

"Grand, Sir."

"When the bombers have done their job, they will turn for home. So will we, and continue to keep with them if we can. Don't stay too long. Remember that the enemy's tactics are usually 'Hit and run'.

"If you are reasonably sure, in the course of combat, that you have got your man, don't follow him down, for you will be asking for trouble. We are not interested in individual score sheets. We are interested in destroying as many enemy fighters as possible. Have your squirt, and let it be a useful one. If you have hit the enemy, he will crash just the same whether you are looking at him or not, and while you are looking at him, somebody else may crash you.

"If you are out of ammunition, get home as soon as possible, or tuck yourself under a friendly formation. If you're in trouble, call for help; but again I say, do not forget your individual call signs. If you have to come down in the sea, there are plenty of people standing by to fish you out of it, provided you do the proper things. See that your Mae Wests are blown up. Don't get into a flap about your dinghies, and Operations Room will put matters in motion to have you picked up and brought home.

"On the return from the target, you should find plenty of other Spitfires to back you up if there is any trouble about.

"So that you have a complete picture of what is happening, there will be an attack proceeding on enemy shipping over the coast. This will be going on during our particular operation. The anti-flak Hurricanes and the bomber Hurricanes will be conducting it, with a squadron of Spitfires as escort. In the meanwhile there will be a similar attack to our own taking place at Derdrier, so the enemy should have a pretty busy morning. . . . Have I made myself clear, Wing Commander?"

"Yes, Sir."

"Ogilvie?"

"Yes, Sir."

"David?"

"Yes, Sir."

"Charles?"

"Yes, Sir."

"Are there any questions?"

There was complete silence. For another few seconds the Group Captain stood and faced the assembly. The Intelligence Officers had been jotting down particulars, and they closed their notebooks and put their pencils away.

"Very good," the Group Captain said. "Ogilvie, your take-off time is 0930 hours. There must be no delay."

The crowd parted again to make a lane, and the Group Captain and the Wing Commander walked for the door and to their waiting car. It started up and quickly receded from sight round the perimeter road.

The others split into their squadrons, some walking, some getting on bicycles or into small cars, and they made for their own Dispersal Points.

Roger stood for a little while in the corner of the hut, watching those who remained. There was an epidemic of yawning, always indicative of an approaching strain. Maps were looked at and tucked inside flying-boots. A few people asked last minute questions of the Intelligence Officer, and there was a general movement to put on flying-coats. Strangely enough, nobody smoked.

Then, when all were ready, they went out slowly towards their aircraft. Each pilot took up his parachute harness, and willing hands lent their assistance as he pulled it over his shoulders, and then strapped it up between his legs to the big safety fastener round his waist.

They had all gone now, except for Roger and the Intelligence Officer.

"Are you staying here?" Roger asked him.

"No. I'm going down to Operations."

"Will you be passing the Watch Hut?"

"Yes. Can I drop you?"

"If you would."

So they, too, came out, and as the pilots within sight were climbing into their aircraft, they drove away.

At the Watch Office the Intelligence Officer dropped Roger. To the left, between two of the hangars, stood the Group Captain's and the Wing Commander's Spitfires. The same large car in which they had driven to the conference was standing by, with the W.A.A.F. Corporal, expressionless, at the wheel.

The Wing Commander had donned a fisherman's old white jersey. It was very grubby. He had already climbed into his cockpit. His flying-helmet was strapped under his chin, and his head was moving from side to side, as he looked at his controls and instruments.

The Group Captain, in white overalls, was being helped into his harness. When it was safely on, he stood for a moment by the wing of his aircraft. With the rectangular container of the parachute hanging behind him, and the tightness of the straps across his shoulders and between his legs, he stood, slightly bent, and because of his posture, his arms looked longer than usual. Then he put his right foot up to the foothold on the fuselage, swung his left foot on to the root of the wing, and climbed into the cockpit.

He adjusted himself carefully, while a mechanic climbed on to the wing after him to attend to his wants. He settled himself as more straps were put over his shoulders and round his waist and locked with a safety-pin, so that now he was part and parcel of his Spitfire. He took off his forage cap, and the mechanic handed him his flying-helmet. Unhurriedly he put it on his head, and slowly and thoughtfully fastened it under his chin. His goggles lay, like an up-turned visor, on the forehead of the helmet.

He moved the control column, and the elevators at the tail flapped up and down. He pushed left and right with his feet, and the rudder on the tail moved to and fro. He asked a question or two of the mechanic and seemed satisfied with the answers, and then he, like the Wing Commander, sat and waited.

Roger was standing on the asphalt road, with his back to the Watch Office, facing the aerodrome. He glanced at his watch, and turned round to call to Bywaters.

"What do you make the time?"

"Nine twenty-nine," was the answer.

For that final minute everything was quite quiet. The shimmer persisted, and the Spitfires in the distance danced a little in the heat.

At nine-thirty precisely, the roar of aircraft engines sounded from left and front and right, and immediately all the stationary Spitfires broke into movement.

To the right, Cygnet Squadron were so placed that they

had no distance to travel to reach the point of take-off. With Ogilvie in front, the first four came taxi-ing into position. Their wheels rolled across the ground and stopped while Ogilvie gave one final glance round—and then, as hands eased the throttles forward, the Spitfires' wheels revolved again, faster and faster, till the bodies of the aircraft were horizontal to the ground, the tails some feet above it, and racing across Roger's front, the four aircraft rose into the air. Their undercarriages hung like the legs of birds in flight till, with a leisurely movement, each wheel lifted itself and was tucked safely away and lost to view in the underside.

As the first four left the ground and climbed away over the aerodrome boundary, the roar of four more followed, transporting them before Roger's vision.

Falcon and Heron were in motion too. The Wing Commander's aircraft had started up, and he swung out and to the right, taxi-ing along the verge of the grass some yards in front of Roger, who could see the lean profile above the dirty white jersey. And one by one, around the boundary and past Roger, came the others of the two squadrons.

It was an unforgettable sight of absolute beauty of power and cleanliness—cleanliness of line, cleanliness of sound, cleanliness of endeavour.

As Cygnet Squadron, in its fours, took off in the middle of the field, so the individual aircraft of Falcon and of Heron passed in single file between Roger and the squadron taking off. One after the other, with some yards' spacing in between, the Spitfires rolled along the grass verge, as race-horses that parade before the start of a classic contest. There was roar after roar, as the fours took off, and the passing forms of aircraft cantered in the opposite direction to take position on the ground.

There went Glebe, his face intent on the instrument panel. The Gauleiter, sitting without expression, and even in the fleeting view Roger had of him, looking very white. Max, grinning at something which seemed to amuse him. Wishart, with a helmet that seemed so big for him that his face appeared diminutive. Teddy Ryan going by, bobbing about in his cockpit seat, and turning a laughing face to Roger. As he passed, he put both hands over his head and clasped and shook them as a boxer does on entering the ring.

Some of the pilots strained forward in their seats. Others continued to adjust helmets and goggles as they went by. A Sergeant pilot waved to someone in a hangar and then held out his right hand with the thumb upwards. Little Humber crouched in his seat, with only his head visible from where Roger stood.

Still the cavalcade went by. Still the fours ascended beyond them, and as the last taxi-ing aircraft passed the Watch Office, the Group Captain's Spitfire swung slowly from the tarmac and brought up the rear. His head was turned inwards to the flying-field. He was watching his pilots take off. Down to the right—down to the starting tape—the fighters paraded, swinging left and forming into fours.

Here came the leading four of the last squadron. A figure in white was in front. The four of them rolled to a stop. The white figure raised its arms and drew the goggles from the forehead to the eyes. One moment's pause, and then, with ever-increasing speed, the four went forward, tails up, wheels off the ground, wheels tucked away, up and up—the Group Captain leading the last squadron to be airborne.

Already Cygnet Squadron was taking formation behind Ogilvie. It had made one or two circuits of the aerodrome. Falcon Squadron was still streaming across the sky, the pilots finding their positions behind the Wing Commander. Now Lookout had called to Operations Room:

"Last squadron, Heron, Sir, airborne. Group Captain leading."

Bywaters came out of the Watch Office and joined Roger. They stood there, pivoting slowly, as they watched the aircraft up above. Cygnet was in perfect formation. Falcon had all fallen into position and were now closing in on one another, and there, at the back of the hangars, was Heron, the lowest of the three, forming up faster than the other two had done, but with one unhappy straggler appearing to make tremendous efforts to find his place and waste no time.

One more wide circuit Cygnet and Falcon made as their height increased, and then round came Heron on its last circuit. The three squadrons were now all perfectly patterned.

The sun was dazzling with summer brightness. The sky was without trace of cloud or mist. The trees in the distance were ruffled by no wind. Quiet figures moved in the fields, bending and hoeing. The long, conical wind-indicator hung at the end of its tall post.

Heron had set course, Falcon above and behind, Cygnet above and behind Falcon. For a moment or two all thirty-eight of them were clear and bright, but as they climbed their numbers seemed to diminish. Heron passed from view. Then only a few of Falcon could be seen. Then, with keen concentration, Cygnet could be traced, growing smaller as it flew forward . . . and then nothing but the bright blue sky.

The resounding hum that had filled the aerodrome with a rushing sound receded, and when all were out of sight, a faint echoing hum came travelling back from the distance. It was all-pervading, so that in fact Roger imagined he could hear it long after it had ceased.

"That's that," Roger said to Bywaters. "Now we wait."

CHAPTER EIGHT

HAVANA'S CHIN was supported on his right hand, as he leaned forward over the dais looking to the map.

The dais itself was somewhat crowded. Apart from its normal occupants there were added the Station Intelligence Officer and several Officer and Sergeant pilots. Most of these were the new arrivals with whom McBain had been having tea the previous afternoon. He, also, was standing on the dais, still sore that he could not be flying in the sweep.

The tracks of the assembling wings and bombers were winding from point to point in these minutes before the hour of rendezvous. No telephone buzzed, and it was as if there were a tacit understanding that Operations Room should not be disturbed from the outside.

The plotters stood beside their piles of coloured counters, laying them in position as information came to them through their headphones. The tracks were converging, some of them on one point, some of them on another.

"What's Whelan doing?" Havana asked Templeton-Browning.

T.B. replied immediately.

"His squadron and Shamrock did not propose to take off until the actual moment our main show had effected rendezvous. Would you like me to telephone and find out?"

"Get through to them," Havana said, "and tell them the rendezvous should be in a few minutes. What's happened to their Spitfire escort?"

Templeton-Browning telephoned to Whelan's forward aerodrome.

"Put me through to Shamrock dispersal. . . . What's happening? I see. Don't let them take off until you get the word from us."

He hung up his telephone again.

"Shamrock, Sir," he called to Havana, "and Thistle, are all in their aircraft waiting to take off. Their escort has just arrived, and is circling the aerodrome. I've told them to await word from us."

"Good," Havana answered, and leaned forward again, resting his chin.

Two Sergeants on either side of him were intent with their radio telephones to their ears, but there was nothing to be heard, and there might not be anything for some time.

The Signals Officer was standing in a corner with one of his Flight-Sergeants, ready to answer any technical questions or to attend to difficulties.

"Good timing," Havana said, as the converging tracks all met and unified. "Templeton-Browning, get Shamrock and Thistle off."

T.B. reacted as Havana spoke.

"Hallo, Shamrock dispersal. O.K. now. Signal the squadrons to take off."

The Spitfire escort circling above could see the Hurricanes wheeling to their positions and then rising into the air. They were very quick in taking their stations, and they flew low.

Whelan set course North-east, with the Shamrock bombers behind him, and the escort watchful just above.

At that moment the Stirlings, not far from them, turned their noses South of East with their own escort and the screens of Spitfires all about them, and South of the map again, more bombers had turned South-east with escort and cover wings to keep them company, for the third attack of the morning.

Out at sea the high-speed launches had taken up their positions. These beautiful boats had been lying in harbour waiting for just such an occasion as this. Their crews had oiled and tested their machine-guns on their turret mountings, overhauled their tremendous engines, cleaned and polished the floors and gleaming wood and shining brass of their cabins, checked their medicines and bandages and restoratives, and when the order had come they had carved the water into green slices as they came out from the harbour-bar. They lay now off the coast, waiting for the call that would send them charging through a curtain of spume to find the pilot in distress.

Near the coast Lysanders stood with their tanks full, ready to take off and to search from the air for those whom the boats could not readily see. Their pilots and observers rested beside them. The mechanics had insured that coloured lights were stowed away, and spare dinghies that could be thrown out to struggling swimmers whose hope might lie in their arrival.

The three-pronged spear of attack went forward. The boats and rescue aircraft lay behind, and in Operations Room Havana and his crew and visitors watched the pattern of it all.

"Can you arrange for us to listen to some of the other wings?" Havana asked the Signals Officer. "If they look like being in trouble we can always warn our own wing near them, if they haven't already seen it."

"It will be ready in two minutes," the Signals Officer replied.

"Listen out to the others," Havana told the Sergeant on his left, "and let me know anything important. If they are being attacked and we've sighted nothing, I can tell our wing."

There was still no message from the air. The group of visiting pilots was beginning to look a litte bored. One of them glanced round the room and then behind him into the radio cabins where the W.A.A.F. operators were sitting attentive with their log books.

One of the operators looked up. She had blue eyes and fair hair, and that habit of looking up and then down which has never failed to cause a certain commotion. The pilot who had seen her stood transfixed. He nudged the pilot next to him, and slowly, one by one, they all turned their heads.

When Havana next twisted in his chair to see what was happening to his visitors, he found they had all transferred themselves to the radio cabin, where they stood one behind the other, all perfectly quiet, waiting for the W.A.A.F. to write her log-book messages, and gazing at the back of her averted head.

Havana pointed in the direction of the cabin.

"What's she on watch for?" he asked the Signals Officer.

"I've put her on to listen out to some of the other escort, as you asked."

"I see," Havana said. "You might just watch that she's not distracted. I think there's an American Eagle squadron among them. She may find she's listening to more than she bargained for. Their language can be fruity, to say the least of it."

Ten minutes had elapsed since all the tracks had congealed and disappeared eastward. Havana picked up his own radio telephone and listened.

"Dyak calling. Loosen up, boys. Loosen up." It was the Group Captain's voice.

Havana caught Templeton-Browning's eye, and he nodded to him.

"They're across," he said. "The fireworks should start any moment."

The rendezvous had been effected without any difficulty. As well-organised trains might arrive at a junction at the prescribed time, the great bombers with their enormous loads had appeared and circled the pre-arranged spot below, and from North and West and South their attendant fighters had fallen into position.

The three squadrons of close escort had placed themselves on either side and behind the bombers. Group Captain Faversham's wing, squadrons in line astern and each stepped up behind the other, had watched the assembly below them, and in a similar formation the other Spitfire wings, very high in the sky, had waited for their companions underneath to turn towards Proyelles.

Not so many miles away, a similar concentration was leaving the coast behind it as it set its course for Derdrier, and below them all, Whelan and his Hurricanes led the fighter-bombers and escort to flay the shipping out over the water.

At that moment an angry shopper was confronting her butcher with an outraged face.

"But I have always had sweetbreads. I've dealt with you for years, and I've been a good customer, and now you tell me I can't have sweetbreads?"

"But, Madam . . ." the protesting butcher was trying to explain.

"There is no excuse. There's some appalling mismanagement somewhere. I'm going to stand here until I get my sweetbreads."

At that moment a business man in his office sipped the cup of tea his typist had brought him, and he called to her as she was leaving the room.

"What's this muck you've given me?"

"I'm awfully sorry, but there's no sugar."

"But I always have sugar. You've been with me long enough to know that. Get me some."

"But we haven't got any, Sir."

"Has this office gone crazy? No sugar? With the taxes that I'm paying! Take this filth away, and don't come back until you bring me something I can drink. I've had my tea at this time for fifteen years, and I'm going to have it now."

At that moment a shipwright was sitting round a corner, hidden by a fence of corrugated iron. He had been there some time. He had a daily paper in his hands, and a notebook and a little bit of pencil.

"Artemis for the two-thirty," he said, and wrote it down. Each race on the programme gave pause for reflection, and there were still the dog races to be tackled.

At that moment the millions of Britons pursued their daily round. There was no thunder of guns; no blasting of the wrenched earth as homes fell apart and their contents spilled about; no lurking death round each corner and behind each copse; no hunger and thirst that might turn men into lunatic animals; no scorching or whipping of aching limbs in tattered clothes from sun or ice; no blood or ghastly despair or agonising tribulation. The Britons went about their businesses—and those who lived within sight of it, gazed across the summer sea that had moated them in security for so long, and others looked above the sea to the specks of aircraft receding in the distance, not yet ready to believe the moat was dangerous, and that the aircraft vanishing from their sight were crossing the bridge that spanned the old security.

"Loosen up, boys. Loosen up."

The squadrons drew apart, and the sections within the squadrons opened out. Puffs of red smoke hung in the sky.

"Red flak to port."

"It's our old friend the red anti-aircraft shell," Havana said to the Intelligence Officer. "The pointer to show the enemy fighter where the attack is developing."

But again there was a period of silence.

The formation flew steadily forward. This time it was Whelan's voice from far away.

"Line astern. Line astern. Go."

The Hurricanes had sighted their target—two tankers, surrounded by flak-ships, with their anti-aircraft guns instilling false assurance into the minds of their oil-laden charges; for almost before they could put their hands to their guns to fire them, Whelan and his men were on them. A fury of cannon-shell swept their decks, and the flak-gunners fell, crawled and rushed for cover.

The Hurricanes zoomed in the air and returned, their diving attacks coming from every quarter. Streams of machine-gun bullets spattered against bridges, doors and hatchways. The eyes of the Nazi gunners were blind with fear or with bullets carving into their skulls, and as they fumbled madly and desperately, the Hurricane bombers swept in upon the tankers. Little firing met them, for Whelan's vicious, searing attack had blasted the path open for them to bomb and hit and soar to safety. The bombs fell one by one. Fountains of foaming sea rose in the clear air, and then, with detonations not so frightful as the effect of them, the bombs hit clean amidships.

The Spitfire escort was circling above this flurry of crescendo destruction.

Thistle had spent all its ammunition. Shamrock had dropped its bombs. The Hurricanes were darting, weaving like gigantic dragon-flies, across the water and away. The Spitfires stayed for one more moment, before turning to shepherd the Hurricanes in their charge. They stayed long enough for weak anti-aircraft fire to break out from the riddled flak ships. Faint puffs of smoke broke some distance from them, as the Germans, cursing and sweating with terror, returned to take what empty revenge was left to them. But the flak had been silenced at the crucial moment. The bombs had done their work. The tankers were on fire—horribly, awfully on fire. Spreading, leaping rivulets of red flame snaked in contorted paths and poured upon the waters. Huge rolling columns of grey-green smoke built their funeral pyre as it rose for the shores of Europe to see.

The Hurricanes were homeward bound. Whelan permitted himself one message.

"Hallo, Tartan, Thistle Leader calling. Job finished. Quite successful."

High flak had met the large formation as it came in and the dirty, broken patterns of its exploding shells dappled the sky. It made no difference to the sweep. Each pilot now was intent on keeping position and in scanning the surrounding distance for possible attack. The first hint of it came from Collie Dalrymple.

"Hallo, Dyak, Heron Blue One calling. Aircraft three o'clock. Three o'clock above us. Some miles away. Over."

The Group Captain looked downwards and could see the formation of bombers and their fighters outlined against the ground below, but not easy to detect, for their camouflage markings blended them into the greens and browns and russets of the earth's palette of colours. Then he looked to his right and upwards. He could see eight—ten—fifteen minute shapes.

"Hallo, Heron Blue One, Dyak answering. I see them. Keep your eye on them."

The high cover was out of sight somewhere in the dazzling blue, straight above them.

It was Ogilvie who called next.

"Hallo, Dyak, Cygnet Leader calling. Enemy aircraft port beam, three thousand feet above."

The Group Captain looked towards his left. He could see them too—twenty, may be, of them.

"O.K. boys. Keep together. Don't straggle."

Glebe glanced impatiently to his left. There was a Spitfire flying some distance away, detached, and apparently unconcerned either with his own safety or that of anybody else. He thought to himself: "That's Wishart," and he called. "Hallo, Falcon Blue Two, Blue One calling. Close in. Close in."

No answer came from the lonely Spitfire, nor did it alter its course.

Glebe looked at it again with fury and despair.

"Hallo, Falcon Blue Two, Blue One calling. Close in, you ass."

As if in direct contravention to the order given to him, Wishart swung farther away. He was sitting in his cockpit, eyes facing forward, face expressionless; he might have been motoring on the Great North Road, with not another vehicle upon its surface.

"Hallo, Dyak, Cygnet Leader calling. Me.s on port beam. They may be preparing to attack."

"Dyak answering. If they have a stab at you, take care of them, Cygnet Leader, but hold together if possible."

"O.K., Dyak."

Dalrymple was still staring at the specks to the right. They were becoming larger.

"Hallo, Dyak, Heron Blue One calling. Me.s two o'clock now."

"Dyak answering. Watch them."

The twenty Messerschmitts to the left of the wing came closer. Their position was comfortable, for they were three thousand feet above Cygnet, the top squadron, and there were other Messerschmitts far above them, nibbling at the flanks of the high cover to keep it from becoming too interested in what was going on below.

The leader of the Messerschmitts watched the formation closely. Opposite him, and out to the right of the British wing, were the other fifteen which Dalrymple had seen. They also had the advantage of height. But it was not so easy. These Spitfires had very likely seen both of the enemy formations—they had a disconcerting habit of holding on their course until the work in hand was done and they were not often taken unawares. Nevertheless, it was a nice position—a beam attack, with the advantage of height. The Me. leader turned a little on to a course converging with his opponents.

Ogilvie was studying the enemy formation on his left, ready to swing his squadron to a head-on position to meet the expected threat. Behind him, Bill Graves was chewing a piece of gum and cynically watching the Messerschmitts. George Cardew had a little hard smile on his young face. For a minute or two these antagonists flew in their respective positions, the head of the enemy formation somewhat behind, but pointed towards, the head of the wing.

And then the Me. leader, his eyes straying for one moment from the main body of the Spitfires, saw something heartening.

"Hallo, Hans. There is one Spitfire apart from his formation. To their left. Do you see?"

"Hallo, Herr Hauptmann. I see him. Is he for us?"

"Hallo, Hans. Detach three others with yourself, and I make you a present of the Spitfire. Attack. Rejoin us later if you can."

The Me. section leader and three others turned inwards a little towards the Spitfires and away from their own comrades, and with their sticks pressed forward, they dived.

Glebe saw them. He gave a shout.

"Falcon Blue Two. Look out! Look out!"

Wishart never wavered. The Spitfire flew straight and level, its occupant silent and deaf to all outside calls.

"Blue Two. Look out! They're coming in on your tail."

But by that time the rattle of the Me.s' machine-guns had settled the matter. For the first and last time, Wishart's machine changed course. It went into a gentle dive and began slowly to turn left-handed. Its pilot still seemed quite unperturbed, as indeed he was, for he had fallen forward over his stick.

There had been no time for anyone to protect him. If others had left the formation when they originally knew he was apart, the squadron would have been split up into the very fragments which the Me. formation was waiting for, and the sudden dive of the four Me.s in the few seconds that elapsed before their guns had opened fire, had given no one any time to turn in and deflect them.

The Me.s followed through their dive. They went out of sight, turning away so far that eyes could hardly follow them. It was first blood to the enemy and Glebe cursed in his cockpit and squeezed the control column as if it were a neck he would like to break.

The sixteen remaining Messerschmitts to the left had watched the success of their four companions, but the Spitfires still looked too solid to attack again. Perhaps there would be another Wishart in a little while.

And similarly, the fifteen Messerschmitts to the right roamed like hyænas, hoping for the moment that some lame straggler might fall to their yellow jaws.

Nothing had approached the bombers or the fighters nearest them yet and the bomb-aimers were waiting for the exact moment to unload the tons of destruction that should blast the walls and lathes and power-houses of their target.

The Wing Commander's was the next voice heard.

"Hallo, Dyak, Pampas calling. Plenty of them ahead of us. More or less the old herd."

"Dyak answering. I see them. All right, boys. We're very nearly through. Keep together, and I'll try to tell you when you may attack."

It was as if the enemy had guessed what the target was to be, for now groups of them were waiting and weaving in the sky, left, right and in front. But it was not until the first great sheet of flame and plume of smoke sprang from the factory's interior, that the enemy, sure now that this was the destination, swarmed in to harry and prevent the devastation if it could.

The pilots standing behind the W.A.A.F. radio operator with the fair hair in Operations Room bent forward to try to see what she was writing, for her pencil was moving quickly over the log book. But while her face preserved its demure look, she shielded the written pages from too prying eyes.

"Anything happening to the rest of the escort?" Havana asked the Sergeant.

"They're talking a lot now, Sir. I think they're seeing a lot, but nothing's happening. . . . Wait a minute, Sir. A lot of them are talking at once now. I think they're being attacked."

"Hallo, Dyak," Havana called. "Hallo, Dyak, Tartan calling. Your friends below you are being attacked. Your friends below you are being attacked."

"Dyak answering. O.K. So are we."

For now the enemy aircraft were doing their utmost to get at the bombers. Their tactics were almost unvarying. A power dive from a great height through the high cover, through the patterned layers of escorts, and on to the tails of the bombers, firing as they came within range and then continuing their dive till out of sight against the ground.

But the escort of Spitfires closest to the bombers was unwavering. It clustered round and over its charges, blazing at the Messerschmitts as they came headlong, so that, at best, the enemy had little accuracy of aim and could but hope for lucky snap-shooting.

The last bomber had dropped its load and the formation

was swinging left, about to begin the return journey. The close escort clung grimly to the phalanx of Stirlings in the centre. It was not to be persuaded down after the diving Messerschmitts which had passed through the formation, for they might zoom up again in an almost vertical climb and the Spitfires were still there to wait for them.

But other enemy formations had appeared from the direction of the sun to attack the Group Captain's wing and the high cover Spitfires. They did not want them diving after those of their comrades who were attacking the main formation below; so as the layers of British aircraft turned North and West, the enemy pressed forward his attack.

The Group Captain could see the various formations—fours, sixes, twelves and twenties—patterned in all directions.

"Hallo, Cygnet Leader, Dyak calling. Are you receiving? Over."

"Hallo, Dyak, Cygnet Leader answering. Above and behind. Over."

"Hallo, Pampas, Dyak calling. Are you receiving? Over."

"Hallo, Dyak, Pampas answering. Behind you with Falcon Squadron. Over."

"Hallo, Dyak Two, Dyak calling. Are you receiving? Over."

Humber's voice replied:

"Hallo, Pampas, Dyak calling. Are you receiving? Over."

"Dyak answering. O.K., all of you. Keep the bombers in sight if you can. Keep going with them, but fight it out."

The air became full of voices.

"Up sun, behind you."

"Coming down to port."

"Five o'clock. Five o'clock."

"Going down on them now."

"Watch your tail, Red Leader."

The Cygnets, led by Ogilvie, had turned left in squadron formation. Bill Graves took the chewing-gum out of his mouth and stuck it on the instrument board. Fifteen enemy fighters had come in from the sun but they dived past Cygnet. Their objective was the bombers.

"Cygnet Leader calling. Down after them." And Bill Graves called to his number two.

"Hallo, Red Two. Are you with me?"

6—WRAT

"Just behind you."

"O.K., Buddy. Stick like glue."

He selected four Me.s. They were the last of the enemy formation and they were flying line astern. Dropping like winged shells out of the sky, Bill Graves and his companion saw the four go through the bombers and pull up underneath them to attempt an attack from below. But in pulling up, the straightness of that line had wavered, and as Graves eased back his stick, they were soaring upwards above him. There was one to his left. He pulled his nose up, and with the tremendous impetus of speed which his dive had given him, he took his sights on the enemy as his aircraft overhauled it.

At some two hundred yards he opened fire, and he released his finger from his gun-button as he closed to fifty yards.

He ceased firing. A second Me. was slightly to his right, the angle of its approach giving it an upward raking shot into the underside of a Stirling. It had no time to fire, for Graves had come immediately astern. His cannon and machine-guns rattled again, and the enemy aircraft dropped its nose and slowly spiralled as black and white smoke poured from it.

"Hallo, Red Two, Cygnet Red One calling. Are you O.K.?"

"Red Two answering. I'm O.K. You got the first one."

"What happened?"

"His whole tail came to pieces."

Graves looked down. His second victim was still spiralling. It was many thousand feet below, and its gyrations would carry it into the ground. The first had disappeared.

"Look out, Red One!" his Number Two called, for they were being attacked.

All the sections of the wing were now twisting and turning, weaving and firing, but slowly making progress forward along their homeward course.

Glebe had looked over his shoulder. There were spitfires and Messerschmitts diving, climbing, half-rolling, pivoting, and he turned to join battle. An enemy aircraft passed from right to left, and he fired. It was not hit but it dived, and it went towards the ground vertically from twenty thousand feet.

Glebe forgot everything else. The hare was escaping and the greyhound went after it. He fired a few seconds' burst, and then, in his mirror, he saw a Messerschmitt behind. The lines of its tracer ammunition passed in front of him. The long years of his early training came to his aid, for every flying trick he had ever learned he now put into practice.

When he finally straightened out the tracers had ceased, but his dive at five hundred miles an hour found him a little breathless and very much lost. He could see no aircraft, and he was just above the ground. He looked at his compass and steered for his own country, but there were many miles between him and it.

For a few minutes he flew on. Suddenly he found himself directly over an aerodrome. He had little time to notice its layout and particulars, for there were two Messerschmitts patrolling it. Glebe took a hurried glance at them.

"This is no time to start trouble," he thought to himself and he opened his throttle wide, but the Messerschmitts had seen him. It seemed too easy for them. It was a gift from the high heavens above. They followed after.

As Glebe soared across the ground surface, lifting to avoid trees and going down the other side, he could see the two enemy behind him in his mirror and he watched them intently. They were gaining. With his eyes glancing from the on-coming trees to his mirror and back again, he watched until his first pursuer was within firing range, and then suddenly Glebe tugged his stick back hard and turned as tightly as he had ever tried. To his horror he found that the enemy was turning inside his own turn, in position to fire and hit him and he was helpless to fire back. He could not climb away because the Me. was out-climbing him. He could not dive, for he was already so low that any downward motion would have flung him into the ground; and suddenly he realised that he was fighting for his life.

All fear had gone. The realisation that this was the supreme moment of existence gave his mind a clarity and a sanity that swept away all emotions and stilled all apprehension.

"This is a fight for life," Glebe's mind said to him. "How interesting! I may not get home. In a few seconds I am a casualty. In a few seconds I'm one of our fighters who did not return."

He was flying about five feet above the ground. Quickly he jerked his stick back until it would go no farther. He blacked out. The sudden violent change of course at tremendous speed tore the blood from the brain, and a grey curtain, darkening and darkening, descended across his eyes as the blood fell through the veins and arteries towards its pump, the heart.

It seemed as if minutes elapsed. He was blind. He was almost unconscious. Suddenly the veil lifted. Glebe could see again, and before him—not more than ten yards before him—was the enemy aircraft. Even the back of its pilot's head was expressing amazement and rage as it searched for the quarry that had disappeared.

Glebe grinned. The clarity was still within him, but his face creased with an amusement that was almost sardonic.

"This is really funny," he thought. "He was so certain of me, and he doesn't know where I am. I'll let him know." And he pressed his gun-button.

The enemy aircraft in front went mad. It leaped, and rolled, looped and slid. It spun like a demented moth and Glebe followed, for now the tables were turned indeed.

The enemy aircraft performed every evolution that an aircraft could sustain. It was like the old days, when Glebe had sat on the tail of Bo'sun Spritt, as that man of war had taught his junior how to follow and to make sure.

At last the Me. bolted for his aerodrome. Gaping German mechanics saw him tearing down the line of the hangars with Glebe just behind. He turned between two huge buildings below the level of their roof-tops, and Glebe turned with him. Over the flying-field and back again the Messerschmitt turned and rushed, climbed and dived. Glebe hung grimly on. He realised the enemy pilot's last attempt. He could not shake off this fiendish Spitfire pursuer, but perhaps the Nazi gunners at their defences round the aerodrome could aid him. If he could keep alive and trail this *verdammter* Englishman before their noses, surely they could shoot him down.

"Gott in Himmel," he shrieked aloud. "Cannot they fire?"

In sudden desperation he turned his aircraft right over. Fifty feet above the ground he was flying on his back. His fear had crazed him. Glebe was quite deliberate. One long burst and the Messerschmitt split in hundreds of pieces, like a toy smashed with a sledge-hammer in the centre of its own aerodrome. But Glebe's ammunition was gone. He headed for home.

The second of the two enemy aircraft had been unable to follow this wild acrobatic flying between his companion and Glebe, but now he saw the Spitfire turning away. For ten minutes he followed, and every time he came within range Glebe turned to face him with his empty guns. Exhausted and with the faintest hope left in him, Glebe made a last effort. He climbed suddenly, flicked over on his back, and as the enemy shot underneath him, he rolled himself straight again and headed in the opposite direction. There was a little hill he had seen.

He went over the top of the hill, down the other side, turned on his wing-tip, shot round the trees under the level of their waving branches as he twisted, inches over the ground. The Me. had lost him.

For some palpitating minutes Glebe watched all round. A Frenchman in a field waved to him. A few stray shots were fired from machine-gun posts, but the water was in sight. He crossed the coast and in the distance he saw the line of chalky whiteness, sparkling in the summer sun. In his twenty-five years he had never known how well he had loved that land, until he saw her shores with the foam breaking on the beaches where once, as a child, he had played.

"Is anything happening?" the Intelligence Officer whispered to Havana. He did not know, really, why he whispered, except that Operations Room was so quiet and all the figures were so still.

"Plenty," said Havana.

When Glebe had turned to join the dog-fight, Teddy Ryan and others of the Falcons had flown on. For a few moments there was a respite, but some distance in front, below and to the right, Heron Squadron appeared to be in the thick of it.

Teddy looked at the bombers, flying in the distance and making for the coast. They were all together, and as far as he could judge, their close escort was protecting them adequately. The long, straight Routes Nationales of France stretched out of sight to his East. Towns showed like sprinklings of dust, which he could obscure from view by stretching his hand out over them. The sea, pearl-grey and silver, lay to his West, with the darker streaks of channels criss-crossed over it. The coastline of England was clear and definite with its estuaries and river-mouths, and beyond his left shoulder he could see the diamond pattern of the Isle of Wight, like a lozenge placed on a flat porcelain dish.

He seemed to be alone, and heavy anti-aircraft fire broke out all round him. He weaved from side to side for a mile or two, but the bursts were too near him. A crashing, billowing detonation threw him on to his right wing-tip and very nearly turned him upside down. He was nearer Heron Squadron now and he could hear some of their voices in his ear-phones. They had fought almost without cessation from the time the bombers had turned from the target. Teddy's bright eyes watched from above the leather mask which held his microphone and oxygen tube over the lower part of his face. The Herons and the Messerschmitts were milling round and round one another. It was difficult to see where to get in a shot without hitting a friend; but he was not alone, for the Gauleiter had seen the anti-aircraft fire and, watching the track of it closely, he had seen Teddy's Spitfire sliding out of control just after the burst that had so nearly hit him; and the Gauleiter had followed along, in case the other Spitfire should be damaged and have need of him.

He, too, saw the general confusion of the Herons and Messerschmitts, and he was gaining on Teddy as the latter saw his chance to attack. There were two Me.s that had spun temporarily out of the battle and were now climbing up to re-engage. The eyes of the two Germans were on the twisting mass of aircraft above them. Teddy was coming from the sun, and he began to dive. But the Germans were climbing on a course converging with one another. Teddy could not make up his mind at which to fire first. The Gauleiter was diving gently behind Teddy, waiting to see which of the enemy his companion would attack.

The Germans answered the problem for themselves, each so concentrated on the objective of his climb that neither saw the other. They climbed with the full power of their engines, and as they climbed, they met. To Teddy, waiting to choose his target, it was as if an explosion had occurred. At one moment, two Messerschmitts were there. At the next moment they were not. Nothing remained—not a wing, not a shred of fabric, not a piece of metal that he could see. He straightened from his dive, looking at the air where two machines had been and searching below and around for any sign of them that might be left.

The Gauleiter had seen it too, and he had forgotten the discomfort of his body. All the morning he had been flying with chattering teeth, and even at great height, he was suffused with sudden flushes of fever heat. His eyes had ached and his head was throbbing. He saw Teddy straighten out and, like him, he searched the sky around for evidence of the Me.s' sudden extinction. Then through his hot, cracked lips, he gave a warning shout.

"Look out! Look out, behind you!"

He could not distinguish the markings on Teddy's aircraft. He did not know who was in it.

"Look out!" he shouted. "You, Spitfire in front of me. Look out! Coming up on your tail. Look out!"

But those were the calls that Teddy had been hearing from the Herons in their dog-fight. He paid no particular attention to them. The crash he had just seen was still filling him with amazement.

The Gauleiter was shouting again, "Look out!" as the Messerschmitt behind Teddy fired from fifty yards away. For a fatal second Teddy was too astonished to do anything. The Messerschmitt fired again, and passed just over the hood of his cockpit.

The last conscious movement that Teddy made was to pull his stick back. The nose of his Spitfire pointed up. It climbed as far as its speed would carry it, and then it shuddered in the air and its tail slid downwards. There was no one now to control it. As it slid backward, its nose fell forwards, and, with engine pointing to the earth below, the Spitfire started its final whirling spin for the ground.

The Gauleiter had seen no more of Teddy since the staggering upward climb, for he was already on the tail of the attacker. He came in from the enemy's right rear. His eyes were watering, and suddenly his teeth had seemed as if they were crumbling tusks of ivory that were locked and choking him. The Messerschmitt had a yellow shout. He concentrated on this fleeting splash of colour. He used his cannon only. A strange hallucination came into his mind—the green cloth of the billiard table, the strong light shining over it. The coloured balls of a snooker game. Pot the yellow. Careful with the cue. There's the yellow. There's the pocket. Pot the yellow. He fired.

The enemy's engine cowl broke off, and flew by, over and behind him. Sparks flickered in the front of its engine—or was it the Gauleiter's eyes?—and then the enemy's cockpit and its hood fell to pieces as if a great iron hand had clenched over it, gripped, and let fragments trickle out.

It was some five minutes later that a Nazi working party, trenching and draining a gun site, found Teddy's Spitfire and the Messerschmitt. What was left of them lay within a hundred yards of one another.

"Are they out of it yet?" the Intelligence Officer whispered to Havana.

"No," Havana said, and his mouth was twitching slightly in a very set face.

"Is there much action?" the Intelligence Officer went on.

"Oh! For God's sake!" Havana said angrily. "What can we do about it, even if there is? Be quiet!"

Templeton-Browning called across to him, softly.

"Can you speak to Group, Sir?"

Havana nodded, put down his radio telephone and picked up another instrument.

"Controller here."

"Have you any spare pilots standing by?"

"In what way, Sir, spare pilots?"

"Well, this is rather a busy morning. If you've anybody spare, we'd like them at readiness for air-sea rescue. Just in case, you know—just in case."

"Well," Havana said, slowly, "the spare pilots that are available have only just been posted here. I don't know that they're exactly ready for anything serious."

"How many can you muster?"

"Nine or ten, I suppose."

"But you say they are not operational?"

"I wouldn't say they're not operational, Sir, but they've never flown together yet, nor with their squadrons."

"Even so," said the voice from Group, "we may need everybody we can lay hands on. There's plenty of action going on the other side, and if some of our boys go into the drink, we want to get them out again."

"I know, Sir," said Havana, soberly.

"There's the position. Do what you can."

Havana put down the telephone. The Group Captain and the Wing Commander were in the air with all the Squadron Leaders; any of these might have given a decision. But Havana was the senior officer left on the ground.

He looked behind him. McBain's face was thrust forward as he stared at the floor below. Havana drummed for a moment with his fingers on the desk.

"You're not operational yet, are you, McBain?"

"As much as I ever will be," McBain growled.

"Would you like to do a job?"

"Who with?"

"Have all the new pilots come in here?"

"Yes, I believe so. They're all stuck round in that radio cabin."

"How many are there?"

"About nine, I think."

"Can you lead them?"

McBain's eyes were wide.

"Lead them on what?"

"Air-sea rescue, if wanted."

"Heavens, yes! When?"

"Any moment now."

"Rather! What are our orders?"

"Collect the pilots this minute. Get them off to the aerodrome. Pinch any aircraft you can find, and stand by for orders."

"O.K.," said McBain, turning on his heel.

"Wait a moment," Havana called out to him. "Stand by in Heron's dispersal. Taxi your aircraft over there and be ready to take off. I'll give you the details when they come through."

McBain was striding for the radio cabin.

"Come on, you rookies," he was shouting. "You're wanted."

"Hey!" shouted Havana. "That'll be your call sign."

"What?" said McBain.

" 'Rooky'. You're Rooky Leader. Now go and form your squadron, and may it not be your last."

The radio cabin had emptied in an instant. The blonde turned her inviting eyes to the audience that had been making her feel that a woman's life was worth living. But the audience had gone, and McBain was running, several yards ahead of them.

CHAPTER NINE

THE WING COMMANDER and his Number Two were flying line abreast. They had made many attempts to come to close quarters with enemy aircraft, but these had invariably dived out of the way to safety. The two of them were overhauling the bombers, who were now meeting the full concentration of anti-aircraft fire from the coastline.

Number Two, a New Zealand Sergeant with a soft and diffident voice, twisted in his seat. The Wing Commander was watching him and saw him break violently to his left as an enemy aircraft tore past at a steep angle, firing at the empty space where Number Two had been a second before. The Me. was going too fast.

"Let him go," the Wing Commander thought.

The Sergeant re-formed into line abreast once more. But Me.s seldom attack by themselves, and just as the Wing Commander saw Number Two come into place on his left, the second Me. dived on his own aircraft. The Sergeant had seen it. He shouted a warning, and his quiet voice had a note of extreme urgency in it.

The Wing Commander broke outwards to his right and up, and, as with Glebe's earlier fight, he blacked out with the suddenness of it. The veil did not lift from his eyes till he had flown in a complete circle, and he found himself behind the Messerschmitt, which was between him and the Sergeant; and they were all flying on the same course. It was impossible to fire, for the shells and bullets that might have hit the Messerschmitt could equally have hit Number Two.

The Messerschmitt was gaining fast. The Wing Commander gave one short call.

"Falcon Red Two. Break to starboard."

The Sergeant swung quickly upwards to his right. The Me., momentarily nonplussed, overshot the position where his target had been, and the Wing Commander fired. He could see the strikes of his shells and bullets entering the enemy machine. It wobbled violently. Its occupant threw back his cockpit hood as if to free himself for a parachute jump, but this time the Sergeant shouted a warning.

"Hallo, Pampas. Break away!"

There was no doubt as to what had happened. A dozen Messerschmitts were attacking them pair by pair and diving from above. From fifteen thousand feet to five thousand, the Wing Commander and the Sergeant, breaking to right and left like the outward feathers of the Prince of Wales' crest, escaped each diving attack; out and up and back again, line abreast—out and up and line abreast, as they waited for a chance to shoot. But no more chances came, and performing these rhythmic evolutions with Messerschmitts diving on them in pairs, they came out over the sea, where another friendly wing was waiting for the homeward-bound; and its leader, seeing the Wing Commander and his Sergeant down below, shouted the "Tally-ho" that brought them their relief.

The Group Captain was then not far away from them, had he but known it. In the dog-fight which Teddy had seen, Humber had spun out to avoid a close attack. The immediate sky was full of aircraft. Maltese crosses and British roundels flashed in every direction.

The Group Captain had the advantage of height. He circled once or twice over the general mêlée, and a Messerschmitt broke out of it. It was aflame in an instant, for when the Group Captain fired, he never made mistakes. He knew the value of his ammunition with his expert eye behind it and he wasted very little.

It was as if he had destroyed a man who mattered, for a concentrated attack developed on him and he, like Humber, span to escape it. He fell twelve thousand feet and headed for the bombers' presumed course. The flak at the coast put up a curtain of fire at him, but he was used to it. Changing direction and height from moment to moment, he passed through the steel belt and out to the sea beyond.

The relief wing was just diving to the Wing Commander's rescue. There was no friendly aircraft near the Group Captain when six of the enemy dived on him from behind. He met their determined attempts head on. The Messerschmitts were in one another's way. In their eagerness to shoot down the Englishman, they jostled one another and missed. It was so stupid, for he could not hope to escape.

"Hallo, *Jagdstaffel Drei*. It is the Leader calling. Attention. You, Klaus, will attack this *Schpitfeuer* from behind. I, myself, will attack him from in front. The other four can watch."

"Zum befehl," came Klaus' voice.

"Understand," the Leader went on, "I do the attacking. You, Klaus, will wait. If, by any chance," and the Leader chuckled with an arrogant lilt, "I should miss—you, Klaus, will get him as he breaks away, for it does not matter whichever way he goes."

The tilting yard was set. In the crystal distance the billows of smoke from the burning tankers spread across the water. No man could go to their aid, for they were white-hot hells on the cool sea's surface.

The Group Captain looked about him. In his mirror he saw a Messerschmitt coming into position from astern. He looked forward, and there was a Messerschmitt dead ahead of him, coming straight towards him. If he broke away they could follow his every movement; and there were four others, like draughtsmen, waiting to huff him from whichever square he might occupy.

The closing speed between the two antagonists was over six hundred miles an hour. Klaus, stationed behind, held his breath, waiting for the result. The enemy Leader and the Group Captain fired simultaneously, as knights that shivered their lances when the chargers met in the field.

But the enemy Leader had missed. Not so the Group Captain. His cannons and machine-guns had fired at short range. At the speed at which the fighters were meeting, the guns needed but a touch before he ceased firing and the Messerschmitt Leader's aircraft was upon him. It was actually a foot or two above him when it exploded. Klaus saw his Leader fall in ribbons to the sea.

The Group Captain jerked violently, for Klaus' first cannon shell had burst in the fuselage behind him. He felt stinging pains in his left arm and his thigh, and he turned up into the sun. But the heart had gone out of the Messerschmitts. The Leader's confident voice was stilled, and Klaus had not avenged it.

They tried to get on the Spitfire's tail, but each time they tried, the Group Captain turned to meet them. None of them wanted a repetition of the Leader's violent end.

In their final attack the Spitfire shot for the last time. It was a long, raking burst of machine-gun from the starboard wing, for the port guns were out of action. A Messerschmitt's radiator poured liquid, and below its fuselage oily blue smoke streamed like the tail of a comet. It went into a gentle dive. The others turned for home. The mad Englishman must escape. He was a dangerous maniac. How could one fight lunatics who did not know when they were beaten?

At sea level the Group Captain approached the coast of England. With his uninjured arm he drew the goggles above his helmet again. His left leg was growing numb and the aircraft was behaving strangely. Suddenly his grim mouth relaxed. He crinkled his nose and his eyes closed, as the Group Captain threw his head back and gave one great shout of laughter.

"It must be nearly over now," the Intelligence Officer said, watching the plots appear over the English coast again. "I'd better get back to dispersals before they arrived. Anything you want me for, Sir?"

"No," said Havana, paying no attention. And then, turning round to see who had spoken to him, "No, thank you."

"Red Two. Red Two. Where are you?"

Whose voice was that? Why did he give no call sign?

"Red Two. Red Two. Are you with me? I'm going down."

Havana tapped with impatience. The voice was very agitated.

"Red Two. For God's sake! Can you hear me?"

It was George Cardew's voice. He was in trouble.

"Hallo, Cygnet Red One, Tartan calling. Can I help you?"

George was not listening for Tartan. He had been hit. He did not know how or where, but his engine was seizing. It shook the whole body of the aircraft, as if it would tear it apart.

"Red Two. Red Two. I'm going doing. Where are you?"

"Hallo, Cygnet Red Two, Tartan calling. Are you receiving?"

But Red Two was silent.

"Hallo, Cygnet Red One, Tartan calling. I am receiving

you. Can I help? Can I help?"

"Red Two. Red Two. Where are you? Keep near me. I'm going down."

It was the last Havana heard of George's voice.

"Hallo, all aircraft, Tartan calling. Cygnet Red One is in difficulty. Can anyone assist?"

As he switched over to receive, Havana could hear a voice humming a song. He switched on again.

"Hallo, all aircraft, Tartan calling. Keep quiet, I say. Keep quiet. Cygnet Red One is in difficulty. Is anybody near him?"

Ogilvie called back.

"Cygnet Leader answering. I cannot see him, but I'm having a look."

Ogilvie turned back from the friendly coast and swept out to sea again. He climbed, but though he saw pairs and small formations of Spitfires coming from the coast of France, no one appeared to be in any trouble. He turned in wide circles, looking for any tell-tale signs upon the sea.

There was something flying low. From his height he could not distinguish it clearly, and he dived to make sure. He had never found an easier victim. It was a Messerschmitt, and at the first burst of Ogilvie's guns it plunged into the water as cleanly as a diver from a springboard, and the foaming swirl of its immersion subsided.

"Hallo, Tartan." It was a very faint voice calling. "Cygnet Red Two calling. Are you receiving?"

Havana gripped his telephone hard.

"Hallo, Cygnet Red Two, Tartan answering. Receiving you very faintly."

"Hallo, Tartan, Cygnet Red Two answering. I can only just hear you. I saw Red One go in."

"Hallo, Cygnet Red Two. Why did you not answer him when he called?"

"Hallo, Tartan, Red Two answering. My R.T. is faulty. I can only just hear you. I say again, I saw Red One go in."

"Hallo, Red Two. Can you see him now?"

"He's in the water, just below me."

"Hallo, Red Two. Did he bale out?"

"Please say again."

"I say again, did he bale out?"

"He baled out very low."

"Did his parachute open?"

"I can't hear you."

"Oh! For God's sake!" Havana muttered to himself. Then he took a steady breath. It was no use betraying the tenseness of his feelings to Red Two.

"Hallo, Red Two. What did Red One do?"

"Hallo, Tartan. He baled out very low. His parachute had just opened when he went in."

The voice trailed away.

"T.B., tell Group that George Cardew is in the water. I haven't got his position yet. We'll pass it the moment we can find it. . . . Hallo, Red Two, Tartan calling. Are you receiving?. . . . Hallo, any aircraft. Any aircraft over the sea. There's a friendly aircraft in the water. Please do your best to find him."

"Everyone standing by," Templeton-Browning said. "Group are only awaiting the position to get the boats cracking and to send over the Lysander."

"Hallo, Red Two, Tartan calling. Are you receiving?"

"Hallo, Tartan, Red Two calling. Were you calling me?"

It was not Red Two's fault. Perhaps he, too, was hit. He could not help it that his radio system, at this critical moment, was proving faulty.

"Hallo, Tartan, Red Two calling. I can still see him."

"Hallo, Red Two. Is he in his dinghy?"

"Damn!" Havana thought. "I don't believe George carries one."

"No," Red Two's voice answered. "I can see him in the water, and his parachute is floating some distance from him."

"Hallo, Red Two. Can you give me a position?"

For five minutes the patient attempts at communication went on. Time after time Red Two's messages faded away or he received nothing, but Havana persisted.

"At last!" he said. He scribbled on a piece of paper. "Here you are, T.B. There's the position. I'll go on trying to check it."

From Group to the coast the news flashed. From the coast to the boats, and from the ground to the air, as the Lysander and its escort took off seawards.

Time passed.

"Hallo, Red Two, Tartan calling. Can you see anything?"

"He is just below me."

"Can you see any boats?"

"Not yet."

More minutes passed.

"Hello, Red Two. Have you any news?"

"I'm short of petrol, Tartan."

"How much have you got left?"

"Only a few gallons."

"Hang on, Red Two, if you can."

All other aircraft were silent. They had heard the conversations. They knew that any talk from them might blot out a vital, necessary message.

"Hallo, Tartan, Red Two calling. I've only a few minutes' petrol left."

"Can Group give us any news, T.B.?"

Havana looked down to the map. The plots of homecoming fighters and bombers were all over it, and marked with a large counter was the position in the sea which had been obtained from Cygnet Red Two after so much difficulty.

"Group say everything's being done that's possible," T.B. called to him. "The boats are out on the course given them, and the Lysander was approaching the spot some minutes ago."

"Hallo, Tartan, Cygnet Red Two calling. I'm sorry. I must go in now. I'll land on the first aerodrome I can find, if my petrol holds out."

"Hallo, Red Two, Tartan answering. Can you see any rescue craft?"

"Hallo, Tartan, Cygnet Red Two answering. I can see a boat coming towards me now. It's about three miles away."

"What about Red One, Cygnet Red Two?"

There was a long pause.

"I can't see him, Tartan. I can't see him any more."

Havana put the telephone down in front of him.

"Hallo, Red Two. Where are you?... Red Two. Where are you?" He could hear George's voice as it had called for help. "Red Two. Where are you? For God's sake! Where are you?"

He looked at the large counter placed on the seaward side of the map. There was a faint hope yet—a very faint hope.

But mentally, he called:

"Hallo, Cygnet Red One. Hallo, Cygnet Red One.... Good-bye, George.... Good-bye."

"What on earth's happening?" Roger asked Bywaters.

During the last hour he had walked round the perimeter road, watched some small-arms firing on the range, taken part in it himself, and then returned to the Watch Office to await the incoming aircraft. He could never get rid of the old habit of counting them as they returned, and hoping that any deficiencies would be happily explained by subsequent telephone calls.

Twos and threes of Spitfires that had been standing at dispersals were now taxi-ing across to Heron's Dispersal Point.

"What's it all in aid of?" Roger repeated his query to Bywaters.

"I think we've just time to run round and find out. If you like to get into my car...."

In the Heron pilots' rest-room they found McBain haranguing nine rather dazed pilots. His forage cap was pushed to the back of his head, and he was gesticulating to all corners of the compass as he explained what he wanted of them.

"There are ten of us," he said, "so that will make five sections of two. Let me see. Who'd better fly with me? Who's junior here?"

They looked at one another, and appeared as if they were about to go into a lengthy conference.

"Never mind. Never mind. You'll do," and he pointed at a long, lean youth who was standing with his hands in his pockets, and smoking a cigarette. The youth removed the cigarette, flicked the ash off it, and regarded McBain with a glint of amusement.

"What am I called?" he said.

"Rooky Red Two. I'm Rooky Leader, but I'll call myself Red One. Now for the rest of you. We want yellow, white, blue and green sections. Which is the senior of you?"

Again the members of the conference eyed one another askance.

"Oh Hell!" said McBain. "We're getting nowhere. You'll do," and he pointed to the same long, lean youth.

"But you've just made me Rooky Red Two."

"Damn! So I have. Well, you then."

This time it was a creature with the appearance of an all-in wrestler, who grinned like a friendly bear.

"You'll be Blue One. I may call you Blue Leader, or I may call you Blue One, but whichever I call you, it's you."

"Now we'll fly this way. Me and my Number Two in front, Yellow and White behind and on either side, and Blue and Green immediately behind them. That's until we get down to the coast, and then I may put you in sections line astern. Don't forget the order—me first, then Yellow, White, Blue and Green as I've said them. It all depends on circumstances. Let's detail the respective sections."

His hand waved vaguely across and about them, as if he were conducting a silent "eeny, meeny, miny, mo" game of childhood. The telephone orderly called to him.

"You're wanted, Sir."

"Hallo," McBain said. "Yes, it's McBain here.... What, now? O.K. I've nearly sorted them out. Where to?... What for?... We'll be off in about five minutes. Good Lord! Don't worry about us. I'll look after them."

He put down the telephone and turned to his substitute squadron.

"There are one or two in the drink. We've got a dual rôle. We're to go out and fly low enough to see if we can spot anything, and to keep off any enemy aircraft that may try to attack our rescue craft. Let's detail you."

He sorted them out into four pairs, leading one of each pair by the arm and placing him in a different spot in the room.

"There you are, chaps," he said. "Now, have you got that? Here's me, out in front with my Number Two. There's you. That's the position in which you'll form up after I've taken off. Don't belly-ache too much on the R.T. unless you're in trouble. Listen to the Controller, and listen to me. All set?"

"O.K.," the chorus replied.

"Get cracking. We take off in the order I told you, and set out in the formation I've shown you."

There was a concerted dash for the door. Bodies jammed against one another and forced their way through. Roger and Bywaters had remained completely unnoticed at the far end of the room and they had to flatten themselves against the passage walls to avoid being trampled underfoot.

Roger went over to the telephone.

"Hello, T.B., MacMurray here. Is Havana free a moment?"

"I'll put you through."

"Oh! Hello, Havana. I've just been listening to McBain briefing his pilots. They'll be all right."

"Do you think so?" said Havana's anxious voice.

"I'm sure so. I think they're still a bit dazed, but it's a completely happy form of daze. They are, in fact, mildly intoxicated with their sudden importance. Is it a difficult job for them?"

"Well, it all depends," Havana said. "There are one or two in the drink."

"Some of ours?" Roger asked, quickly.

"I'm afraid poor George has gone."

"What, in the sea?"

"Yes."

"Any hope?"

"I'm afraid not."

They said nothing to one another, while they both thought their own thoughts.

"He's the only one," Havana continued, "of our lot that I know of, but there may be one or two more from the other wings. McBain's lot will be useful searching, and keeping off the Hun."

"How long are they going to be at it?"

"Not very long. It was rather a sudden arrangement and Group will be relieving them almost as soon as they get there."

"From what I've seen of them, that won't suit them."

Havana laughed. Then he said, "Pity about George."

"Yes," said Roger, "a great pity," and suddenly he remembered that he had never had that drink last night after all.

Bywaters and he emerged from the hut as the ten Spitfires were moving to take off. McBain and his lanky supporter led the way, to be followed in quick succession by two other sections. Then there was a pause, and Havana could hear an argument between the last two sections as to which should take off first. He cut in on it.

"Don't chatter so much. Blue Section, get going."

All ten Spitfires were now in the sky. McBain was circling the aerodrome, waiting for his pilots to fall into position. There was still a little confusion, however, as if a mild form of musical chairs were taking place, except for two austere Spitfires, who kept well out of the way to the right, and flew sedately by themselves.

"Hallo, you blighters on the right," McBain called. "What section are you?"

"White," replied one of them promptly.

"Yellow," replied the other.

"Oh! For God's sake!" McBain's voice said.

"O.K., Rooky Leader," said another voice. "We're Yellow Section. Behind you to starboard."

"Hallo, you two on the right. You're White Section. Please understand. You are White Section. Cross over to port. Get behind me to port."

They made three more circuits of the aerodrome, and smilingly, Roger and Bywaters watched the formation take rough shape at first, and then, all doubts resolved, it settled into a squadron that might have been flying together for many months. It flew off to the South-east.

The two observers on the ground went back to the Watch Hut.

"The wing should be coming in soon now," Bywaters said, and sat down again at his telephones.

Lookout, from his high post, was scanning South and East with his field-glasses, and he gave his first sighting report.

"One Spitfire approaching from the South-east."

" 'Allo, Tartan," Max's voice called. " 'Allo, Tartan. I am Falcon Black One. I am coming in to land, but my air pressure system has gone."

"Hallo, Falcon Black One, Tartan answering. Are you O.K. otherwise?"

"Otherwise what?"

"Is everything else all right? Are you all right?"

"I am very O.K., Tartan, but I must land without my flaps, and I think I have no brake. Do not worry, Tartan. I come in now."

"Get the Watch Hut," Havana said. . . . "Aircraft landing

without flaps or brakes. Liable to overshoot. Ambulance and fire-tender ready."

Bywaters leaned out of the Watch Hut window.

"Ambulance," he yelled, "fire-tender, stand by!"

The engines of the vehicles started immediately and they moved forward a yard or two on to the perimeter road, to be ready to start in any direction.

Max made one or two circuits, and then he came in on his glide to land.

"His flaps are not down," Roger called to Bywaters.

"That's the trouble," Bywaters called back.

Max seemed to be coming in fast, and although he was so near the ground, his aircraft would not settle. At last it touched down, but it ran—how it ran! Its speed still seemed frighteningly high. It ran to the uttermost edge of the aerodrome and straight into a high embankment. The sound of the thud and of rending, crashing metal, echoed back to the anxious watchers. Ambulance and fire-tender tore off down the road.

But Havana, in Operations Room, was grinning. A voice had sounded in his ear a moment before.

" 'Allo, Tartan, Falcon Black One here. I have landed—but not so good, you know. I am very O.K. Switching off to you."

And when the ambulance arrived first, it was to find the big Max standing with his mouth open, looking at the ruins of his beloved machine.

Other aircraft were now appearing, singly or in twos and fours. As they came in to land, the watchers tried to see if the covers over the gun apertures in the wings had been shot away, for if these covers, which had protected the guns in flight had disappeared, it meant the aircraft had fired and had been in action.

"He's fired," excited mechanics would remark. "Good old Nobby", or "Good old Buster", or whatever their irreverent but affectionate names might be for the pilots whose interests they served. "I'll bet he's got one."

"I'll betcher my bloke's got two."

"Garn! Your bloke couldn't hit a haystack!" So the chaff continued, as they ran to greet the landing machines.

The Wing Commander landed, with his New Zealand

Sergeant, and the latter taxied away into the distance, while the Wing Commander slowly moved back to his original starting point between the hangars on Roger's left. Eager hands gripped the wing-tips, and he swung his aircraft to face the aerodrome. He ran his engine for a little, and then, with staccato coughs, it stopped.

He sat quite motionless, as if in thought. The old jersey, the lean, aquiline face, were outlined against the dark grey hangar, just as they had been not much more than an hour ago. Then he unpinned his straps, swung over the cockpit, and jumped to the ground.

By the time Roger had strolled over to join him, the Intelligence Officer was jotting down what scraps of information the Wing Commander was giving him. It seemed a tiresome procedure to have to take these details from the pilots while they were still breathless and nerve-strung from battle, but every scrap of their news was wanted elsewhere as soon as possible, and in their short, quick descriptions which they gave immediately after the events, the Intelligence Officers could often piece together more accurate information than after a rest had given time for impressions to become blurred.

As he threw his words at the I.O., the Wing Commander was watching the flying-field and the aircraft landing.

"Thank you, Sir," the I.O. said, closing his notebook. "I'll be off to the others."

Roger hesitated to speak. It seemed impertinence to ask unnecessary questions from such men at times like this, but the Wing Commander turned and smiled at him.

"What sort of an outing, Sir?"

"Pretty hot today."

"Did you have much action?"

"Quite a lot, I should think, but I had to make a bolt for it."

"Did the bombers get back safely?"

"They were all there when I last saw them."

"Get anything yourself, Sir?"

"Just one."

"Good, Sir."

The Wing Commander was paying no attention. He was concentrating on the aircraft once more.

"I hope the Group Captain's all right," Roger heard him mutter.

"Is there any reason why he shouldn't be, Sir?"

"Er . . . what?" the Wing Commander said, not realising Roger had heard his spoken thought. "No. . . . No. He'll be all right. We all got rather split up, that's all."

Glebe was down—a beautiful landing. Then Humber came in.

"That's the Group Captain's Number Two," the Wing Commander exclaimed. "Can you see Dyak?"

They looked round the sky. There were Spitfires circling round, but at that distance there was nothing to help them to distinguish them individually.

"Get on to the Controller, Roger, will you? Find out if the Group Captain's all right."

Roger ran to the Watch Office.

"Controller, please," he said. "Havana, Roger here. The Wing Commander's just landed. He wants to know if the Group Captain's all right."

"Hang on, Roger. He's just coming through. . . . Hello, Roger. Are you there? The Group Captain's just called up. He's wounded and his machine's damaged. He thinks he can just make it, but have everything on the top line. Will you tell the Watch Office?"

"All right, Havana. . . . Bywaters, the Group Captain's wounded, and he may have difficulty in landing. What can we do?"

The ambulance and the fire-tender were returning round the perimeter road from Max's accident. There was nothing the matter with Max, but he had taken the opportunity of a ride in the ambulance. Bywaters called to one of his orderlies.

"Stop them both outside. Have them ready to go out, and I'll get through to Sick Quarters. . . . Hallo, Sick Quarters. Give me the Station Doctor. . . . Oh! Doc. Can you get here at once? The Group Captain may need your help. I can't explain anything more. Thank you. . . . Doc's coming now," he said to Roger.

A Spitfire had just made a poor landing. One wheel had touched down first, then the machine had jumped in the air, and, bouncing and rolling, it seemed that every moment would turn it on its nose; but at last it was on the ground safely.

"It's the Gauleiter," Bywaters remarked. "He doesn't usually land like that."

Out in the middle of the aerodrome the Gauleiter's engine had stopped. He was passing his gloved hand across his eyes. He could hardly see and each movement of his limbs seemed to be wrenched from him. Bywaters rushed for the telephone.

"Controller, please. . . . Oh! I say, Sir, could you get through on the loudspeaker to Falcon's ground crew to get out and move the Gauleiter's aircraft from the aerodrome? His engine has stopped, and it looks as if he's stuck there. I'm thinking of the Group Captain landing."

"Hallo," boomed Havana's voice on the loudspeakers. "Hallo, Falcon maintenance crew. Falcon maintenance crew. Remove Spitfire on the aerodrome as quickly as possible. Can you assist the aircraft in the middle of the aerodrome to move out of the way as quickly as possible? This is an urgent message. Switching off."

Figures in the distance began to run out over the grass field. A large lorry with a travelling crane aboard it lumbered over the ground. Other aircraft were still landing.

"Hallo, all aircraft," Havana called. "Beware obstruction in centre of aerodrome. Exercise caution on landing."

Bill Graves was down. He had removed the chewing-gum from the instrument board a long way from home and put it back in his mouth. Now he threw it from his open cockpit.

Dalrymple and Halliwell came in together. Their sections had fought almost wing-tip to wing-tip. High over the English coast as they came in, they had called one another.

"Are you all right, Bob?"

"I'm all right, Collie. Are you all right?"

"I'm all right, Bob."

Ogilvie landed in great haste. His aircraft taxied like a racing motor-car to his dispersal. He wanted news of Cardew.

One by one all the Spitfires in sight had come down.

"Thirty-one, thirty-two, thirty-three," Roger counted. He peered into the distance and turned his head from side to side to try to hear the sound of engines.

"Thirty-three," he said. "The Group Captain, thirty-four.

Four more to come. Thirty-five," he said, thinking of George.

But thirty-six was Cygnet Red Two, whose pertol had been so low that he had landed elsewhere; and thirty-seven was Wishart, imperturbable and seemingly so negative; and thirty-eight was Teddy Ryan, whose little painted racehorse, with its jockey riding for the post, was lying with its colours glowing on a field in France.

Rooky Squadron had been put into échelon port by McBain. That is to say, the other four sections were formed up on his left, one behind the other, so that McBain's was the forward section and the remainder spread diagonally backwards. He was leading them up and down the waters, watching for any dinghy floating on their surface.

The leader of Blue Section, away to his left, called out to him.

"There's something below me now."

"Close in on Blue Section," McBain ordered, and the ten Spitfires were soon forming a protective circle round a yellow patch below.

Lying on his back in his rubber boat, a pilot was smoking a cigarette and watching McBain and his fellows overhead. He had baled out from the wing which had gone to the rescue of the Wing Commander some thirty minutes previously. He had pulled the metal handle on his left-hand side, and the parachute had opened reassuringly. He floated down with the dinghy container still attached to the parachute harness, and when he hit the water, he had disengaged the harness by turning its large circular safety catch resting on his diaphragm. The straps of it fell away between his legs, and he wriggled quickly out of the shoulder pieces. As it drifted off, it pulled the container of the dinghy with it, but this could not go far away, for a stout lead was attached to it with the other end buckled round the belt of the Mae West which was keeping him afloat; so that, as the parachute pulled away, it ripped at the container, and the rubber dinghy unfolded itself from within.

The pilot reached till his hands could grip the little carbon dioxide bottle, and one turn of its screw caused the dinghy to inflate miraculously. With splashings and heavings, he had climbed into it. He searched it carefully and discovered three bullet-holes. He had not realised that he himself had been so nearly hit. He found, stored away, some little conical rubber wedges with which he plugged the holes. The dinghy was now secure.

The sea was too calm for him to need the baling cup which dangled on the end of a piece of cord, so he let out his little sea anchor, found a packet of chocolate in the boat, ate it with relish, and then lit a cigarette. He was rather enjoying his boating adventure. He had a vision of hundreds of these dinghies, bobbing in the water off some holiday centre, with vari-coloured costumes swimming all around them.

McBain had reported his find to Havana, and was now talking to his squadron.

"Rooky Leader calling. If anyone sees a rescue boat, call me immediately."

He had not long to wait.

"Hallo, Rooky Leader, Rooky Green Two calling. Rescue boat to starboard."

"Whose starboard?" McBain replied. "It may be your starboard, but not anyone else's. We're going round and round, you ass."

"Sorry, Rooky Leader. Rescue boat approaching from the North-west."

"That's beter," growled McBain. "Hallo, Rooky Green One. Detach your section. Make contact with the rescue boat and lead it here. Keep us in sight."

The high-speed launch was making no error in the course that had been passed to it from the first sighting report which McBain had given to Havana.

The two aircraft of Green Section flew towards it, turned over it, pointed towards the dinghy, and repeated their manœuvre several times. McBain could see a figure in the rescue boat waving, and the arm of the pilot in the dinghy raised in reply.

"Hallo, Rooky Leader, White One—I mean, Yellow One—Damn it! Who am I? Anyhow, it doesn't matter. Aircraft ahead of you now. Two aircraft."

"Follow me," said McBain. The other nine turned after him.

Sliding over the surface of the water, two Messerschmitts

had appeared, hoping that their camouflage would screen them sufficiently for a short, sharp attack on the rescue boat before they could scurry for the shelter of their own coast.

"After them, boys!" McBain yelled, and the ten of them came down like an avalanche. Nobody worried about formation any longer. It was each for himself. One of the enemy aircraft turned immediately. His sudden retreat seemed to puzzle the other, for it weaved to and fro like a snake.

The Rookies were all firing at once. The splash of their ammunition threw up the water as if a hail-storm had descended, but the enemy did not seem to be hit. He slid all over the sea. From up above he looked to McBain like one of those skating water-beetles which he used to watch on the pond at home.

"Steady, boys," he called. "No need to be in a hurry." But the other nine were past caring for any sort of cohesion. They had all climbed up again after their first attack, and now they all came down on their second dive. But before any one of them had fired, the Messerschmitt tried a steep turn. Its wing-tip hit the water. It cartwheeled completely and was gone. For a moment one of its wings rose like a shark's fin from the surface of the sea, and then subsided to the safe-keeping of the bottom.

"Re-form!" McBain ordered his squadron, but it was not the same pattern that flew back as had flown out. In long, swaying, see-sawing Indian file, the Rookies followed their leader home.

"Re-form," McBain called, despairingly. "We can't let them see us at home like this." His lean, lanky Number Two replied to him:

"It's all very fine you telling them to re-form, Rooky Leader, but by now none of them knows which is which."

McBain gave it up.

"I think I can make it, Tartan. I shall be over base in a few minutes."

"Hallo Dyak, Tartan answering. Everything is ready for you."

"I may have difficulty in landing. My undercarriage will not come down, and half my controls are shot away. Is the aerodrome clear?"

"T.B.," Havana called, hurriedly, "have they moved the Gauleiter's machine?"

"Yes, Sir. Just got it clear."

"Hallo, Dyak. Everything all clear."

Roger saw a Spitfire some four miles away. The pencilled outline of its lovely form was headed straight for the centre of the aerodrome.

"Group Captain coming in," he said to Bywaters, who nodded in reply.

He was flying at some five hundred feet. He could not manage to do anything other than a flat turn for one circuit, for half his elevator and rudder controls were shot away. He came in for his final glide. Everything on the aerodrome was motionless, except for the fire-tender and the ambulance vibrating behind their engines. The Doctor pulled the self-starter of his car.

The Spitfire came in low over the outer boundary. No wheels came down, nor did any flaps. It seemed to Roger to be travelling at tremendous speed. The Group Captain was holding it about four feet off the ground. Its tapered fuselage shot past Roger's front, and he could see the figure in white sitting in the open cockpit.

"It's never going to touch down," he said to Bywaters.

As he spoke, the whole underside slid on to the earth like a gigantic sleigh. The metal blades of the propeller tore into the ground. The body of the aircraft whipped like a wounded whale as it tried to throw itself over on to its back. Soil and lumps of turf foamed at this mighty ploughing. The aircraft jerked and jerked, with the figure in white crouching for the final impact. The fuselage gave one last heave, but the twisted propeller blades had bent themselves like steel runners, and they held the aircraft on its course until it stopped.

Roger could see the figure raise its hand to unstrap the flying-helmet, and as he took it off his head the Doctor's car drew up alongside him.

"How are you, Sir?"

"Oh! Is that you, Doc.? Nice of you to meet me. Just a bit stiff."

"We'll help you out, Sir."

"That's all right," the Group Captain said. "I think I can manage it."

He pulled the pin out of his safety belt, and then let his parachute harness fall off him. He winced a little as he put his left leg over the cockpit on to the wing resting on the grass. The medical orderlies from the ambulance were beside him, but he waved them away. He was looking at something. It was a piece of torn Messerschmitt fabric clinging to his wing. He bent, and pulled it off, holding it in his hand, and thinking.

"I want to see what I add up to," he said after a pause, and he walked a few paces, moving his arms, and turning to face the Doctor.

"Nothing much wrong with me," he announced. "It's only superficial."

"That may be, Sir, but for once you're under my orders. You will get into that ambulance immediately."

It was lunch-time again. Roger had relieved Havana, and he was standing beside Havering, reading a message that was being taken down. It was the state of the squadrons as ordered by Group for the rest of the day. Roger took up a spare telephone to listen.

"Sorry we can't release them yet," a voice at the other end was saying, "but the enemy has had a good stirring up this morning, and he may take it into his head to come over and see us for a change. We'll see what we can do later."

A W.A.A.F. was putting coloured discs on an indicator to show the states.

"Heron Squadron: One flight readiness. One flight available. Cygnet and Falcon Squadrons: Available in the Mess."

Roger asked for the Wing Commander.

"MacMurray here, Sir. I thought you'd like to know the squadron's states for the time being."

"Yes. Tell me, Roger."

Roger repeated them. "I would have told the Group Captain, Sir, if he'd been available."

"Why didn't you?"

"Well, I mean to say, Sir. He's wounded."

"It hasn't stopped him from having lunch."

"Where, Sir?"

"In the Mess. I was sitting beside him when you called."

"Is he all right, Sir?"

"He looks as if he's suffering from a strange disease with all the iodine they've dabbed over him, but otherwise he's all right."

"But isn't he going sick, Sir?"

"Good gracious, no! You know his views about that sort of thing. Once you get into the hands of the quacks, they never let you go. He's not falling for that."

They rang off.

The Intelligence Officer came into the room. "What's the final result?" Roger asked him.

"For our wing? Seven destroyed. Two probables. Four damaged. Group will let me know the other wings' results later—of course, there's the one that destroyed itself dodging the McBain outfit. We may as well credit them with one-tenth each to start them off on their fighter careers."

"And our own wing?"

"Three missing."

A fair proportion, Roger thought, if only one could exclude the personalities. A fair proportion for a nation fighting back against the greatest armed might in the history of man. Seven to three, apart from those others that could not definitely be claimed. "That will do," Roger said to himself. "Seven to three. Seven enemy to every three British. Keep it up long enough, and we shall have shot them out of the sky; and when that day comes the Army can sustain the battle, and we shall begin to see the end of it all, and have a chance to figure out why it happened, and to begin to plan that it shall not happen again."

One patient had fallen to the Doctor's net, but he was very submissive. The Gauleiter had pneumonia, and he was lying, cool and quiet at last, in his hospital bed.

Some figures were sprawled, fast asleep, on the couches and chairs in the anteroom. White flannels moved backwards and forwards on the tennis court.

"What about dinner in town tonight?" a voice called outside the window.

"Fine. If we're released in time we might get in at the flicks first."

The Wing Commander was standing on the lawn in the middle of the garden, watching Tom clipping dead blooms from the flowering profusion all around.

The swing chairs, with their coloured canopies, were rocking to and fro as their occupants swung lazily in the warm afternoon. The sound of a record came from the open window of a downstairs room, where Glebe was sitting in his shirt-sleeves, smoking his pipe, and listening to Sibelius.

The Group Captain was lying on his bed. His arm and his leg had stiffened and were giving him some pain. He was drowsily watching a flock of birds wheeling, rising and falling, beyond the tall tree in his garden, outlined against the blue sky.

The recurrent pat-patting of the tennis balls came to his ears—shouts and calls from far away—the noise of a motor car diminishing into the distance, the tick of his clock on the bed table beside him, the swell of the Sibelius harmonies as the light breeze carried them towards his window, the clopping of a horse's hooves on a road outside the camp, the rattle of an electric train, and the far-away sound of a ship's siren—all the normal, natural, happy noises, blending and merging into one continuous song—the song of a summer day. The birds were still wheeling and rising. He saw them through his half-closed eyes.

The Group Captain fell asleep.

The little elderly man tending his onion-bed, straightened his back and pushed his old panama hat off his eyes.

His wife had appeared at the opening in the fence. "Dinner-time, John," she said. "You and your old vegetables!"

He smiled at her. And he looked up. The big, white clouds were sailing slowly on their way.

"Quiet up there," he remarked, "nowadays."

"Very," she answered.

They walked together along the path towards the kitchen door.